Damian's Windsor

Damian's Windsor

By

Ebony Farashuu

Cover design: Jae Slae of Eight Three Designs, www.83designs.com

Printed in the United States of America

Metamorphosis Ink Publishing
2608 W. Kenosha #537
Broken Arrow, OK 74012
www.metainkpub.com

Dedication

For all the little black girls who have been told they aren't enough.
You are…
More than enough.
You are beautiful.

Other Books by Ebony Farashuu

Butterfly Kisses: Poetry for the Many Faces of Love
Slow Burn
Erika's Diary
Slow Burn: Deluxe Edition
Orchid's Nectar

October

He knew me
Biblically
Mythically
Rhythmically
Thoroughly
Purely
Surely this couldn't be real.
Life comes at you fast
He made me cum faster
Harder
Bombarding my body with sensations I can't explain.
It was beautifully profane
Pleasure and pain
The sting of being spanked just right
His hand on my throat, but not too tight
We fucked long into the night.
And I
Knew him
Without knowing anything but his name
Damian
And he
Knew me
Without knowing anything but my name
Windsor.

Ebony Farashuu

Chapter 1

Damian Lawrence Anthony

Last night was… interesting.

Okay, maybe it was a little more than interesting.

It was… strange.

It was beautiful.

She was strange.

She was beautiful.

Beautiful and strange.

Strange and beautiful.

She was… an aspiration.

She was something to strive for.

Something to work towards.

Something to place on a vision board if you're into that kind of shit.

She was… the least likely to end up in my bed, and yet, there she was… in my bed, licking me, sucking me, fucking me like I'd never been fucked before. Curling my toes, breaking my back, draining me of my very essence.

She was gazing down at me with big chocolate eyes… dark eyes… so dark it was hard to distinguish her irises from her pupils. Her soul was on full display, and as she hovered above me, looking down at me while biting her lower lip, I could see the wheels turning in her head as she contemplated how to torture me next.

Her waist length locs tickled my ribcage like tiny fingers, stroking me until the hairs on my arms stood up.

It had been an hour already.

She wouldn't let me cum.

She wouldn't let me touch her.

She wouldn't let me kiss her.

It was torture.

It was beautiful.

It was… strange.

It was the most profound night of my life and I had no idea if I'd ever see her again.

I didn't even know who she was, this… beautifully strange woman.

I only knew her first name.

Windsor.

Windsor with the long black locs. Windsor with the wide hips. Windsor with the thick thighs. Windsor with skin so dark she could dip her fingers in her pussy and write her name all over my chest with the ink of her juices. Windsor with the overflowing handfuls of breasts she dangled in my face without taking off her lacy black bra, smothering me between them, but not allowing me the pleasure of snatching that bra off and sucking the beautiful nipples I got peeks of through the lace.

Windsor with the beautiful smile that blessed her face every time she made me cry out in pleasure.

I felt like a shiny new toy.

I wanted to bury myself in her box and pound her into the mattress, but she was in control. She was the one on top. She was the one doing the talking, pressing her fingers to my lips every time I tried to speak.

"Shh," she would say. "I only wanna hear you moan."

And moan I did… all night long.

Her voice was soft, gentle, like a sensual tickle to the eardrum.

Her touch was intoxicating.

Her pheromones were overpowering, lulling me into a trance as I inhaled her sexual perfume.

Her pussy was poetic.

Being inside of her felt like a privilege.

What the fuck did I do to deserve this?

Sweat poured from her body and mingled with mine, pooling where our loins connected, and dripped down onto my bed, creating a wet spot I'd gladly sleep in if only she'd allow me the pleasure of cumming inside her.

But she wouldn't allow it.

Every time she felt the slightest tension in my body, she would calm the rhythmic movement of her hips, slowing to a pause and then lifting her body until her pussy hovered over my dick, close enough to touch, daring me to lift my hips. Daring me to try plunging inside of her, just to hear her say, "No."

"Please, I just wanna…"

"Shh," she put her fingers to my lips. "I only wanna hear you moan."

I shut up, but my mind was racing… until she slid her pussy over me again, entombing me deep inside of her, burying me within the swollen walls of her sexual cave until I thought my dick would choke. All thoughts of touching her left my mind as I closed my eyes and lost myself inside of her.

"Open your eyes," she whispered huskily.

She unsnapped her bra, and as it tumbled to the floor beside my bed, a little black rock fell onto my stomach. Windsor scooped it up and carefully placed it on my nightstand before licking her lips and smiling down at me.

I stared up at her as she slowly wound her hips in a sensual rhythm, keeping in time with the music softly playing in the background. I watched, in awe, as she slid her hands over her naked breasts, caressing them, pinching her nipples until they stood at attention, begging to be licked and sucked.

"Do you want to taste them?" she asked.

I nodded vigorously, like a toddler who'd just been asked if he wanted a lollipop.

She smiled teasingly and then cupped both breasts in her hands, lifting them as she dipped her head down and slowly flicked her tongue over them.

She was sucking her titties.

She was sucking her own damn titties.

That shit was sexy as fuck.

My mouth hung open and I could feel a small pool of saliva forming under my tongue and dripping down the side of my mouth, gathering in my ear, and making her words sound muffled as she slid one hand down the length of her body and began gently caressing her clit.

Her slow grind never stopped.

Her mouth never left her nipple.

Her eyes never left mine.

"Sit up," she said softly. "And wrap your arms around my waist."

I did as I was told. She slid her arms around my neck. I heard a sharp gasp escape her lips. I knew this position put my dick at an angle that hit the most sensitive nerves inside of her. It pleased me to know she was enjoying this as much as me.

"Keep still," she whispered as she placed both legs over my shoulders and wound her arms even tighter around my neck.

Her waist beads rolled against my stomach… the sensation was too much…

Oh my god.

She used my neck as an anchor as she slid back and forth against me, pounding my dick into her pussy until I thought my pelvis would break.

"Fuck me," she whispered.

And I did.

Flipping her over onto her back and slamming my body into hers as all the frustration and deprivation I felt while under her spell, gathered up and exploded inside of me.

She lifted her hips, meeting every thrust, crying out in pleasure, never closing her eyes. She was smiling at me, biting her lip, becoming more exhilarated with every stroke.

I could feel her walls swelling and gripping my dick so tightly, I feared she would spontaneously push me out, so I dove deeper, hit it harder, pushed against her in a powerful quest for survival.

I was fighting for my life.

"Let's cum together," she screamed as an intense spasm gripped her body.

A tsunami spilled out of her and I fought against the current, stroking her harder and harder until her screams were in concert with the savage moans gurgling in my throat and spilling out of my mouth in one ragged breath.

She kissed me then.

She pulled my face towards hers and parted her lips as I slid my tongue inside of her mouth, kissing her as if I'd known her my entire life.

Kissing her as if I loved her.

But I didn't even know her.

I only knew her first name.

Windsor.

Chapter 2

Windsor Elaine Bradley

He had a big dick. I could tell by the way he walked into the gallery and leaned against the wall, shifting ever so slightly, trying to adjust himself without blatantly using his hands. Of course, looking like you're packing and *actually* packing are two different things, so I studied him a little longer, watching him as he watched everything going on around him without actively participating.

He was invisible. Blending into the wall like an odd piece of art, not catching the eye of anyone in the room, but seemingly unfazed by the lack of attention he received as the women at the event gravitated towards the trendier pieces.

He was... cute in a nerdy kind of way.

He was wearing jeans and a blazer in a room full of men in tailored suits. His black framed glasses sat snugly atop his broad nose in subtle contrast to his coppery brown skin.

Discovering him in the crowd felt like finding a shiny new penny laying face up on the sidewalk. I wanted to pick him up and put him in my pocket for good luck.

He looked tall from where I was standing... taller than me. Not that it mattered, but I loved wearing heels and, at five foot nine, some men felt intimidated by a woman who towered over them. I'd done my fair share of wearing flats and slouching for the comfort of a man who wasn't worth the effort. Going into my forties I promised myself I'd never make myself small to cater to the insecurities of any man. Never again.

I was keeping that promise to myself.

So as several men approached me with self-serving compliments and mindless conversation, mostly about themselves and why I should choose them, my eye was on the guy leaning against the wall, obviously out of place, yet unintimidated by the people who thought they belonged there.

I stared at him, silently willing him to walk over, rescue me and allow me to appraise him. I wasn't unreasonably picky, but I did have a few non-negotiable requirements. First and foremost, he had to have a big dick. I don't give a damn what anybody says about the motion of the ocean. I don't want a tugboat. I want a fucking yacht.

Secondly, he can't be judgmental... of me, himself, or others. I hate men who put themselves on a pedestal. It makes me want to kick the base from beneath them and watch them crash land to the floor where they belong.

I need a man who will look me in the eyes and honestly like who I am on any given day, not someone who wants to try and mold me into his version of the perfect woman. I've had enough of men who act like they're doing me a favor by dating me. It took years, but now I understand... *I'm the prize.*

And while there are many other qualities on my check list, I would be remiss if I didn't mention... you can't have a big dick and not know how to use it. I'm just saying, don't get my mouth all watered up for a steak and then serve me chicken nuggets. I will knock all this shit over!

He noticed me staring at him and looked around, trying to figure out if I was looking at him or one of the other men in the vicinity.

I stifled a laugh. I understood. I'd made the mistake of thinking a man was waving at me, only to have him walk right past me and talk to the pretty girl standing behind me. Growing up I'd become accustomed to being chosen by default. I was always the blackest black girl in the room and my complexion wasn't always on trend. I didn't grow up seeing women who looked like me idolized and revered as the standard of beauty.

I was on trend now. Men who passed me up years ago were suddenly sliding into my DMs, as if I would somehow forget how they frequently made fun of me and chose the lighter sistahs when it came to *actual* romance. I was just for practice back in the day.

I once heard a boyfriend's mother tell him it was okay to mess around with me, but to marry a light skinned girl so his children wouldn't be black.

Ironic. Now my black ass is the white rabbit at the dog track.

"I'm sorry, I see someone I need to speak to," I told Eugene.

"I'm trying to get to know you," Eugene said lustfully.

"I don't wanna get to know you," I said firmly. "Please leave me alone. This doesn't have to be a scene." I looked around for Marissa, but she wasn't in my line of sight. Eugene wrapped his hand around my arm. Disturbed, I pulled away from him.

I must have looked distressed because a deep voice suddenly exclaimed, "Hey, baby. Sorry I'm late, who's your friend?"

It was the mystery brotha in the jeans and blazer. I smiled appreciatively as he put his arm around my shoulders and kissed my cheek. In an ordinary situation this would have earned him a swift kick in the nuts, but this was not an ordinary situation.

He looked at the hand on my arm and then looked Eugene in the eye.

"Are we gonna have a problem?" the mystery man asked without flinching.

Eugene let go of me and walked away without another word. I stared at his retreating back as he walked away in a huff. I briefly wondered how he'd try to spin it if I said something to Marissa. My mystery man took his arm from around my shoulders and smiled at me. I liked the way his brown eyes lit up behind his glasses.

"Thank you," I said laughingly as my nerves settled. "I thought I was gonna have to Chun Li that fool."

"Ahhh-You-Kit!" he laughed with a subtle sideways kick that had folks in the area looking at us like we were crazy.

Sense of humor… *check.*

Our laughter calmed and I found myself looking up at him. He was taller than me. In heels.

Check.

Looking up at him this way, I realized he was more than the nerdy little cute guy from across the room. He was sexy. I could tell from the way his blazer hung on him; he was no stranger to the gym. He did just enough to stay fit and didn't have a ridiculous amount of muscles stretching the fabric of his shirt. He was built like a point guard, tall and trim. His closely cropped hair was so wavy I got seasick just looking at it. It was obvious he slept in a durag but didn't seem the type to carry a brush in his back pocket or obsess over doing wave checks at any given moment. His fingernails were manicured but his hands were a little rough. I knew that from his touch.

He smelled like earth, woodsy, spicy… heavenly.

Well groomed, possibly works with his hands, smells good.

Check. Check. Check.

"You were looking at me," he told me.

"Yes, I was," I admitted. "You heard my subliminal plea for help."

"Do you know him?" He jerked his head towards Eugene who was staring at us from across the room.

"He's my best friend's boyfriend," I answered.

He raised an eyebrow.

"Oh, God, NO!" I said, shaking my head vigorously. "I would *never*. He seems to think I should."

"Have you told your best friend?"

"I've tried, and been accused of thinking every man wants me," I admitted.

"Don't they?" He was staring at my lips. I involuntarily licked them. "I'm sorry... I... that was corny, right? It just came out."

I smiled.

"Admittedly, I thought you were looking at someone else," he chuckled.

"Now, why would you think that?"

"I'm a bit out of place," he said with a smile. "I like art, but I don't normally do the whole art show gallery thing."

"I love art shows," I told him. "I can't afford anything here, but it gave me a reason to dress up."

I liked him immediately. There was something about him that made me feel comfortable enough to let down my guard. I was invited to the show by my best friend, Marissa, who promptly left me hanging when her new boyfriend showed up. I had no idea he was invited, but I should have known. Marissa and Eugene had been joined at the hip since they met at church three months ago. Suddenly our girl's nights disappeared, and our twosome became an awkward threesome. Eugene was a good, church-going man who didn't approve of me because I lived my life free and unapologetically. He didn't want that to rub off on his new girlfriend. Little did he know, his prissy little girlfriend was the one who pushed me to be the free and unapologetic woman I am today... she was the same way until she met him.

When Marissa invited me to Harlem Ali's big art show, I thought it would finally be an opportunity for us to dress up and drink, while staring at art we couldn't afford. Instead, I was left alone the moment her knight in shining armor showed up unannounced.

I was mad for many different reasons, but had I not been standing alone, being accosted by that good, church-going man, I wouldn't have been rescued by... whoever he was.

"Let's be out of place together," I told him. "I'm Windsor, by the way."

"Windsor," he said softly, studying me for a moment. "I like it. It suits you."

"How so?"

"You're regal... like a queen," he said simply. "Why wouldn't you be named after a castle?"

Well, damn.

Quick on his feet.

Check.

"I'm Damian," he said.

"Damian," I repeated. "Should I be worried about Satan strolling up in here and tapping me on the shoulder?"

He immediately picked up on my horror movie reference and started laughing again. "Nah, you're safe… he gave me the night off from world destruction and mayhem. My next shift doesn't start until tomorrow morning."

"Then dance with me tonight."

"Dance?" He raised an eyebrow. "There's no dance floor."

"Be adventurous," I told him.

Without waiting for an answer, I led him to a secluded corner of the room and wrapped my arms around his neck, pulling him close as he rested his hands on either side of my waist. He had a firm grip, as if he wanted every man in the room to know there would be no cutting in on this impromptu dance.

I liked his rhythm. Liked the way his hips moved with mine. Liked the sound of his voice as he sang in my ear. His voice was smooth, like milk chocolate dripping onto a strawberry, enveloping it in a rich creamy sweetness that made you savor every bite.

Sexy voice.

Check.

"Do you sing to all the girls," I asked him.

"Oh no, I didn't even notice I was singing out loud," he said, blushing. "I thought I was singing in my head."

He was truly embarrassed. I thought it was cute.

"I like it," I told him. "Keep going, it's sexy."

He kept singing softly as his body continued grinding with mine. His hands moved from my waist to my back, gently pulling me closer until our bodies felt like one unit under a sensual groove. His erection introduced itself and I felt a slow smile forming on my lips.

It's a yacht.

Check.

I giggled.

"Do I sound that bad?" he asked.

"Nooooo, I wasn't laughing at your singing," I told him. "I was just… thinking about something."

"Care to share?" he asked.

He pulled away and looked down at me with an amused expression on his face. He opened his mouth to speak but I put a finger to his lips.

"Shh," I whispered. "I just wanna hear you sing."

He pulled me close and began crooning again, softly, sensually, performing a concert for my ears only.

I smiled again, licking my lips as his erection pressed into my center, moisture already forming in my panties. Damian didn't know it yet, but I was gonna fuck the shit outta him.

Chapter 3

Damian Lawrence Anthony

She fucked the *shit* outta me.

There's no other way to explain it. No other way to describe it. No other way to make sense of the carnal escapades that took place in my bedroom a few hours ago.

I woke up alone… in the wet spot, her name on my lips as I reached over to find an empty space where her beautiful body once rested, sitting up on one elbow, tracing lazy circles on my chest with her fingernails.

Her conversation had been casual, as if she hadn't just fucked the shit outta me.

"What made you bring me home?" she asked.

"You told me to," I answered with a grin.

She laughed, "Do you always do what you're told?"

"Not usually," I answered truthfully. "This is definitely a first."

"Why now?" she asked.

"Why me?" I countered her question with one of my own. "Of all the men in that room, why me?"

"Because. In a room full of uptight men pretending to be above it all… you were just you," she said simply. "Plus… you stepped up when no one else did. Do you have anything to eat?"

"I have an antipasto tray I was gonna eat later," I told her.

"Where'd you buy it?"

"I made it."

"Go get it." She sat up and looked down at me.

I rolled into her, placing a gentle kiss on her rib cage before swinging my legs over the other side of the bed and walking naked to the kitchen.

"Do you want some wine?" I called from the kitchen as I washed my hands.

13

"Red, please," she called back sweetly.

"Red it is," I mused, grabbing the tray, the wine, and two glasses before heading back into the bedroom.

We sat, naked in the middle of my bed, feeding each other cheese and kalamata olives while drinking red wine and playing a guarded game of twenty questions, making up the rules as we went.

No personal questions.

No questions that needed a detailed answer.

"Yes or no questions," I offered.

"Okay," she agreed.

"Have you done this before?" I asked her.

"Yes."

"Does that turn you off?" she asked me.

"No."

She smiled. "Your turn."

"Can I kiss you again?" I asked.

"Yes."

She tasted like kalamatas and wine, salty and habit forming. It was a nice kiss, almost timid. Nothing like the ardent kisses we shared in the throes of passion. This kiss was sweet, like the first kiss after a first date, where both parties are wondering when they will see each other again. I gave her lips a subtle lick and took a small sip of my wine.

"Your turn," I told her.

"You didn't tell me I'm pretty when you met me," she said suddenly. "Why?"

"That's not a yes or no question," I observed.

"Am I pretty?"

"Yes," I answered. "Don't you get tired of men telling you that the moment you meet them?"

"Yes," she responded. "Can we alter the rules?"

"You're asking *me*?" I laughed.

She laughed at the irony.

"Sometimes, that's all people see. A pretty woman. That's all. That's it. Even when they're complimenting other aspects of my personality... pretty works its way into it. Pretty and smart. Pretty and talented. Pretty and, Pretty and, Pretty and," she sighed. "Back in the day, men told me I was pretty to get what they wanted. They knew I wasn't used to compliments. Now it's just tiresome because I never know what the *real* motive is. Does that make sense?"

I nodded. It made a lot of sense. "Wanna know what I see?" I asked her.

She nodded.

"Confidence." I picked up her hand and dipped her fingers in my wine before slowly suckling each one. "Passion," I continued, moving the antipasto tray out of the way as I leaned in for a slow kiss. "Unapologetic acceptance of yourself, wit, humor." I slowly eased her down onto her back and loomed above her, staring into her eyes as I said, "But I would be blind if I didn't acknowledge you're the most beautiful woman I've ever met."

Windsor's eyes fluttered and then closed as my hand cupped her dripping wet mound of pleasure. I began softly tapping her clit with my index finger, loving the sound of her soft moans as they filled the room.

"She feels so good," I whispered, sliding one, and then two fingers inside of her, stroking her gently from within.

"Ooohhh, shit…" she moaned.

"Shh…" I whispered, removing my fingers from her secret place, and gently placing them against her lips. "I only wanna hear you moan."

She bit her lip and I smiled.

Now it was my turn to fuck the shit outta *her*.

I parted her legs with my face, licking her slowly, reveling in the way she tasted, sweet like honey, an abundant oasis providing all the juices I needed to quench my insatiable thirst for her. I dipped into her with my tongue, lapping her essence like a dog at his water bowl… quickly, slowly, pausing whenever I felt her curled toes gripping the sheets beneath us.

I didn't want her to cum.

Not yet.

Her moans sounded like a symphony to my ears, and I was the conductor, twirling and swirling my tongue against her clit like a baton, directing her moans as they began to crescendo under my expert tutelage.

I slid my finger inside of her as my tongue wreaked havoc on her clit. Two instruments working together to create musical moans in low tones until her screams echoed off the walls in surround sound. A river of juices pushed against my face, drenching me in her nectar as I continued feasting upon her. She squeezed my head between her thighs and tried to scoot away but my grip on her was tight.

I wasn't finished yet.

She grabbed me by my ears, pulling at me until we were face to face.

She lifted her legs as I kissed her, wrapping them around my waist, guiding me inside as I began stroking her slowly, pulling out completely and then plunging back in, harder, deeper, faster until I had to grip the headboard to steady myself. She met each thrust without pausing… her hips lifting higher and higher, matching my tempo, absorbing my intensity… twisting and circling around my dick as if she were performing an erotic dance.

15

It was too much, and as I came inside of her, I thought I saw a burst of red energy explode all over the room.

I collapsed on top of her, spent like a crisp new twenty.

Her legs were still wrapped around me. Her feet, hooked at the ankles, were holding me in place, not allowing me to disengage. I was glad. I didn't want to lose the connection, and as I felt her Kegel muscles gently squeezing me, I buried my face in her neck and exhaled loudly.

"Yes or no question," I whispered breathlessly. "Is it my imagination, or did you have a rock inside of your bra?"

She laughed and reached over to grab the little black rock from the nightstand. I rolled off her, losing the physical connection, but the mental connection was equally as strong. I watched as she held the smooth rock above us between her thumb and forefinger, admiring it as I admired her.

"It's a crystal," she finally said.

I reached out to touch it, but she slapped my hand away. "No, don't touch it."

"Why do you have a rock—"

"Crystal," she corrected me.

"Crystal," I repeated. "Why do you have a crystal in your bra?"

"It's a labradorite," she told me. "It has healing properties. I carry it with me always."

"Why your bra?" I asked.

"Because it's close to my heart," she whispered.

"What do you need to be healed from?" I asked her.

"Too personal," she whispered as she put a finger to my lips.

She kissed me gently and laid her head on my shoulder. I pulled her closer and buried my face in her locs.

We fell asleep that way…

When I woke up, Windsor was gone.

Chapter 4

Windsor Elaine Bradley

My body was sore. I hadn't performed that level of sexual gymnastics in a very long time. My yoga sessions were great preparation, but when Damian turned the tables on me, I was totally unprepared for the way my body reacted to him.

I lost control.

I lost my mind.

I damn near lost my voice.

I coughed slightly and then laughed hoarsely. It was unlike me to fuck the shit out of a dude and then turn around and allow him to do the same thing to me. I'd planned on leaving immediately after riding him into the sunset, but I felt so comfortable with him I ended up sitting in the middle of his bed, drinking wine while he fed me.

If that wasn't enough, I had the nerve to open up to him... and then allow him to open me up with his tongue.

Chile, when he told me he only wanted to hear *me* moan...

I smiled at the memory. He'd taken my words and effectively used them against me, while making me cum until I was screaming in octaves I didn't even know were in me. He had me gripping the sheets so tightly I thought I'd leave one of my fingernails buried in his mattress.

It was good.

It was better than good, and I'm not sure they've come up with a word to describe the way my body still trembles when I think about it. In fact, my legs were so wobbly when I was trying to get dressed, I thought I'd collapse while sneaking out of his house.

I said I wanted a yacht.

Goddammit I got one.

Shit.

I wanted to take another ride. Sail out into his ocean and ride those orgasmic waves until my voice was nothing but a distant memory.

He made me cum so hard.

Multiple times.

Now, I don't wanna say I'm dick whipped but, dammit I'm dick whipped, tongue whipped, finger whipped, whipped cream, hell what other kind of whips are there? I'm all of them. All. Of. Them.

I'd been nastier than usual with him. Somehow, I knew he could appreciate it with no judgement. Feeling sexually uninhibited was the most freeing experience ever. Being able to touch myself, taste myself, make him watch as I enjoyed myself and all I had to offer while his big dick was just… chilling inside of me, caressing my g-spot while I caressed myself.

I started trembling again.

I crossed my legs and squeezed tightly.

I could cum just thinking about him… thinking about Damian.

"You devil dick muthafucka," I whispered.

"Ummm?" the Uber driver looked up into the rearview mirror and made eye contact with me. "You okay?"

"Hey, when I request an Uber does it give you the address or just navigate you to my phone? Like, if I wanted you to take me back… could you?"

"Now, Sis…" the Uber driver raised her eyebrows and tilted her head to the side.

"I know," I groaned. "But it was so good."

"I'm not taking you back over there," she laughed. "Trust me, I've had good dick. It's nothing but the devil. I'm saving you from yourself."

I laughed at the irony. She was right, of course. I only knew a few things about this man and none of those things included his last name, relationship status, place of employment… you know… the basics.

I knew he had good dick, though.

I knew I wanted to see him again.

I knew I needed to take my ass home.

"You're right. Thanks for talking some sense into me," I said, placing a hand on the Uber driver's shoulder.

"We have to take care of one another, Sis," she said. "Make sure you give me a good rating."

I gave her the same rating I gave Damian's dick.

Five out of Five stars.

***

I woke up a few hours later, not fully refreshed, but full of pent-up energy that needed to be worked off... and since Damian wasn't conveniently lounging in my bed, I had to make do with jumping on my treadmill and doing a brisk walk as I cracked up laughing at Nathan Lane and Robin Williams while I watched The Birdcage on the flatscreen in my basement. I walked until the movie was over and then carried my tired sweaty body back upstairs. I was tempted to lay across my bed, but I'd just changed the sheets and didn't want my workout sweat mingling with the lavender spray I spritzed on my pillowcases.

"Alexa, turn the bathroom lights blue," I said as I walked into the bathroom and turned on the shower.

The room suddenly darkened as a peaceful, blue glow settled over the space. I sighed softly as I undressed and walked into the glass shower, letting hot water trickle over my body while imagining I could see the steam rising from my skin. I closed my eyes and took several deep breaths, in through my nose and out of my mouth, the whole time internally whispering words of affirmation with each inhale as negative thoughts and feelings were released with every exhale.

My body relaxed as I stood in silence. Only the sound of the water pounding the small shower tiles beneath my feet penetrated my thoughts. It sounded like rain. It felt like rain as I stretched out my arms and placed my palms against the wall, leaning into it and bracing myself as the hot water pounded my back in a hard, staccato rhythm.

On a normal, sleepless, ass crack of dawn morning, that showerhead would have been disengaged from its roost and strategically placed for a more 'personally stimulating' massage, but this sleepless morning wasn't going to be fixed with a cup of chamomile tea and a water pressure induced orgasm.

If my life were a Lifetime movie... this would be the commercial break. This episode of Black Windsor is being brought to you by Damian whatever the fuck his last name is. Black Windsor. That name used to make me cry. My daddy used to call me Black Windsor. My older sister, the mahogany brown one who looked like him... he called her Red Paris.

It was no secret he didn't think I was his... even though his mama was blacker than me. In his eyes... a red skinned man and a dark-skinned woman made mahogany babies. I wasn't a mahogany baby. I was a tar baby... another name I learned to loathe when my clueless... and by 'clueless,' I mean racist, white teacher decided to read that dreadful book to my first-grade class at a predominantly white private school. And when I say predominantly white... I mean my sister and I were only half of the black population at that school.

After reading that story… Everyone forgot my name. Windsor was too regal for a little black girl on scholarship. My new name was T.B, and it took my mother going up to that school and cussing everybody out for it to stop.

I opened my eyes… of all things to think of under my blue light…

Why were the most painful memories from my childhood bubbling up and flooding my thoughts? I'm over that. I've been over that. That racist teacher is probably dead, those little racist first graders are probably raising little racist babies of their own, and my daddy… well, I guess he's wherever the fuck he is. He left when I was ten. I used to miss him.

Maybe that's why it was so easy for me to get caught up with Ian.

I closed my eyes again.

Breathe in through your nose.

Breathe out through your mouth.

In through your nose.

Out through your mouth.

My mind began to relax again as I struggled to quiet my racing thoughts. I sat on the built-in bench in my shower and placed my hands in my lap. I relaxed with my back against the wall… eyes still closed… still being mindful of my breathing… still trying to figure out why the tragedies of my life were invading my mind when all I wanted to do was rehash my adventure with Damian, meditate, and forgive myself for the hoe-ish tendencies that sometimes took over when I least expected them to.

I'm not mad at myself… far from it, but in the back of my mind I feel like maybe I should be… mad at myself. Like, maybe I should feel ashamed for not… being more… what's the word? Remorseful? Reflective? Sorry?

But I wasn't.

Once I quieted the painful thoughts of my distant past… I felt nothing but giddiness. The only thing I felt any semblance of remorse about… was not waking Damian up and doing more of what we'd been doing all night… and then leaving while he was awake so he could watch me walk away.

But… maybe that's why I left the way I did. Maybe I didn't want him to look at me differently once the fun was over. Maybe I didn't want to feel ashamed by looking at myself through his eyes the morning after.

I can't remember the last time I cared enough about what someone else thought of me, to care about how it would affect me if they harbored a negative opinion. I certainly didn't give a fuck about Eugene's negative feelings about me… but it hurt to see my best friend slowly walking away from me as his judgement of me, and his secret lust, slowly morphed into her hatred of me.

I shook my head as I thought of the conversation we had in the bathroom at the gallery last night.

"Did I really just see you slow dancing with some dude at an art show? Last time I checked, there wasn't a dance floor."

I laughed, "We weren't the only one's dancing."

"Right, but no one else started dancing until you started dancing. It's not that kind of event. Why do you always have to get the party started? Why can't you just chill out sometimes? Eugene is trying so hard to like you, Windsor, but you aren't making it easy."

I paused with my lipstick barely touching my bottom lip and stared at her through the bathroom mirror. Whatever she was trying to say... I needed her to just spit it out and stop beating around the bush. Was dancing in public something else I needed to stop doing to make her lame ass boyfriend like me?

What Marissa didn't understand was... her boyfriend liked me just fine. He just didn't like that I turned him down... repeatedly. He was so fearful of me telling Marissa he tried to get in my pants... he was painting a horrible picture of me in her mind. It was just a matter of time before he flipped it and told her I was trying to take him away from her. That's how it works. Poison her mind and she'll believe anything he has to say about her best friend.

Facebook may have disappearing inbox messages... but I have a quick trigger finger. When the inevitable occurred... I would be ready with screenshots.

"You and Eugene don't have to worry about me embarrassing you any more tonight. I'm leaving." I touched up my lipstick and then turned to face her. "This was fun. Thanks for the invite."

"You're leaving? How? I was hoping you'd drive my car so I can ride home with Eugene."

The nerve of this bitch.

I shrugged. "Sorry," I said, not really meaning it.

I didn't wait for her response. I walked out of the bathroom, past Eugene who was looking at me the way he always looks at me when Marissa isn't watching, and walked up to Damian, planting a soft kiss on his surprised lips.

"Let's go," I told him.

"Where do you wanna go?" he asked me.

"Do you live with your mama?"

"Nope."

"Take me to your house."

A blast of cool water hit me, waking me from my thoughts. I hadn't realized I'd been in the shower long enough for the hot water to run cold. I yawned loudly and shut the water off before walking, naked, into my bedroom and collapsing on my bed.

November

Sometimes a one-night stand
Is just
A
One
Night
Stand.
I understand.
I overstand.
I can't get this girl off
My mind is in total disarray.
I can't even play
She's got that
Good good
Got me wishing she
Would
Find me
Wind me up
And play with me again.
Biblically it's a sin
But hell would be a win
If I could just taste her again.

Chapter 5

Damian Lawrence Anthony

I was so distracted I didn't notice I was still wearing my glasses until they fogged up in the shower. I had to laugh at myself. Three weeks later, and I was still feeling a little discombobulated from my night with Windsor. It wasn't my first one-night stand, but it was the first time I'd ever been turned out.

Some freaky shit went down that night. Shit so freaky, the younger version of myself would have called up my big brother, Devin, and yelled, "bruh, she sucked her own titties!"

Thirty-nine-year-old me didn't want to tell anyone about it. I wanted to keep it to myself and savor the memory without having to hear Devin clown me about being pussy whipped on the first night.

The only problem I had with Windsor was the way she left me. She left like a thief in the night. She stole my sanity.

I only knew her first name, and while I knew there probably weren't many black women in Tulsa named Windsor, I didn't know how to search for her without looking like a stalker... so I didn't.

Sometimes a one-night stand is just that... a one-night stand.

I was going crazy wondering how in the hell she ended up in my bed, and how I could possibly get her to come back. It wasn't that I wanted to fuck her... well, yes, I wanted to fuck her. I wanted to make love, I wanted to taste her and let her taste me. I wanted to taste me on her, and I wanted her to taste herself on me.

I wanted the opportunity to take off my shoes and tiptoe through the palace of her mind while my dick probed the depths of her temple... I wanted to experience every part of her.

I hopped out of the shower and wiped condensation from the mirror, staring at myself while trying not to smile like a virgin who just got his first piece of ass. My scratches had faded, but I still had ten tiny little puncture wounds where she'd dug her nails into my chest as she rode me.

My dick stood at attention just thinking about it.

I closed my eyes and tried thinking unsexy thoughts. My mind went back to that night at the gallery.

I had no idea what to expect when Harlem invited me to his gallery opening. Since my brother was married to his sister-in-law, it was inevitable that I'd be trapped into attending one of those hoity toity affairs where rich folks mingled and paid outrageous prices for art they couldn't understand.

Harlem's art was understandable, though… and if I could afford it, I'd have his work hanging all over my walls. I appreciated the invitation, but I never knew what to do with myself in those kinds of crowds. I was out of my element. I knew it the moment I showed up in jeans and a blazer while every other man in the room was wearing a suit.

"Man, I feel underdressed," I'd told Harlem the moment I found him in the crowd.

"Shit, I'm so ready to take this suit off and put my sweats back on," Harlem said with a laugh. "Hell, at least you're comfortable. I've gotten too used to running around with paint all over me."

I liked Harlem. He was one of the coolest brothas I knew. He was making more money than he could spend but he was still wearing the same sweatpants he got in high school. I once asked him why, and he told me he wasn't spending a bunch of money on some shit that was just gonna get paint all over it.

I could only respect that. His money was reserved for taking care of his beautiful family. His family was my family now, and I was hoping to convince Harlem to let me have a book signing in his spacious gallery when my next book dropped. We were actually working on a collaboration we hadn't told anyone about yet. My books, his paintings… each one would depict a scene from my book, with a part of the proceeds going to pay for a neighborhood playground in North Tulsa, where we both grew up.

"Yo…. you see that woman across the room? I think she's looking at you," Harlem said, nudging me with his elbow.

I followed his gaze and found myself locking eyes with the most beautiful woman I'd ever seen. Surely, she was looking at Harlem or some other well-dressed man in the vicinity. I turned my head. Harlem was gone. I was standing alone… and she was still looking.

When I saw a man aggressively vying for her attention, the discomfort on her face caused me to spring into action without hesitation. It was like me to intervene… my father instilled that kind of responsibility in me… but it wasn't like me to slow dance at an art show with no dance floor. It wasn't like me to sing to a woman as we danced… It wasn't like me to lose myself, but in that moment, I lost myself.

When she told me to take her home… my home… I obliged and then continued to lose myself inside of her eyes, her lips, her long supple legs, her cup ran over for me and I drank of her… gorged myself on her flesh… fed her from my hands… fell asleep in her arms, my face buried in her locs… my arms lacking when I woke up a few hours later… sans Windsor.

"Windsor," I said her name out loud and chuckled.

I woke up confused on the morning after, wondering if my late-night tryst had been a beautifully vivid dream. Had I tossed and turned so much that my sheets were completely pulled away from the bed… or had she really gripped them, holding on for dear life as I plunged into her over and over and over again? Had I eaten my antipasto tray alone in a drunken stupor… or had I really fed her from my hands as she sat naked in the middle of my bed?

I felt that tell-tale stirring in my loins again. I didn't have time to jack off, so I tried to think of anything other than Windsor as I hurriedly dressed, grabbed my backpack, and sprinted out the door.

My Uber was waiting, and as I climbed into the back seat, I noticed the driver staring at me with an odd expression on her face.

"You're heading to the airport? I just wanna confirm," she said.

"Yeah," I told her. "You don't have to rush. I've got plenty of time. My flight doesn't even board for three hours, but I'm flying standby so…"

"Ugh, I hate flying standby. Tulsa is so hard to get out of."

"Yeah, hopefully leaving on a Tuesday makes a difference."

"You work for the airline?" she asked.

Chatty Uber drivers usually annoyed me, but she seemed cool, and honestly, I could use the distraction.

"My cousin works for Delta and hooks me up from time to time," I told her, "I'm headed to a writer's conference in Philadelphia," I added before she had a chance to ask.

"And you're flying standby?"

I laughed, "I'm not a celebrity so no one is paying my airfare. I'm lucky I'm getting a room comped. I'm praying I sell enough books to cover my meals. Breakfast and a couple of dinners are covered, but I'm on my own for lunch and anything else I wanna do while I'm in town. I'd truly be a starving artist if I didn't have a job."

"So why do you do it?" she asked.

"I love it," I told her. "Words have always been easy for me. I understand words. Women on the other hand…" I let that hang in the air, surprised I'd even made mention of something so intimate… even if I didn't go into detail. "My bad," I told her. "I'm acting like this is Taxicab Confessions."

"Well," she said jokingly. "It can be, if you need it to be."

I took a deep breath and briefly caught her eye in the rearview.

"I met this woman at a gallery opening a few weeks ago. One thing led to another and now I can't get her off my mind. It's driving me nuts," I confessed, feeling lighter once I'd gotten it off my chest.

"Turned you out, huh?"

I laughed loudly and nodded in defeat. "I cannot tell a lie. She put it on me. She's tall, like a Supermodel, and she has these… locs that hang down to her waist, and her skin… oh my God, her skin… it's so dark… like Mother Africa birthed her to remind us how beautiful we are as a people. But more than that… she's… deep. Like, I want to get to know her on a spirit level… I wanna know if the things I saw in her are real or if it was just my imagination."

"What did you see in her?"

"Don't laugh."

"Never."

"I can't believe I'm saying this out loud," I chuckled. "I feel like I saw… her aura. Like…I'm not even into that shit but… I just saw these… bursts of red and I immediately knew I was seeing her energy. And I know she must believe in that shit because she had a black rock in her bra… labradore? Laborite?"

"Labradorite," the uber driver said as she nodded slowly. "And it's not a rock. It's a crystal.".

"Yeah! You're into that shit too? No offense. I didn't mean to call it shit."

"You got a little time?" she asked me.

"Yeahhhh," I said slowly.

"You mind if I pull over?"

I looked up and we were approaching the airport, but I still had a lot of time to spare. It should have felt weird… confiding in this woman, but it didn't. It felt normal… and that… in itself… was weird as hell.

"Sure, go ahead," I told her.

She pulled into the parking lot of the Radisson hotel and turned around to face me. She studied me for a moment and then began speaking to me as if she could see into the depths of my soul.

"You're gifted. When I look at you, I see purple energy with flecks of gold scattered here and there. You're creative, but you're sensitive. You absorb other

27

people's energy, and you have gifts you haven't even tapped in to. You're a great writer because you feel every emotion you put on paper," she revealed. "And, before you say it… I know you already told me you're a writer, but you know what I'm saying is true, don't you?"

I nodded.

"That wasn't the first time you've seen something in someone you were intimate with."

I nodded again. "About a year ago… I slept with a woman I'd been dating and saw… darkness. Like there was a black cloud hanging over her."

"How did you feel when you were with her?"

"Hopeless."

"What did you do?"

"I let her go. On my happiest days, one look from her had the power to suck all the positivity from my very bones."

"She hated you," she told me. "She was jealous of the things you wanted out of life. She had no aspirations of her own and didn't want you to have any either. Your misery made her happy. I'm glad you got away from her."

I stared at her in awe. She'd just told me, verbatim, every thought I ever had while dating Priscilla. She always seemed to revel in my defeat and usually found a way to make me feel bad about the good things happening in my life. It was so bad, that when we broke up, my sister-in-law came over and smudged my entire house with sage just in case my ex left any residual energy.

"I already know the answers to these questions, but I need to hear it from your mouth," she said thoughtfully.

"Shoot," I said, waiting for her to hit me with it.

"Are you married?"

"No."

"Do you have a girlfriend?"

"No."

"Boyfriend?"

"What?"

She held up her hands. "Hey, I have to ask."

"No," I laughed. "Not that there's anything wrong with that."

"Okay, is there anyone out there who *thinks* she's your girlfriend?"

"Really?"

She shrugged. "You know how men are."

She was right. It was a question that needed to be asked.

"No," I said emphatically. "No girlfriend, no fuck buddy, no nothing."

"You absolutely saw Windsor's aura," she said evenly. "But you were seeing her sexual energy, yours too. I saw the purple in her."

I blinked and jerked my head abruptly. "How do you know her name?"

She shrugged. "I picked her up from your house. Midway through the ride she asked me to turn around and take her back to you."

I leaned forward. "She did? Why didn't you?"

"She was being led by her sexual energy... and I saw something in her I wanted to protect," she said matter-of-factly, as if I should agree with what she just told me.

For some reason... I did.

"You're not being led by sexual energy. Not now anyway," she told me. "You're being led by something deeper, and I like it... I like you. I can't tell you her last name or where she lives... that would be intrusive. But if you want me to... I'll give her your number."

"You'll do that for me?"

"Absolutely. Now let's get you going. Your spot on the standby list is safe, by the way."

She pulled out of the parking lot and took me to departures. Before getting out of the car I made sure to give her one of my business cards.

"Don't forget to give me a good rating," she laughed as I closed the door, still in awe of our conversation.

I held up five fingers and smiled before opening my Uber app and giving her five stars. She deserved that and more.

Chapter 6

Windsor Elaine Bradley

She stood on my porch, peeking around me as if she were looking for something or someone other than me. I stared back curiously, wondering why the Uber driver who wouldn't take me back to Damian's house was standing in front of me when I hadn't ordered a ride. It was a little unnerving, and as I searched for words, she opened her eyes wide and tilted her head like, "Well, are you gonna let me in or what?" We hadn't even spoken yet, but I stepped aside and watched as she walked past me into my foyer.

I stood there, with my hand still on the open door, wondering what it was about this woman that allowed my trust to be given so easily. It wasn't like me to invite strangers into my home, but there was some small part of my brain that felt safe with her. Still, I needed to know what the hell she was doing at my house.

"I didn't order an Uber, and don't you guys usually wait in the car?" I asked, closing the door, and turning to face her.

"What were you doing?" she asked. I wasn't sure if she was purposely avoiding my question or if she caught sight of a shiny thing and got distracted as she looked around the foyer curiously.

"Come on," I sighed,

I led her to the basement door and slowly walked down the stairs with her following close behind.

"This is where you work?" she asked, looking around appreciatively.

"Yes. Welcome to Windsor Noire Enterprises. This is my home office, photography studio, soap factory, corporate headquarters, gym, you name it," I said, spreading my arms wide and pointing out different aspects of my space.

"You make soap?" she asked, staring at the rows and rows of multicolored soaps lining my shelves like books in a library.

"Yeah, I make soap, I take pictures of my soap, I sell my soap..." I laughed, "You want some?" I grabbed a freshly cut bar of sweet temptation, a jasmine scented soap made with milk and honey... a soothing blend that cleansed the skin while acting as an aphrodisiac whether you were bathing your lover or showering alone.

"Whoa...this smells..."

"Sexy?" I finished for her. "Yeah. All of my soaps make you feel sexy or... pretty...or free... like washing all your inhibitions away while giving yourself a layer of raw energy."

"You do this full time?"

"Yep, but you still haven't answered my question," I reminded her. "What are you doing here? Not that I mind, but... you don't find it a bit strange?"

"Oh, I almost forgot. I have something for you," she said, reaching into her purse.

"Did I leave something in your car?" I asked.

"Well, you could say that." She smiled as she handed me a business card. It was face down.

I flipped it over and gasped as I realized who it belonged to.

"You didn't!"

"I did."

"Damian Lawrence Anthony," I read aloud slowly, allowing his name to linger on my tongue like the last kiss we shared. I looked over at the Uber driver. "How did you get this?"

"He got an Uber this morning. I recognized the house and realized he must be the dude that had you squirming in your seat that night."

I laughed. "Your name is Malika, right?" I asked, hoping I remembered her name correctly.

"Yeah, but all my friends call me LeeLee. You can call me LeeLee." She smelled the soap again and smiled. "Well, my work here is done. I'd better get going."

"Aw naw, Sis." Now it was *my* turn to raise my eyebrows and cock my head to the side with my hands on my hips. "You gotta tell me how you got this man's business card." I grabbed her hand. "Come upstairs. I have a pizza in the oven. It should be ready by now."

"Ohhh, that's what I smelled when I walked in," she said. "I was wondering if you were gonna offer to feed me cuz it smells divine."

I playfully rolled my eyes and led her back upstairs into the kitchen where the timer on my stove was going off. I sliced the tomato basil pizza and set it down between us at the kitchen table. I watched as she took her first bite and closed her eyes in ecstasy.

"Right?" I asked with a grin.

"Girl, you can cook," she complimented me. "So, let me tell you about the conversation I had with Damian this morning…"

She told me what he said about me… how he wanted to get to know me on a deeper level and had thought of me constantly since the night we spent together. She told me she had just dropped him off at the airport, and that he was spending the week in Philly at a writer's conference.

"He's a writer," I mused.

"And you make soap," she said proudly, as if I was family.

"Yeah, I do," I said smiling back, trying to absorb all the information she just shared. He was a writer. He wasn't married. He didn't have a girlfriend, and he was yearning for me in more than a sexual way.

"He's different, Windsor," she told me. "He's not someone to play with."

It was a subtle warning. Now she sounded like she could have been *his* sister.

"I sensed that," I sighed. "Look, I have no problem admitting my original intentions." I shrugged. "But somewhere between riding the shit out of him and then… him burying his face in my hair and falling asleep in my arms… he felt different… inside of me… and more than a few men have been inside of me."

"What felt different?"

"I don't know… it felt like a transference of energy. Like every time he pushed inside of me… I don't know how to explain it. I felt naked."

"You *were* naked." She smirked.

"Noooo, I mean… like, I was *naked*. I did things with him I don't do with anyone else. I let my hair down. I exposed myself and he… he wasn't disgusted by me. He wasn't turned off or ready for me to go… that dude fed me from a fucking antipasto tray he made with his own two hands. He didn't treat me like a one-night stand, and I found it hard to keep treating him like one."

"That's why you snuck off," she said after swallowing another bite of pizza.

"I didn't know what to do with that… so I left it there." I took a sip of my wine and watched as LeeLee took a small sip of water. "I wanted to go back but you wouldn't take me," I reminded her jokingly.

"Trust me, that was the best thing I could have done for you. You were still in the afterglow of that… what did you call it? Devil dick?"

I laughed so hard wine came out of my nose and she tossed me a napkin.

"So, what are you gonna do, Sis?" she asked. "Seriously."

"What do you mean?"

"Are you gonna go get him?"

"In Philadelphia?" I asked with my face screwed up. "Chile, I was just gon' call him or… leave him a voicemail or text or something."

"I mean, I guess… if that's how you wanna play it. I just got a more adventurous vibe from you."

"You want me to fly all the way to Philly for some dick, LeeLee? Girl, are you crazy?"

"I want you to fly to Philly and get yo man, Sis. That's all."

I stared at her thoughtfully before saying, "Okay, hypothetically speaking…"

"Strictly hypothetical," she responded.

"Philadelphia is a huge city. I don't even know where he's staying."

"I googled him," she told me.

"Of course, you did," I sighed, throwing my hands up in defeat.

"He's at The Johnson Hotel. It's downtown… and he's a guest speaker at the Kobalt Writer's Association Authors Convention."

"You want me to—"

"He's actually speaking tomorrow at 5pm," she interrupted. "If you caught a flight tomorrow, you could make it there in time to hear him speak. I mean… you'd have to sneak into the ballroom, of course. Oh, I know. You can pretend you're his assistant and you're dropping off some notes he forgot."

I was impressed. She had it all figured out. It was crazy as hell but… I had to hand it to her. She was a great little schemer. I stared down at my empty plate as I twirled one of my locs around my finger. I couldn't believe I was actually sitting here, contemplating flying to another state to see a man I'd left hanging after seducing him for the hell of it.

"Southwest has a special going," she coaxed.

"Oh my God. Who are you?" I asked in exasperation. "Why are you trying to force this? You don't even know me!"

"I'm sorry," she sighed. "I just wanna see you win. Sis. This is exciting! It's not every day I get to be in the middle of a love story."

"LeeLee, this is hardly a love story," I said with a twist of my lips.

"Okay, whatever," she mumbled as if she knew something I didn't. "So… I'll pick you up around 8-ish tomorrow morning for your flight?"

"I ain't even checked for tickets yet," I hissed defensively.

LeeLee made a sweeping motion towards my phone. I begrudgingly picked it up and opened my Southwest app. Sure enough, there was a wide-open flight to Philly that started boarding at 10am. I had a strong feeling she already knew that.

"You want me to help you pick out something to wear?"

"I'm not doing this with you, Lee Lee," I told her.

"Are you sure? He looked really handsome this morning. You do remember what he looks like, don't you?"

I couldn't forget his handsome face if I tried. Images of his face plagued my dreams as I squeezed a pillow between my knees at night. I looked across the table at her. I wanted to slap the smirk off her face, but instead, I took a deep breath and said, "I'll see you at eight."

Chapter 7

Windsor Elaine Bradley

The hotel was fully booked, which was just as well. The shit was expensive, and if things went well, I'd be sleeping in Damian's room tonight... that is... if he didn't think I was a batshit crazy stalker who flew in all the way from Tulsa to see if his devil dick was still as dickmatizing as it was the first time I sat on it.

But I digress.

The attire for the dinner was formal, and Natalie, the sistah at the front desk, took pity on me and allowed me to take a quick hoe bath and get dressed in the employee bathroom. I didn't have time to fully beat my face, so I applied foundation, my favorite highlighter, and heavily lined my eyes, making them look even darker as my carefully applied eyelash extensions made up for my lack of eyeshadow. I added a nude gloss for effect and smiled at myself in the mirror.

I hoped he would approve of the long red dress I was wearing. The plunging neckline enhanced my breasts, showing just enough to tease, but not enough to cause a scandal. This dress was made for the red bottom heels I found at a consignment shop for ninety dollars. I loved nice things, but being on a budget taught me I didn't need to spend thousands of dollars on clothes when thrift stores and consignment shops existed.

My long locs were piled on top of my head in a mass of ringlets that took forever to form. I stayed up all night washing and conditioning my hair. LeeLee helped me finger part my hair into sections before twisting it into tight bantu knots. I sat under a hot ass hair dryer for almost three hours, and then, being paranoid about the curls falling throughout the day, I tied a scarf around my head and didn't take my hair down until the plane began making its descent into Philadelphia International Airport.

It was worth it just to see the look on Natalie's face when I walked out of the bathroom, looking nothing like the mess I was when I walked into the hotel lobby.

"Your boyfriend is going to freak out when he sees you," she told me. "You look stunning!"

"You don't think it's too much?" I asked, hoping I wasn't overdressed for the event.

"I just saw a few women walk in wearing ball gowns... they can't hold a candle to you," she told me. "I'll keep your bags locked in the closet and you can come get them later, okay?" she added with a wink.

"Thank you so much, you saved my life, truly," I said, handing her a gift bag with three of my special soaps. "I make these soaps and sell them online. Please accept this as a 'thank you' for what you did for me today."

"You make these?" she asked after smelling them. "You gotta tell me how to order more, cuz I'm not sharing these with my roommates."

"My card is in the bag, Sis," I said with a wave as I made my way to the ballroom.

I walked in alone, unchecked by the watchdogs at the entrance. I hadn't even needed to use the elaborate lie LeeLee and I came up with on our way to the airport. I looked like I belonged there, even stopping to take a few pictures on the red carpet before finally walking into the ballroom and making my way to the open bar. Tables started filling up and I stood there, lemon drop martini in hand, watching until it became evident which seats had been reserved by no-shows. I made my way to the closest empty chair and asked the couple sitting there if the seats were taken. They seemed completely unbothered as I sat down and discreetly licked the sugar from the rim of my martini glass.

"How are you enjoying the conference so far?" the gentleman sitting next to me asked.

"Can I tell you a secret?" I asked, leaning in, and lowering my voice.

"Sure, you can," he said, grinning from ear to ear.

"I'm here to surprise my boyfriend," I told him. "He has no idea I'm coming. I told him I couldn't make it... but I didn't think things through. Him thinking I wasn't gonna be here means he has no plus one." I lowered my voice a little more. "I'm afraid I won't be able to sit with him and it's breaking my heart. I'm trying to figure out how to get his attention."

"Who is your boyfriend?" he asked curiously, tapping his wife on the shoulder so she could listen.

"Damian Anthony," I whispered with a giggle, almost believing my own lie. Actually, I wasn't even going to call it a lie... more like a... manifestation. I was speaking Damian into my existence.

"Oh, he's very handsome," his wife said sweetly. "And a really nice guy. What's your name, sweetie? I'm friends with the organizer of this event. The only reason we're sitting in the back is because I hate sitting so close to the sound system. It gives me a migraine. I'll be right back, let me see if I can get you closer."

Are you fucking kidding me?

Things were falling into place so smoothly it was almost scary. I watched as the woman walked over to a tall brotha in a tux and began speaking excitedly while glancing over at me from time to time. She pointed me out and I raised my hand timidly. The man she was talking to stared at me from across the room.

There was something about the way he looked at me. He knew I didn't belong there. I knew the jig was up, and as he walked towards me, I braced myself for the embarrassment of being escorted out of such an elaborate event.

"Hello, Miss?"

"Bradley. Windsor Bradley," I extended my hand and he grasped it firmly before motioning for me to stand up.

"Nice to meet you, Miss Bradley," he said, still grasping my hand. "I'm Cedric Mixon, president of Kobalt Books and Entertainment, come walk with me and we'll find you a seat."

"Seems like a nice event," I said, making small talk as we walked to the rear of the room, out of earshot of anyone else.

"We both know you're crashing the party, Windsor Bradley," he looked at me with a knowing expression. "It's really funny too. I know your last name and Damian... he has no idea."

I wondered how much this Cedric person knew about my night with Damian, but I was afraid to ask for fear of further exposing myself. A strikingly beautiful sistah with long, dark curly hair approached and tapped Cedric on the shoulder.

"There you are, babe, it's about to start. You have to introduce the keynote speaker," she said with a smile, while looking at me curiously.

"Honey, guess who this is?" Cedric made a dramatic motion towards me and I tried to look unbothered.

I was failing.

"Who?" she asked.

"Tell her who you are," Cedric said with a smirk on his face.

I extended my hand slowly, silently cursing this man who seemed hellbent on making a mockery of my presence. "Hi, I'm Windsor," I said cautiously.

"No way!" She looked over at her husband in shock, and then turned her attention back to me. "You're Windsor? *The* Windsor?"

"He's talked about me?" I asked hesitantly, inwardly cringing, hoping they hadn't been given the wrong impression of me.

37

I was relieved to see a huge grin on her face.

"Oh my God! Damian kept going on and on about you over dinner. Honestly, I was beginning to think you were a figment of his imagination," she said sweetly. "So, *you're* Windsor, no last name."

"Bradley," I extended my hand again, and she grasped it with both of hers. "Windsor Bradley, party crasher, as your husband so eloquently pointed out."

"Girl, don't pay him any attention. I'm Holly and you're sitting with us," she said, hooking her arm through mine. "I can't wait to see the look on his face when he sees you," she added as Cedric stood there laughing.

It became obvious he had no intention of throwing me out. He just wanted to make me sweat a little. I felt like Damian painted me in a positive light, so I relaxed a tad as Holly led me to their table... directly in front of the stage.

Nerves couldn't possibly describe the butterflies in my stomach as I waited for Damian to enter the room and take his place at the podium. According to the program I was holding, Damian Lawrence Anthony penned his critically acclaimed novel, *Three First Names*, while sitting at a job he hated.

I was impressed. I'd never heard of Damian Lawrence Anthony, never read his critically acclaimed book, never imagined he was as revered in this space as he'd been ignored in the space where I met him. If I had any reservations, any regrets, any thoughts of pushing my chair back and running for the door, they disappeared the moment I saw him cross the stage and take his place at the podium.

He looked so... confident. So sure, so... in control of, not only himself, but every person in that ballroom. They were listening intently to every word he spoke.

He was an animated speaker, full of life, full of jokes, full of entertaining anecdotes that kept the audience laughing as he gave a speech I could barely concentrate on, because I was too busy admiring how sexy he looked wearing a traditional black tux.

I stared at him, willfully sending telepathic signals to him. I needed to lock eyes with him to confirm I hadn't made a mistake by coming here on a peer pressure fueled whim. I wanted my presence to make a difference... in a good way. Wanted him to notice me sitting there and smile as if he'd been waiting his entire life for this moment.

And then I was staring into his eyes, praying he was as happy to see me as I was to see him. Damian stumbled over his words. Momentarily losing his place, he apologized to the audience as he glanced down at his notes. A sneaky smile appeared on his lips before he continued speaking.

I could feel heat rising from my neck to my chin and I wondered if anyone else could see the blush taking over my face.

I glanced over at Holly and Cedric. They were staring at me with knowing smirks on their faces. I smiled, not caring who saw the way his reaction affected me. The most popular guy in the room was happy to see me. If this was the only interaction Damian and I had the entire rest of the weekend… it was worth it.

The sound of deafening applause snapped me out of my reverie. I watched as Damian walked off the stage and disappeared behind a curtain. I wanted to go after him, but uncharacteristic nervousness kept me rooted to my seat.

"You okay?" Cedric asked me.

"She will be in five, four, three, two, oh, hey, Damian. You did a great job, didn't he, Windsor Bradley?" Holly said sneakily, looking above my head.

I stood and turned just in time to see Damian approaching in slow motion. The program I'd been holding in my hand fluttered to the ground as he stood in front of me with a happy, yet puzzled smile on his face.

"You found me," he whispered, kissing me before I had a chance to respond.

It was just as well. I was at a complete loss for words, and I'd been dreaming of this kiss since the last time I kissed him. Now it was his turn to blush as he realized the continuous, thunderous applause was now a reaction to the deeply passionate kiss we had yet to break.

I don't remember anything about dinner. They could have been serving beanie weenie and it would have tasted like Oklahoma Style Barbecue as long as Damian was sitting beside me and holding my hand beneath the table.

The water in my glass was more hydrating, my wine tasted sweeter, the music sounded more intoxicating as dinner ended and the dance floor began filling up with a bunch of fancy folks gyrating to the beat. Damian took my hand and led me out of the ballroom, pausing to pose with me on the makeshift red carpet before pulling me into a secluded corner and kissing me again.

"Twenty Questions," he whispered once we came up for air.

"Yes or no," I responded.

"Have you done this before?"

"No," I answered breathlessly. "Does that turn you on?"

"Yes," he told me. "Can I kiss you again?"

"Yes."

"Where are you staying?" he asked between kisses.

"With you."

I didn't know enough about this man to be making out with him in a hotel lobby like a horny teenager on prom night, yet there I was, all hugged up in the corner, looking around but not really caring if anyone saw me.

"I need to get my bags, they're holding them for me," I told him.

I grabbed his hand and led him to the front desk. Natalie, the young lady who so graciously allowed me to use the staff bathroom, smiled approvingly the moment she saw me holding hands with Damian.

"I see you found your man," she said with a subtle wink.

"Will you please send up some of that double chocolate cake and a bottle of red wine?" Damian asked as she wheeled my luggage from behind the counter.

"Absolutely," she said. "As a matter of fact, why don't I just have someone bring up the luggage as well? What room are you in, Sir?"

I was impressed when Damian casually rattled off a room number on one of the executive floors. He led me to the elevators where we waited impatiently for the doors to open. Our silent prayers were answered when no one boarded with us, leaving us alone as the elevator made a slow ascent to our floor. Oddly, we weren't touching. We just stood there, leaning against opposite ends of the elevator, staring at one another in disbelief as we stared at our own reflections in the mirrored walls.

My lip gloss was a distant memory. I licked my lips slowly, not trying to be seductive, but loving the way he licked his own as if he couldn't wait to taste mine again. I could feel a smoldering fire sparking at my toenails and slowly rolling over my ankles as it leisurely made its way up my thighs until the flames settled between my tightly closed legs.

The dripping moisture in my thong acted as an accelerant, feeding the fire, causing it to spread to my stomach, fanning upwards until it settled in my eyes. I couldn't stop looking at him. He must have seen it, the burning flames, the desire, because he held out his hand in an invitation to join him on his side of the elevator as his other hand hovered above the "stop" button.

"Have you ever?" I asked as he slid one arm around my waist, pulling me close enough to feel his beautiful erection poking me through my dress. The slit in my dress was dangerously high, it would be so easy to slide his hand over my thigh and pull my thong to the side if only he had the nerve to push that button.

"Have you?"

I bit my lip and shook my head.

I had *never*… but I wanted to.

I slid my hands down to his zipper and slowly unzipped his pants before pulling him out and wrapping my fingers around him. He inhaled sharply and slammed his hand against the stop button. A shrill bell sounded, and a loud voice came over an intercom, "Do you need assistance?"

We both jumped.

"Naw, my bad. I accidentally leaned against the button." Damian said hurriedly as I buried my face in his neck, trying desperately to quiet my laughter.

The elevator started up again and we burst out laughing as I tucked him back into his pants and zipped him up. We were still laughing when the doors opened on his floor.

I hugged him from behind as he fumbled with the card key, pressing my breasts against his back, and whispering all the nasty things I wanted to do with him once he got that damn door open. The door wasn't open two seconds before his hands were on me, his fingers caressing my exposed thigh as I lifted my leg until my knee was resting on his hip.

There was an urgency in the way he tugged at my thong, but the fabric was durable. Seeing that he couldn't tear it off, he deftly pulled it to the side just as I pulled him out of his pants. I jumped into his arms and wrapped my legs around his waist as he slid inside of me.

I was suspended in the air as Damian gripped my ass, holding me tightly as he lifted me up and down, slowly at first, as if he were curling a heavy set of weights. He curled me.... up and down... down and up... gradually increasing his rhythm as I held onto him with no fear of falling.

He slowly walked us over to the bed where he gently sat down on the edge, being careful not to lose our intimate connection as he gripped me tighter, grinding me against him, and kissing me to drown out my screams of pleasure.

My breath quickened as I felt an intense pulsating sensation. He continued thrusting upwards, not being careful with me at all. He was, theoretically, beating the pussy up, and I was doing my darndest to match his intensity. The first orgasmic wave took me by surprise, and I bit his shoulder to keep from screaming out. That was his cue to hit it harder, faster, stroking me with a raw determination that made me want to give him everything I had. I wanted to do things for him I'd never done for anyone else... things I couldn't even pronounce. I wanted to open the Kama Sutra and perform every position with absolutely no regard for anything but the way he felt inside of me.

"Oh my god, I wish you could just hold me in your lap and fuck me every day," I whispered aggressively as I grinded on him.

"You like that shit, don't'cha," he slid his hands through my carefully crafted high bun, watching as a mass of curls cascaded down my back. He grabbed a handful of my locs and gently pulled my head back, exposing my neck and nibbling gently as he fucked me harder. The stark contrast in the multiple ways he was managing to handle me turned me on in a way I couldn't even explain.

My eyes rolled to the back of my head as I came again, gushing all over his lap until I was slipping and gliding against him like his dick was the big slide at a waterpark. Damian's body tensed up and I knew it was my turn to control the rhythm. He gripped my thighs in an ill-fated attempt to slow me down, but I gyrated my pelvis against his in a winding motion, moving faster and faster as I felt his body trembling.

He buried his face in my hair and wrapped his arms around me, holding me close, locking me in place and keeping me from moving in the slightest. We sat that way, wrapped up in each other's arms until his hardness slowly began to lose its position within my swollen walls. My body reluctantly released him, and I felt a huge sense of loss as he lifted me up and off his lap, gently placing me on the bed beside him.

There was a knock at the door and Damian pulled his pants up before going to answer it. My dress was bunched up around my hips and I walked into the bathroom where I swiftly undressed and braided my hair into two long ponytails before stepping into the glass shower.

I turned the water on full blast, as hot as I could stand it, and stood there with my eyes closed as the water washed over me like a sexy baptism, rinsing me clean of all traces of Damian, but leaving the pulsating sensation between my legs as a not-so-subtle reminder of the devil dick that had me screaming in pleasure. He slid in behind me and I leaned backwards into him as he kissed my shoulder.

"That was your luggage." He lifted my hair and kissed the back of my neck. "And our cake." He turned me around to face him and I snaked my arms around his neck as he kissed me and said, "And our wine."

"Mmmm," I murmured as he dipped his head and began suckling my left breast while his fingers held my right breast in the palm of his hand, squeezing gently. I took a step backwards, finding myself sandwiched between Damian and the shower wall as hot water poured all over our naked bodies.

"You see that shower bench behind us," he mumbled against my breast.

"uh huh," I whispered.

He lifted his head, put his face close to mine and said seductively, "Go sit down over there… facing me."

He backed away from me as I walked over to the bench. I gasped as an unexpected showerhead rained down on me from above. I sat down and watched as he got on his knees in front of me.

"I've been dreaming about eating your pussy for three weeks," he said as he put his hands between my knees and parted my legs like Moses parting the pink sea.

I was completely exposed, and as he buried his face between my thighs, I leaned back against the wall and put my feet on his shoulders, letting my knees fall to the side as I opened up to him like a flower to a honeybee.

"You taste so good," he whispered against my clit as he licked me with the broad strokes of a painter putting the finishing touches on his greatest masterpiece.

It didn't take long to make me cum, and as he looked up at me with a big grin on his face, I couldn't tell if his face was glistening from my juices or from the water in the shower. He sat next to me on the bench and held onto my ponytails, guiding my head up and down as I leaned over his lap and wrapped my lips around his dick, sliding my mouth up and down on it, damn near swallowing it as it hit the back of my throat before sliding my hands down the shaft to control the depth of his involuntary thrusts.

Unlike the first time I licked and sucked him, I didn't stop when I felt his body tense up. I continued stroking him with my mouth, even as he tried to pull me away.

"Ohhhh shit!" he yelled loudly, spreading his arms, and bracing against the shower walls as the inevitable pumped out of him and slid down my throat.

I kept going, the suction of my lips pulling him in as far as he could go while my tongue swirled around and around like I was enjoying a juicy popsicle. I kept going until he had to literally grab me and pull me off his dick. He leaned back against the wall and threw an arm over his face, breathing heavily, his body jerking as if he was having aftershocks from the seismic head he'd just received.

"Damn, girl," he said breathlessly. "Got damn, got damn, got *damn*."

I was still sitting between his legs, catching shower water in my mouth, and playfully spitting it at him as he smiled down at me with eyes so glazed over, he looked like he'd just hit a blunt.

"You're bad," he said with a chuckle.

"You like that shit, don't'cha?" I laughed watching as his tremors lessened and his curled toes slowly relaxed.

"Hell yeah." He put his hand on the back of my head and drew me to him, sliding his tongue inside of my mouth as he kissed me passionately. "Thank you for *cumming*," he whispered provocatively. "And thank you for coming too," he added in a gentler tone as he pulled away to stare into my eyes. "Looking out into the audience and seeing you sitting there… I wish I could fold that feeling up and put it in my pocket so I can carry it with me and take it out when the world feels like it's crashing down around me."

"I was so scared," I admitted.

"You? Scared? Scared of what? Scared of me?"

"I was scared you would think I was crazy," I laughed.

"A little crazy never hurt nobody," he told me with a smile. "I'm curious though. What brought you here?" He pulled me into his lap and held me like I was the most precious thing in his world. I lay my head on his shoulder, loving the way his arms felt around me as water washed over us from multiple angles.

"LeeLee stopped by and told me all yo business," I told him.

He started laughing and held me tighter. "She's extremely insightful. For some reason, she sees something in us that… I don't know… transcends all practicality and reason."

He was right. I had the same feeling when talking to LeeLee. I didn't really know her, but I felt like she knew me. She knew the me *I* didn't even know yet.

"What do we do with this, Windsor Bradley?" he asked, intertwining his fingers with mine and kissing the back of my hand.

"I don't know, Damian Anthony," I replied.

I closed my eyes and allowed myself the luxury of fully relaxing in his arms, sinking into him, and letting him swallow me up within his embrace. My body was exhausted. All the preparation and anxiety over this trip was finally catching up with me. I'd embarked on this adventure blindly. I had no idea what would happen when he saw me. Now I was here, in his arms, in his lap, in his shower while he held me like a baby.

I didn't wanna move.

"Don't fall asleep," he whispered. "We have cake."

"Cake," I opened my eyes and kissed the side of his neck. "And wine."

"And questions," he said softly. "So many questions…"

I lifted my head and looked at him, before slowly saying, "I'm sorry I left the way I did."

"I wasn't mad, just… confused," he said seriously. "When I woke up and you were gone… I kept staring at the empty space next to me and wondering if it had all been a dream. Why did you leave without saying goodbye?"

"You made me feel special. I was afraid you'd look at me… differently when you woke up. I didn't want to ruin the experience with introspection and regret."

"Did you regret it?"

I shook my head, no.

"You came all the way to Philly for me." There was a measure of happiness in his voice that I'd never experienced a man directing towards me.

I smiled. Hearing him say it out loud really put things into perspective for me. I hadn't come to Philly for his dick or his hugs or his kisses… I'd come to Philly for *him*… for Damian… and it didn't feel as crazy as it would probably look to someone on the outside looking in.

"Twenty questions," he said softly.

"Am I the only one?" I asked, praying his answer wouldn't have me immersing myself in a river of lies if I decided I couldn't let him go. LeeLee assured me he was single, but I needed to hear it from him.

"Yes, and it will stay that way… as long as I'm the only one," he answered, cleverly sliding another question into the conversation.

"There's only you," I told him. "As long as there's only me."

"I don't need anyone else," he told me. "I don't know how I know that… but it's true."

I didn't know how I knew it either, but oddly enough, I wasn't scared of it.

Chapter 8

Damian Lawrence Anthony

She was wide awake, standing naked in the window as the moonlight bathed her skin, giving it a sexy blue glow. She'd taken her hair down, letting it hang to her waist, brushing against the tops of her round hips as she stood there, arms folded, face looking up at the stars as if she were asking the cosmos a serious question. I joined her at the window, following her gaze, trying to see what she was seeing. I saw a bright moon, I saw a light sprinkling of stars, I saw darkness.

"I didn't ask you the most important question," she whispered nervously, for the first time, appearing vulnerable and unsure of herself in my presence.

"What question is that?" I asked, placing a hand on her cheek, and urging her to look at me.

"Remember that first night?" she began. "You asked if I'd ever done that before."

"You said, yes," I remembered.

"Have you?" she asked.

"Yes," I said truthfully.

"Ok, so… I said, 'yes' but… that was only partly true," she sighed softly and turned her gaze upward again, staring at the moon like she was silently willing it to perform a miracle. "I've never not been… careful, Damian. We weren't careful. I don't know why I'm just now thinking about that. I've never been so caught up in the moment I haven't used protection. Not ever. Have you?"

Her confession gave me pause. I was also usually more careful than I'd been with her. That first night… I hadn't even hesitated at the thought of sliding inside of her completely bare. I was so overwhelmed by my need for her, protecting myself… protecting *her*, hadn't even crossed my mind. I thought of the past few hours with her… on the bed… on the couch… in the shower… on the bed again…

"I don't want you to think I'm just out here in these streets fucking every man I meet," she told me. "I'm not. I mean... I know I'm a free spirit and I run around with crystals in my bra, but I never intended to... do so much with you. For what it's worth after the fact, I got tested about a month ago at this HIV/AIDS awareness symposium I was vending at. They were offering free tests and I figured, 'what the hell? might as well,' ya know? It was negative by the way... and I haven't been with anyone but you since that test."

I didn't realize I'd been holding my breath until I exhaled louder than I intended to. I knew my status. I'd had a full STD panel about six months ago... after finding out my ex-girlfriend cheated on me a few times. We'd already been apart for several months, and she told me there was nothing to worry about, but I needed to know for sure... for my own peace of mind.

"I'm negative too," I assured her. "I can show you my results. I keep them in my wallet to remind me to be careful."

"A lot of good that did," she said jokingly.

It was good to see her worry replaced by a smile. I turned on a bedside lamp and got my wallet. I pulled a folded piece of paper from behind my driver's license and handed it to her. She held it in her hand for a moment before unfolding it and releasing a relieved sigh of her own.

"My purse is on the nightstand. Will you hand it to me?" she asked, handing my results back to me.

I refolded my test and placed it back in my wallet before going to get her purse. I handed it to her and watched as she pulled out a swanky lady's wallet with L's and V's all over it.

"Fancy," I said observantly.

"Trust me, it's old," she laughed. "My accountant would have a fit if I spent all my money on fancy shit, but I like nice things. I do a lot of shopping at thrift stores and consignment shops."

I was relieved in more ways than one. The hotel had comped me a beautiful suite, but on Tuesday I was going to be sitting in an airport praying they called my name and didn't bump me from my flight home. I hoped she wouldn't be too disappointed when she found out I was just another starving artist who needed an actual 9-5 to survive.

"Here it is," she exclaimed, pulling a folded piece of paper out of her wallet and handing it to me.

As expected, she'd had an STD panel done a month ago and her results were negative. We were both disease free, but today alone, we'd had the wildest unprotected sex I'd ever had in my life... several times. The reality was... there could be a baby inside of her right now if she wasn't on some form of birth control.

"Do you think there's a chance you're pregnant?" I asked hesitantly.

"Maybe we should come up for air long enough to talk about a few things," she suggested.

She was right. We needed to know more about one another. A *lot* more. We weren't going to be able to cover everything in one night, but we needed to at *least* break ground before we started laying the foundation of a relationship with someone we only knew biblically.

It seemed strange to think of building with a woman I barely knew... but I've never been the kind of man that needed a bunch of women. My father was a one-woman man and his example shaped me into the man I am today. I'd had my fair share of one-night stands, but once I decided I was truly interested in a woman... I was all in.

I looked at the clock, it was a little after midnight. I didn't need to be downstairs until eleven for the workshops, panels, and autograph sessions, but I did have an early morning meeting with Cedric.

"Did you bring pajamas?" I asked her.

"I sleep naked," she admitted. "I just figured I wouldn't need any," she added, almost shyly.

"There's a pajama party on the last night of the conference," I told her. "But we'll go shopping. In the interim... put this on." I handed her a pair of my boxer shorts and a wife beater.

She put them on, and my dick immediately hardened. I hadn't expected her to look so... cute. The way my boxers hung on her in contrast with the way her breasts stretched the top of my undershirt had to be the sexiest thing I'd ever seen.

"Here," I said, trying to think unsexy thoughts as I tossed her a hotel robe. "We need to have a question answer session and... I won't be able to concentrate if you're looking all... sexy and shit."

"Well, since we're keeping it real," she quipped. "Maybe you should cover ya dick before I sit on it."

She looked down at my crotch and I could do nothing to hide my erect penis, standing straight out like Pinocchio's nose after telling several lies.

I grabbed a pair of pajama bottoms from a drawer and turned my back to her as I slipped them on. She followed me into the living room where I put water in the Keurig, making us both a large cup of coffee as she got comfortable in a corner of the couch. I handed her a mug before sitting at the opposite end of the couch, staring at her as she took a tiny sip.

"Could you be pregnant?" I asked again, finding it easier to dive right in instead of hem-hawing around and acting shy about the things we needed to know about one another.

"No," she said looking me in the eye.

"You're positive?" I asked.

She paused, a thoughtful look on her face. I could tell she was struggling with something. I gave her a moment to figure out what she wanted to say and how she wanted to say it.

"I can't have children," she finally said. "I had a hysterectomy a few years ago," she explained.

"Do you have any kids?" I asked softly.

She smiled sadly and slightly hesitated before shaking her head. "No," she said simply.

She clapped softly, as if to jar herself out of a painful memory, and then smiled at me. "What about you? Do you have kids?"

"I have a little boy," I told her. "His name is Daniel. He's an only child and the first grandchild on both sides so…"

She laughed, genuinely. "Spoiled?"

"Rotten," I laughed. "But he really is the best little boy. He lives in Dallas with his mama and his step-father."

I grabbed my phone and showed her my lock screen. Daniel stared back at her with a twinkle in his eye and a smile that screamed "cheese."

She smiled, tracing a finger over his face. "How old is he?"

"He's four."

"He's been here before," she said softly.

"Yes, he has," I agreed. "He's an old soul."

"He's beautiful," she said. "He looks just like you."

"That's my little sidekick," I said proudly. "I talk to him every day. I try my best to see him every other weekend. His mama and I… it didn't work out, but we have a good relationship. You don't have to worry about baby mama drama. I don't even refer to her that way. She's my son's mother. We're actually really good friends… her husband too."

"What happened?" she asked curiously.

It was a simple question with a complicated answer. Felicia and I got along very well, but there was something missing in our relationship. Neither one of us could explain it. We just knew we weren't destined to be together. We loved one another but we weren't *in* love. Our breakup was a mutual agreement, each one of us relieved the other felt the same way. Two months later she found out she was pregnant. We toyed with the idea of getting back together, but neither one of us wanted to raise our baby in a home with two parents just going through the motions. He deserved more than that. We deserved more than that. We decided we were better at being friends.

Windsor listened as I explained, nodding her understanding. She seemed relieved there was no chance of Felicia and I getting back together. Felicia got married two years ago, and she never looked at me the way I've seen her look at him… the way Windsor looked at me when I was giving my speech.

I never looked at Felicia the way I'm looking at Windsor now.

"Sometimes I feel guilty for chasing this dream," I confided in her. "Before Daniel came along… I was only responsible for myself. I wasn't in the right financial situation to have kids. I chose a career that causes me to struggle if I'm not careful. I'm not starving. I have a full-time job and I do a lot of freelance work, but I can't give Daniel everything I want him to have. I can't give him more than I had growing up… not right now."

"Kids don't always need more than we had," she told me. "They just need love and understanding... and two parents who want to give them the best without giving them too much. Don't get caught up in trying to give him the world."

"You sound like Felicia," I chuckled.

"Well, she must be very smart," Windsor told me.

"Did you want kids?" I asked gently.

She nodded. "I don't like to talk about it. You think you have time… until you don't."

Something in her way her voice slightly cracked told me not to push. She wasn't ready to tell me. I had to respect that.

"You should know," she said, her voice suddenly perking up, "I'm forty."

Forty? Where? I was a little ashamed to admit it… but I thought Windsor was late twenties, early thirties at the most… forty? I felt like I needed to see her driver's license to make sure she wasn't lying to me. Was forty going to be a problem for me? Hell naw.

"I'm thirty-nine," I told her.

"Are you serious?" she asked, obviously shocked.

"How old did you think I was?" I asked laughingly.

"Late twenties, maybe thirty," she admitted. "I know, I know… I was prepared to be a cougar."

"Ahhhhh, so you thought you were gonna turn a young whipper snapper out and then disappear," I laughed teasingly.

"I did," she retorted.

"You got me," I laughed. I took a long sip of my coffee before adding, "You got turned out too, though."

"How do you figure?"

"Girl, you hopped a last-minute flight from Tulsa to Philly to get this dick… don't play."

I ducked as she threw a couch pillow at me.

"You stuttered when you saw me," she said.

"I was shocked," I said seriously. "You were the last person I expected to see sitting at my table. I thought I was dreaming at first... that dress... oh my god... you just looked so beautiful. I couldn't wait to finish talking so I could touch you again."

"My age doesn't bother you?" she asked.

"It's only a year, Windsor. You're hardly a cougar... although I did like the way you pounced on me when we got to the room."

The thought of holding her up in the air as I fucked her immediately made my loins tingle, and this time, I didn't try to calm myself down.

"I didn't know you were so strong," she crawled across the couch and straddled me, leaning forward until her titties were in my face.

The conversation was over. There was no way I could talk with a nipple in my mouth anyway. I slid my hand inside the boxers she was wearing, marveling at the way she stayed wet for me. All I had to do was look at her a certain way, say a certain thing, touch a certain place... and she was ready. I slid one, then two, then three fingers inside of her while gently caressing her clit with my thumb. She twisted and gyrated against my fingers, riding them like a dick, moaning in my ear as I fingered her faster, rubbed her more vigorously until she came all over my hand.

She was shivering as I picked her up and carried her to the bed, this time laying her down and slowly sliding the boxers down her long legs before sitting her up just long enough to pull my tank top over her head. I slid her locs through the shirt, being careful not to pull them too hard as the tank top slid away and onto the floor. The lamp was still on. She reached over to turn it off, but I grabbed her hand, kissing her fingers one by one before ridding myself of my pajama bottoms.

"Leave the lights on," I said, looking down at her as she writhed beneath my gaze. "Like the first time... when you wouldn't let me close my eyes... I don't want you to close yours. I want you to see me when I make love to you."

Her eyes grew wide as I gently spread her legs, lingering above her, unwavering as I studied her... the anticipation in her eyes, the way her lips parted, the sheer magnitude of passion in her expression as she waited for me to slide between her legs and fill her up until her juices runneth over.

I entered her tenderly, carefully draping my body over hers as if she were a porcelain doll and any sudden move would break her. It was nothing like the way I'd entered her before... abruptly, swiftly, pounding her with an intensity that caused her entire body to inch further into the headboard. This was different. It was gentle. It was loving. It was... soothing. I felt a tranquility within her body that almost brought tears to my eyes. Never in my life had I felt so calm while a beautiful woman's legs were wrapped around me. Looking into her eyes, I knew she felt it too. Knew she felt the serenity.

She reached out to me, holding my face in the palms of her hands, pulling me towards her and kissing me slowly as I stroked her in rhythms my ancestors must have composed while staring into the night sky and admiring the universe. Slow drumbeats that told the story of … strangers … taking the kind of chances reserved for wandering spirits in search of a passion that can't be found on earth.

The chaos within my mind dissipated the moment she swallowed me up within her sacred walls. Being inside of her was like church.

It was spiritual.

She was my peace.

I was saved.

Chapter 9

Windsor Elaine Bradley

Last night was… different.

It was beautiful.

It was tranquil.

It was… loving.

It was scary.

I was scared, but I was also fascinated by the thoughts and feelings being with Damian were invoking within my scattered mind.

He made love to me.

I loved fucking him.

I loved being fucked *by* him, but in the wee hours of the morning… he made *love* to me and I couldn't make sense of the confusing signals passing from my pussy to my heart to my brain.

Dick wasn't supposed to have this effect on me.

I mean… I've had some good dick in my lifetime.

I've been around for forty years. I can get good dick when I can't get anything else. That's an indisputable fact.

So why was this particular dick making me weak?

It wasn't like he was my boyfriend… at least I didn't think he was. We hadn't had the whole, 'what are we and what are we doing?' conversation yet. I just knew that whatever we were and whatever we were doing… we were only doing it with each other. We made that abundantly clear yesterday.

Sexual exclusivity.

I leaned back against the fluffy pillows and closed my eyes, allowing my mind to travel back to our lovemaking.

I thought I saw tears in his eyes. It could have been perspiration, but there was something about the way he looked at me. Something about the way he said my name as an intense orgasm made him shudder… had him clinging to me.

He hadn't said my name before… not during sex.

I never said his name, not because it wasn't on the tip of my tongue, but because I mustered just enough control to kiss him every time I wanted to say it.

Every time I wanted to say, 'Damian'.

His name would form on my lips and I would swallow it with a kiss, allowing his tongue to push his name to the back of my throat.

I wanted to kiss him now, but he was downstairs having an impromptu early morning meeting with his publisher. I was in the room alone, trying to find the strength to get into the shower and get dressed. He wanted me to come down for breakfast and there was a book signing after lunch. I told him I'd help him set up.

He told me to dress casually so I followed his lead, making note of the jeans and blazer he'd been wearing when he left our room. I chose a long-sleeved denim shirt with an orange front slit tulip skirt. I dressed it down with a pair of white chucks because I knew I'd be on my feet. I loved my Converse and had several pairs in a variety of colors… each with a gel insert tucked inside. Chucks were cute, but they weren't an '*on your feet all day*' type of shoe.

I was just about to head downstairs when my phone started ringing. It was my mama.

Shit.

I hadn't told her I was leaving town.

"Girl, where the hell are you?" she asked as soon as I picked up.

"Hi, mommy," I said apologetically.

My mama and I spoke at least once a day. I'd been gone for over twenty-four hours without calling or texting her. I wasn't her only child, but I was the child she could joke with and vent to. She got on my nerves every now and then with her common sense and shit, but… you know… that's what mamas do.

"What are you doing, daughter?" she asked. "I'm not trying to get in your business, but I usually hear from you by now. Either you're really busy or you're really happy… which one is it?"

"Mama, come on. I call you when I'm happy," I told her.

"You know what I mean. When I don't hear from you for a few days… I worry."

I laughed, "First of all, it's only been one day. Second of all… you *are* trying to get in my business. It's what you do best. I've been grown for a long time. You don't have to worry about me."

Now it was her turn to laugh, but there was still a little worry in her voice.

"Mama, I saw this meme on Facebook the other day that made me think of you. I was gonna send it to you, but I got sidetracked."

"What did it say?"

"It said, '*there's nothing messier than a woman on the phone with her youngest daughter*'."

Mama let out a half shriek, half cackle kind of laugh, and I could picture her vigorously shaking her left shoulder as tears sprang to her eyes. I knew she'd probably call my Aunt Lee a little later and tell her about our conversation while loudly saying, "and girl, I whooped!"

I cracked up laughing with her. That meme summed us up so well I was almost triggered by it. My mama and I talked about anything, everything, and everybody. Our vent sessions were therapeutic for both of us.

"So, what have you been up to?" she asked after our laughter died down.

"Well, actually... I'm in Philly right now."

The phone went eerily silent.

"Hello?" I said. "Mama? Are you there? Did she hang up?"

"Can you hear me now? Girl, this damn phone, I done hit the damn mute button with my face. Can you pick me up a chicken philly?"

"What?"

"You're at Phat Philly's, right?"

I snickered. Phat Philly's was a local restaurant that served cheesesteaks and such.

"I'm not at Phat Philly's... I'm *in* Philly," I told her. "I got here yesterday."

"Philadelphia?" she asked in shock. "PENNSYLVANIA? What? Did you score last minute tickets to a Steelers game or something?"

"I'm boycotting the NFL," I reminded her. "Anyway, I um... I met this guy and he's in Philly for the week, so I flew out here."

"Girl, you flew all the way to Philly for some ding-ding?"

"Mama!"

"You mean to tell me you just hopped a flight without telling anybody where you were going? You ain't called and said, 'goodbye', 'dog kiss my ass' or nothing! And what about your soap? Don't you have orders to get out?"

"I haven't had any orders in about a week," I sighed.

"None?" she asked worriedly. "And you hopped your ass on a flight to Philly?"

Mama had been more than a little worried when I told her I was quitting my job to make soap in my basement. As my accountant, she was horrified. As my mother, she supported my vision enough to not bring negativity to my dream.

"Mama."

She changed the subject, "So, who is this man? Do I know him?"

55

"You don't know him," I told her. "But, Mama…" I sighed. "Mama I just don't know… he's unlike any other man I've ever been with. I barely know him, and I just jumped on a plane to see him. He didn't even know I was coming."

"Oh Lord, you done found yourself some of that devil dick, haven't you?"

"I don't even know how to explain it."

"Your daddy had that devil dick," she chuckled.

"Oh, I do not wanna hear this," I told her.

She ignored me and kept talking. "I fell in love with that man so fast everybody thought I was stupid, but you know what? I can guarantee you I'd have probably popped up on him too… even if it meant flying across seventy states to secure my prize and make sure he knew nobody else could have it."

I didn't like talking about my deadbeat daddy. I didn't know how things were in their humble beginning… but my most vivid memories of my father didn't paint him in a positive light.

"That's not what this is," I told her. "He's nothing like your ex-husband."

"I'm sorry. You know that's not what I meant, but I was once madly in love with your daddy. It took me a while to wake up… and I'm glad I did… but I don't like to remember the bad times. I'd rather hold on to the good times… they brought me you and your sister." She paused and then said, "Are you in love with this man you dropped everything for?"

"I don't even know him, Mama," I told her.

"But your broke ass jumped on a plane and showed up where he was… unannounced?" she asked suspiciously. "All the way in PHILADELPHIA?"

I almost told her about the way we met, but there were some things my mama didn't need to know about me.

"I like him," I told her. "We're getting to know one another."

"Well, I need his full name and a picture of him just in case something happens. Does he live in Philly?"

"No, he's actually from Tulsa. I met him at that art gallery I went to a few weeks ago."

"A FEW WEEKS?" she yelled and then added, "You know what? You're grown, Windsor. Who is this man?"

"His name is Damian Anthony. He's thirty-nine. He's a writer. One kid. Never been married. And, before you ask, I know that's his real name."

She started laughing and then stopped suddenly. "Wait a minute… Damian Anthony… Damian *Lawrence* Anthony? The one who wrote *Three First Names*?"

"Yeah," I said slowly. "You've read it?"

"That's a good book. My book club read it last month and he came to the meeting to discuss it with us. Girl, he is FINE! I told him I had a daughter he needed to meet, but honestly, every woman there had a daughter he needed to meet... or needs they wanted him to meet." She was cackling again. "I bet he left that meeting with a pocket full of phone numbers... oooh, baby. You're laying up with Damian Anthony?"

"Yes, and don't tell nobody."

"Nobody knows?" she asked me. "Not even Marissa?"

"*Especially* not Marissa," I sighed.

"Still?"

"I don't know, Mama. I'm happy for her if she's happy... but this guy... he's no good. She loves him. She loves him so much she tells him all my business and then tells me he doesn't like me because of the things she's told him. I've had to hold my tongue so many times when it comes to him. I don't tell her shit now."

"You and Marissa used to be thick as thieves."

"Well, I'm all for growth and change, but she's pushing me to my limits. Oh... let me tell you the latest. Her boyfriend doesn't want her to talk to me because I worship the devil."

"What the fuck?"

"Right? I'm like... you mean my crystals? My meditation? My YOGA? My spirituality has nothing to do with the devil."

"Wow," Mama chuckled. "Sometimes friends grow apart, Windsor," she added softly.

"I know, Mama, but... this feels like a personal attack. I don't know if our friendship can survive this. I've gone from being mad to just... sad."

"Are you happy with your life and the way you're living it?"

"Yes."

"Then who gives a fuck what Marissa thinks? Who cares what that thick necked boyfriend of hers thinks? Hell, who gives a fuck what *I* think? It's *your* life, little girl, but as your accountant, if you hop another flight trying to chase some dick, Ima beat your ass!"

I burst out laughing, but she was right. Financially, this trip was ill advised... but spiritually... it was just what I needed.

"Duly noted. I love you, Mama. I'm not sure how long I'm staying but I'll call and check in with you tomorrow."

"You don't have to, baby. Just text and let me know when you're coming home. Enjoy yourself. You deserve it."

She made a kissing noise before the line dropped and I smiled. My mama was a great judge of character. If she thought Damian Lawrence Anthony was a catch... he was a catch.

***

Damian was waiting for me in the lobby. He grabbed my hand as we walked into the breakfast buffet like it was the most natural thing in the world. It felt good walking hand and hand until we were forced to let go as we grabbed our plates and silverware. I'm not normally a breakfast person, but after all the physical activity I had over the past several hours… I was ravenous. I put a good helping of potatoes on my plate and then smothered them with gravy before throwing a couple of buttermilk biscuits on top.

"Do you need some grape jelly?" he asked me. "Ketchup?"

"How did you know?" I asked him.

"Woman, that's the only way to eat biscuits, gravy and potatoes," he answered.

I looked at his plate and laughed. We were both eating the same thing.

"I don't eat pork," he told me. "I'm trying to stop eating meat all together but it's hard. I love me some yard bird."

"I don't eat pork either," I said as we found a table near the window and sat down. I spread my napkin over my lap and then said a quick prayer before taking a big bite of one of my biscuits. "Mmmmm, these are homemade," I said happily. "I try to only eat meat once or twice a week. I'm slowly weaning myself. I completely stay away from red meat."

"Same," he said looking at me with a big smile on his face.

"What?"

"You love food, don't you?"

I put my fork down and he put his hand over mine. "Don't do that. I love that you love food. I love food too. I love to cook. I love to eat. I love to watch you eat. I like the way you enjoy it."

I smiled at him, forgetting my momentary bout with self-consciousness. Once upon a time I'd been on the verge of an eating disorder, trying so hard to fit into a world that didn't want to make room for me. It felt good to be in his space.

"Tell me about it," he said softly.

"About what?"

"About your reaction just now. I feel like there's something I need to know."

"There's nothing to know," I told him. "I used to model. I ran away from home thinking I was gonna be rich and famous because some woman approached me in the mall about modeling classes."

"Ohhh, that old scam," he said.

"Right. Imagine being a tall, dark, skinny teenager who was made fun of her entire life. That woman knew what she was doing when she suckered me into paying for those classes. I took a few classes, left my mama a note and bought myself a one-way bus ticket to New York City."

"How old were you?"

"Eighteen," I smiled wryly. "It was one of the stupidest things I've ever done. My mother was LIVID, but there was nothing she could do about it. I was a legal adult. She yelled and screamed and then told she guessed I was gonna have to *buy* my sense."

"My granny used to say that," Damian told me. "Bought sense is better than-"

"Told sense," I finished. "There isn't a day that I don't wish I'd have invested in some of that 'told sense.'"

I learned quickly just how hard it was to survive on my own in a city I knew nothing about. The modeling jobs were few and far between. The jobs I did book… I'd arrive on set and find out I was just a prop. The tall dark girl flanked by two lily white blondes standing too close to me. It wasn't me they wanted. They wanted my skin. They loved the contrast.

"I was starving myself, not on purpose. I was broke… but then it became convenient. I couldn't afford to eat. The modeling agency I was with put me in an apartment with about ten other girls. It was rent free, but it was a brutal environment. We were all competing for the same jobs."

I hesitated, unsure if I should tell him about Ian. It wasn't something I shared with anyone… Marissa only knew bits and pieces. Mama knew. My sister and her husband knew… no one else had a clue about what life was like for me back then.

"I met a man… a photographer. He was really nice to me. He took me under his wing. He told me I was his muse. He was a lot older than me. He was rich. He was 'known' in that world. He let me come and live with him… strictly platonic at first. I was so stupid," I sighed, thinking about how well he groomed me.

Ian introduced himself as my friend, and I desperately needed something… someone to cling to. He took beautiful pictures of me. He taught me how to pose. My portfolio boasted everything from commercial to couture. He found a loophole in my modeling contract and got me out of it. Whenever he had a client looking for something different… he'd introduce them to me. Suddenly I was getting high paying gigs. He didn't seem to want anything in return. He was just helping me out. I was like a pet project to him… an experiment.

I felt like I could finally relax. I was safe. I wasn't living in that cramped apartment. I wasn't living in a hostel or camping out on a park bench. I had security. I had a beautiful room at Ian's fancy high-rise apartment. He taught me how to enjoy the finer things in life.

Mama didn't like it. She told me a man like that wasn't interested in friendship with a teenage girl. She told me Ian wasn't being nice to me for free, but I didn't listen to her. Once again, the *told* sense went in one ear and out the other.

I told Ian what Mama said. He convinced me she was wrong. Told me I was a grown woman, not a baby. I was finally enjoying my life and I shouldn't let my mother tear down what I'd worked so hard to build. She didn't understand my new life. Ian was the only one who understood me.

"Save every penny you make and most of what he gives you."

It was the only advice I listened to before letting Ian convince me Mama just didn't want to see me happy. I want to slap myself every time I think of how I estranged myself from my family during that time. I would later learn that's how it starts.

The transition from friend to girlfriend was smooth. Ian was my first lover. He taught me things about love and sex I'd only read in books. I smoked my first joint with him on the night he took my virginity. I was in love with him, but more than that, I was grateful for him and the life he gave me.

I felt like the luckiest girl in the world. Under Ian's influence, my face was on billboards and in magazines. I walked runways as he sat in the audience admiring his work. He took me to events where I was the trophy on his arm in rooms full of powerful and famous people.

It was almost like a fairytale.

At first.

"He used to hit me," I looked down at my plate. "At first it was just every now and then... I stopped modeling. I was embarrassed. People saw my bruises. I could only walk into so many doors or trip and fall so many times. No one ever questioned me. No one asked me if I needed help. They just... put makeup on me and pushed me in front of the camera."

Damian's fists were balled up next to his plate. I shouldn't have told him. I didn't want it to ruin his day. I didn't dare tell him anything else about that time in my life. It was too much.

"Hey," I put my hands over his and sighed with relief as I felt his hands relaxing beneath mine. "That was a long time ago. I'm okay, I promise."

"Who is he?"

I shook my head, refusing to answer the question. I didn't want to say his name out loud. I never wanted to say his name again.

"How long were you with him?"

"A little over four years. I was almost nineteen when I met him."

"You were just a baby," he said sadly. To my complete and utter surprise... there were tears in his eyes. "How did you get over that?"

"I didn't," I told him. "I don't know that I ever will… but I've moved on from it. I can't let it define me, right? It's just… a chapter of my story I don't like to re-read. It makes me sad."

"I'm sorry I made you talk about it," he apologized.

"I look like I have it all together, but deep down, sometimes I feel like my sock is permanently sliding down in my shoe." I smiled, determined to push all thoughts of Ian to the locked room in the back of my mind.

"The thought of someone doing that to somebody I-" he stopped short.

"I'm ok," I told him. "I'm not wearing socks today."

I squeezed his hand. He cared. He genuinely cared about me. I couldn't believe I was telling him things I swore I'd never discuss again. I told him one of my darkest secrets over biscuits and country gravy.

I trusted him with almost everything.

"Anyway, let's put some drawls on those memories," I said cheerfully. "Today is about you!"

"Put some drawls- I haven't heard that expression in years," he said with a laugh.

"Your granny?" I asked him.

He nodded.

"Mine too," I said, joining him in laughter. "I remember the first time she told me to 'put some drawls on that winda'… I had no damn idea she wanted me to roll the window up."

"You sure know how to lighten a mood," he told me.

"I want you to have a good day."

"I have a feeling any day with you is a good day, Windsor Bradley."

"I'm not gonna tell you you're wrong," I said smiling at him.

"The young lady at the front desk was really impressed with your soap. She stopped me this morning to tell me. I googled it. I'm impressed too. How did you get started?"

"You know, I went from modeling in New York where everyone thought I was living this perfect life, to moving back in with my mama. I had a lot of money saved up, but I was only twenty-three and had never seen a budget in my life. Thank God my Mama took over. She's an accountant. She controlled my finances and gave me a small allowance. I took some classes, but school just wasn't for me, so started working odd jobs… nothing that would afford me my own place until I got sucked into working at a call center. I think I was twenty-five, still living with my mama, miserable… but it was full time with benefits. Mama gave me enough of my savings for the down payment on my house and I started being a responsible adult. I was there for almost fifteen years... just going through the motions, hating every minute of it."

"That's a long time."

"Hell yeah, that's a long time. One day I was at work watching YouTube documentaries, and I ended up in a black hole."

"Oh my god, yeah. You watch a video about llamas and the next thing you know you're watching documentaries about goats in Jamaica," he laughed.

"Exactly. I was watching documentaries about tribal customs in Africa. I think that led to how shea butter is made, and the next thing I knew, I was watching a video of a woman cutting soap with India Arie playing in the background. I was mesmerized. For the first time, in a very long time, I felt... I don't know... at peace. Just watching someone cut soap. After that I started googling and watching tutorials and playing around with different soap recipes until I felt like I had it. I started taking bars of soap to work and giving them away. It was therapeutic at first... but then someone said I should sell them."

"So, you quit your job...just like that?"

"Not exactly. They were getting ready to lay folks off. I'd been there 15 years, so they offered me a package to volunteer. The package was a year's pay, all my accrued vacation and sick time, and three months of medical and dental benefits. I took the package, paid off my house and used the rest to buy supplies. I convinced my Mama to give me more of an allowance from my modeling money. She invested it so there's a lot more to work with, but I want to be smart. I need that money for retirement, and I don't want to dip into my 401K. It's enough to hold me for a few years if need be, but I need to be able to sustain myself for a lifetime. Anyway, that's how Windsor Noir got started."

"Windsor Noir," Damian repeated. "I like it. What made you choose that?"

I laughed. I could actually laugh about it now. "My mother's ex-husband used to call me 'Black Windsor,'" I told him with a shrug. "He meant it for humiliation, and it worked for a long time... but one day I woke up and realized I was beautiful. So, I flipped that shit. What he meant for my demise... I used it for my good."

"Your mother's ex? What did your father say?"

"Oh, he's my father. He doesn't think so and he made no secret of that. I haven't spoken to him in years. Life is better without him, trust me. My sister doesn't even deal with him... and he actually adored her in a weird abusive way."

"I can't even imagine that." Damian looked horrified.

"That's a good thing," I told him. "That means you grew up in a stable home with parents who showed you what real love looks like."

"How do you know that?"

"I can tell by the way you talk to me. The way you touch me. The way you look at me. Someone did more than tell you to be a good man. They showed you *how* to be a good man… led by example."

He smiled.

"My parents were deeply in love." I could tell he was reminiscing.

Were. Past tense. It wasn't lost on me. I stared at him questioningly.

"My daddy died a few years ago… heart attack. It was unexpected," he shared hesitantly.

"I'm sorry," I squeezed his hand. I felt bad telling him I was estranged from my father when his own father, a good man, was no longer with him. "Do you wanna talk about it?"

"One day," he smiled.

I smiled back. "I promise, my whole life isn't a tragedy. This is just shit I had to go through to get where I am today. I'm okay. I love making soap in my basement. It brings me joy."

"And how's business going?"

I knew he thought he was segueing into a more cheerful topic, but I hadn't sold a bar of soap in over a week. My remaining severance was only gonna last three more months before I'd be forced to look for a part time job to pay my utilities.

"It's not," I sighed. "I haven't sold anything in a week. That's a long time to have a bunch of inventory laying around."

"So, you only have three months' worth of bills saved up and you flew out here?" he asked.

He sounded like my mama.

"I wanted to see you," I told him. "I know it sounds stupid."

"No, it doesn't," he replied thoughtfully. He stared at me for a moment before grabbing my hand and saying, "Come with me."

In a matter of minutes, we were in the lobby, standing at the front desk with the young lady who helped me yesterday.

"Hey, soap lady!" Natalie said cheerfully. "I was just telling your boyfriend how much I love the soap. My roommates tried to take it. I told them they had to buy their own. I cut off a little piece for my manager because… well, I like my job and I want to stay on her good side. She loves it too. Said she's gonna order some on payday."

"Oh really?" Damian said with a smile. "Is your manager here? I bet my girlfriend would be willing to sell the hotel small bars of soap at wholesale. The soap in the rooms now… I mean it's okay, but… it's not Windsor Noir."

"Let me call her," Natalie said cheerfully. "If you can get in here… it would be huge. Even if they just put your soaps in the gift shop. I'm gonna talk you up."

63

"Girl, if I can get into this hotel, I will send you free soap every month," I told her.

"Deal!"

She called her manager, and the next thing I knew, I was sitting with the buyer, telling her about my soaps and promising to send samples immediately. If she liked them, she'd see about starting them off in the gift shop and then possibly branding them to place exclusively in the executive rooms and suites.

I immediately got on the phone with my mama and asked her to gather multiple bars of soap, put them in a box, and overnight them to me at the hotel. She sounded excited and I was glad something about my soap business could make her smile.

Maybe this trip wasn't so crazy after all. After the conversation with the buyer, I could officially list it on my taxes as a business expense.

Plus, I lied and called Damian my boyfriend when I was trying to hustle my way into his event… but he just publicly called me his girlfriend and I wasn't sure if he was saying that for show or if he really meant it.

The way he held my hand as we went to set up his table for the book signing could have been a clue, but I was no longer into assumptions. I didn't want to scare him away, but I wanted to know what the end goal was… soon.

Chapter 10

Damian Lawrence Anthony

I sold fifty books yesterday. Thank God I purchased them wholesale from the publisher. My twenty percent royalty was far above the industry standard, but it was hardly enough to keep the lights on, yet alone feed me if I wanted to eat something besides ramen noodles next week. I walked into this conference with lowered expectations so selling fifty books was more than I expected. The hardcover retailed for $25. My profit was $12.50 per book. I was leaving the conference with $1,250, but $875 of that covered my costs. That left me with a profit of $375 and 20 books in inventory. I felt successful and regretful at the same time. If I was forced to buy a ticket home…it would take a big chunk out of my earnings… maybe all of it.

I loved writing… loved reading excerpts to people who hung on my every word… loved signing autographs. What I didn't love were the expectations many entities had when inviting authors to events.

Kobalt paid me a modest fee to speak and gave me a nice room… a rarity for an author who doesn't have an agent and hasn't yet landed on the New York Times Bestseller list. Aside from my book sales today, that fee would pay off some of my bills and, coupled with my job, I'd finally be able to put some extra money in Daniel's college fund.

So often, hosts expected an author to pay their own way, book their own room, and speak in front of an audience for that overrated thing they call, 'exposure.'

That worked when I was in my twenties and eager to please anyone who would give me a chance to sell books or spit a poem at an event, but as I got older, I realized exposure was cool… but it didn't take care of my son. I wasn't starving, but at times, I was barely breaking even, and that's not the most comfortable position to be in.

I needed to figure something out. There was no way I could continue traveling on buddy passes, trying to make it to every event I was invited to. This was supposed to be my weekend with Daniel, but instead of sitting on the couch with him watching Disney movies… I was miles away from him… hustling backwards. I wanted better for him. I needed to do something that would fully establish me as my own boss and give me complete control over my work.

I wanted to self-publish but the thought of branching out on my own was a little scary. Yes, I'd have 100% control of my work and reap 100% of the profits… but I'd also be responsible for 100% of the production and marketing of my book. I'd be the one trying to set up interviews and put my books into the hands of the folks who could get more people to buy and read my work. I'd be doing more than just writing. I'd also be doing all the groundwork.

It was a tough decision. My heart wanted it, but my brain was afraid. I needed to stop playing around with the idea and just do it before my brain could step in with misguided logic and self-doubt.

Cedric and I discussed it early yesterday morning, and although he hated to see me go, he understood my need for growth.

I still left that meeting undecided.

I wanted to discuss it with Windsor, but didn't want to burden her with a decision I needed to make for myself. Didn't want her to think I lacked the courage to step out on faith the way she did. I admired her for that… admired her tenacity… admired her willingness to take risks, to take chances.

She took a chance on me. Picked me out of a crowd and said, "that one."

I wasn't naïve enough to think she had anything but lustful intentions… initially. My intentions had also been lustful, and the moment she slid her arms around my neck and laid her head on my shoulder as we danced, I knew I was leaving that party with her.

I didn't know how happy I'd be to see her again… until I saw her again… smiling up at me as I stood on stage, grinning and stuttering, trying to compose myself before everyone in the room could see the effect she had on me.

I didn't know I would fall in love.

I lost more than my composure when I saw her… I lost my heart.

I don't even think I knew it then. I honestly don't think I knew until she told me about her past… about the man who…

I didn't want to think about it.

I almost told her then… in that moment when she was trying to fight her way through the memories of her past so *I* could have a good day. She wanted *me* to be okay.

I love that woman.

I love the way she speaks to me as if I'm the most important person in the world. The way she shows interest in what I'm saying, the way she looks me in the eye when I'm talking to her.

Everyone loves her and it's more than her stunning beauty… it's her.

It's the way she carries herself, the way she smiles and laughs, the way she allows herself to be approached… the way she treats other people with kindness and grace.

People talk to her. Complete strangers walk up to her as if they know she can be trusted with their deepest secrets. I noticed it as I watched her practically skipping up and down the line of people waiting to get their books signed yesterday… engaging with them, writing their names on sticky notes, opening their books to exactly where I would be signing and instructing them to keep the book open to that page to make things easier for me… it was the most beautiful thing I'd ever seen. People were moved by her, and at that moment, I understood it wasn't just me.

She has a power within her, and I don't think she's aware of it.

I thought back to what LeeLee told me. She said she saw something in Windsor she wanted to protect.

I want to protect it too.

I know she's been hurt… horribly.

So, to see the person she is today… to see her spirit preserved in such a way… it makes me want to be the one to keep that smile on her face.

It's funny. Yesterday, people kept walking up to me and complimenting me on, not only my book, but the beautiful woman they assumed was my girlfriend. I didn't tell them otherwise, merely nodded my head in agreement and smiled proudly.

"Yes, I'm blessed," I said each time someone told me how nice she was, how pretty she was, how lucky I was…

Was she my girlfriend? We hadn't discussed it, but the word slid out of my mouth so easily as I spoke to the front desk clerk, and then the manager, as I spontaneously tried to set up a meeting between Windsor and the buyer for the hotel.

I wanted to see her win. I wanted to win with her, but I needed to make sure I was bringing more than my dick to the table.

My cell phone beeped, letting me know I had a new email. I glanced down at my phone and realized the email was from Cedric. I was stunned. The email contained every file he had on my book with a note telling me I now had full publishing rights to my work.

It was mine. He'd given me the reins. He just wanted to see me succeed and if it meant pushing me into the decision of my heart then, so be it.

He also included a hilarious P.S. about wanting to be the first person to get an invitation to my wedding. I laughed out loud, but in the back of my mind I could totally see myself putting a ring on Windsor's finger… and I hadn't felt that way about a woman in… never.

I read the email several times before responding, "Thank you for taking a chance on me when no one else would… and thank you for encouraging me to take a chance on myself."

Windsor swept into our room just as I was sending the email. She stood in the doorway, breathlessly giggling when she noticed what I was wearing. It was the same blazer I wore the night I met her. That small detail wasn't lost on her as she practically ran towards me and kissed me excitedly!

"Guess what?" she said, jumping up and down like a kid waiting on a piece of candy.

"Chicken butt," I responded, pulling her into my arms.

"Ha," she said, giving me another quick peck on the lips.

"You left with a big box of beautiful soap and you've returned to me empty handed so…" I coaxed teasingly.

"So, my full-sized soaps are going to be sold in the gift shop… annndddddd-" She paused for dramatic effect- "branded mini soaps will be placed in all the executive rooms and suites in the hotel along with my lotions."

"What? Are you serious?" I picked her up and swung her around, loving the infectious excitement in her voice. I suddenly had a sobering thought. "Baby, you don't make lotion."

"They don't know that," she laughed. "I'm going to go home, and experiment until I perfect that shit, and then I'm gonna to sell the lotions to the hotel and on my website!"

"I am so fuckin' proud of you!" I told her.

She couldn't stop smiling, especially when I said, "I may or may not have ordered more of that chocolate cake in celebration of your win."

"You just made that up," she laughed. "You had no idea I was gonna win."

"Well, it was gonna be a celebration cake," I said with a kiss. "Or it was gonna be a 'cheer you up' cake." I kissed her again. "But either way, we were gon' eat some cake."

"Ahhhhhhh, let her eat cake," she said dramatically. "The man knows the way to my heart."

"Yes, and now I need to make my way downstairs to this workshop. Are you gonna be okay here alone?" I asked her.

"Yeah, I just came back to the room to change into something more comfortable. They gave me a spa day and they told me I could bring anyone I wanted, but you're gonna be busy all day," she said with a cute little pout.

"Aw man, you mean I'm gonna miss out on having cucumbers on my eyes while drinking water with mint leaves floating in it?" I asked jokingly. "How about... you go have your spa day, and then later, after dinner, we can come back here, and you can give me a spa night?"

"I believe that can be arranged," she told me. "But first I need to talk to you."

"Yeah, I need to talk to you too," I told her.

Both our tones became serious.

The mood in the room changed.

It was our first awkward moment.

"Okay," she said, kissing my cheek and then walking into the bathroom before I could say anything else.

"I'll see you at dinner," I told her.

"Okay, have fun," she called back sweetly.

I wasn't sure what she needed to talk to me about... but I hoped it didn't contradict what I needed to talk to her about.

Chapter 11

Windsor Elaine Bradley

We sat on opposite ends of the couch, staring at one another, both anticipating what the other had to say. The room was silent aside from the tick-tick ticking of the decorative clock hanging on the wall. I looked away from him and stared at the clock, wondering how long it would take him to muster up the nerve to say what he had to say… wondering how long it would take me.

I looked over at him.

"Windsor…"

"Damian…"

We both spoke at once and then laughed nervously, each encouraging the other to start first.

"What were you expecting when you came here?" he asked hesitantly.

"I don't know," I answered truthfully.

"What were you expecting when you saw me?" I asked him.

"I wasn't expecting this," he told me.

"And what is… this?"

"I'm in love with you," he blurted it out like he needed to say it before he lost his nerve.

I couldn't look away from him. He wouldn't look away from me.

He looked like he meant it.

"What did you want to talk about?" he asked nonchalantly, as if he hadn't just professed his love for me.

"Ummmm, it feels stupid now," I stammered.

"Try me," he coaxed.

"I was gonna ask you what we're doing…"

"What are *you* doing?" he asked.

"I'm waiting for the punchline," I mumbled.

"You don't believe me?"

It wasn't that I didn't believe him. In fact, it was the opposite. I believed him… and I couldn't believe I, well, believed it. He was supposed to be a one-night stand, but our connection was otherworldly. The first time we were together… that first slow dance… I swore my heart skipped a beat and altered its rhythm to match his. It was like our hearts synched up… like they'd been waiting for one another.

I didn't know what it was then… but I know now.

"I think I love you too," I whispered, laughing at the audacity of it all. "I think I'm in love with you, and I don't think I knew that until now."

I cocked my head to the side and stared at him thoughtfully.

Love.

It was such a… strong word, such a… robust word.

It made no sense.

But it made sense.

"So… I mean… if I'm in love with you and you're in love with me…" he said thoughtfully as he slid closer to me on the couch. "What are we really doing here?"

"I don't know." I leaned into him and laid my head on his shoulder. "You don't find this the least bit absurd?" I asked. "How is this even possible? We just met. Don't you think this is crazy?"

"Yep," he agreed, gently kissing the top of my head. "But I've never felt this kind of connection with anyone. When I woke up that morning… and you were gone… I felt like a piece of my soul was missing. I felt lost, Windsor. I wanted to look you up… try to reconnect with you… but I didn't think you wanted to be found. I didn't want to stalk or harass you so I just…."

"I thought about you every day," I said softly. "I prayed I would run into you again. I wrote my intentions down and whispered your name into the wind. Maybe I thought you'd hear me, or maybe the ancestors would carry the message to you."

"When LeeLee took me to the airport… I don't even know why I told her about you. It's like I knew I could trust her with it. Now I know it's because she was like… the bridge to our connection. Like, I needed her to get to you." He paused thoughtfully. "She knew things. Things she couldn't have known."

"She told me she was excited to be part of our love story," I laughed. "I thought it was crazy to show up here unannounced, but she convinced me it was saner than calling or texting you."

Damian twirled one of my locs around his finger. "She was right. Sometimes you have to take a chance, just in case the risk has a reward. Think about it. Your severance is running out. You don't want to dip into your retirement. You hadn't had any orders in a week, but you still took a chance and jumped on that plane for me." He hugged me closer to him. "Not only did you get your man, but you got a contract with this hotel. Now your cross-country dick expedition can be classified as a business trip."

I laughed so hard I started choking on my own spit. Damian handed me his bottle of water and I took a few sips and tried to catch my breath.

"Windsor," he whispered my name, and I lifted my head to look at him.

"What is it?" I answered raspily, my throat scratchy from my coughing fit.

"Will you be my girlfriend?" he asked me.

"Oh my god, we are doing everything so assed backwards," I told him.

"We really are," he agreed. "But I'm serious. Just because we have this connection… just because we're at the beginning of this beautiful love story… I don't want anything between us to be left open to interpretation. I'm making my intentions known right now. So, I ask again, will you be my…"

"Yes," I answered before he could finish.

"Girlfriend, damn," he laughed, determined to finish his sentence.

"Yes," I said again, sliding my hand underneath his shirt and placing my palm on his bare chest.

I could feel his heart quicken beneath my hand, and I closed my eyes as he kissed me slowly, willingly absorbing the multitude of emotions rushing through my brain at once.

I felt high.

Floating above us as I watched myself look him in his eyes and unexpectedly whisper, "Please don't hurt me."

And there it was.

The reason I had sworn off actual relationships and settled for occasional sex and dinner dates… and it wasn't really settling. Every now and then, as my past stared me in the face, I needed a release to keep myself from diving into a deep depression. It worked for me until I met Damian. Now, all the sudden, I was opening my heart to someone who had the power to break it... again. It was terrifying.

I was taking a huge risk with him, and as whimsical and as beautiful as it felt in the moment… I was afraid. More afraid than I'd ever been in my life. I'd just handed this man my heart in its rawest state. As is. Damaged. Carefully reconstructed after the few before him had taken my precious gift and thrown it against a wall, shattering it into a million tiny pieces, shards scattered as I desperately worked to find every fragment and put myself back together.

I'd given him my body, unafraid of the difficulties that could arise from such an intimate physical connection. I'd given him my secrets, somehow trusting him with the keys to the hidden chambers deep inside of my mind.

My heart, though?

My heart I gave both eagerly and hesitantly at the same time.

I'd never fallen this hard… this fast.

It made me question whether I'd ever actually been in love before now.

Had I just been falling into a pattern with the others? Going through the motions, doing what I thought I was supposed to do to fulfill my dreams of two kids, an SUV, and PTA meetings?

When those dreams were dashed, I fell into a pattern of loving only myself and doing what was necessary to fulfill my need for pleasure without the worry of falling in love again.

Again? There was no… again.

That couldn't have been love. It didn't feel like this.

It felt nothing like this.

Nothing like this mature, knows what I want, doesn't give a shit about what anyone else thinks kind of love.

This is different.

This feels like sitting at the top of a roller coaster, anticipating the drop, screaming with exhilaration as gravity pulls me towards the ground only to lift me again… higher and higher until the ride comes to an abrupt stop, jolting me back to reality.

This is a rush I'd do anything to feel on a constant basis, and I had no regrets behind loving him. I regretted the potential of him not loving me enough to handle my heart with care.

So, asking him not to hurt me… it was more than a request.

It was a plea.

My heart was literally begging him to take care of it, and as unintentional tears slid down my face, there was nothing more for me to say.

He said nothing, merely pulled me closer and spread out on the couch with me cradled against his chest like someone he needed to hold on to… someone he needed to protect.

Someone he loved.

I had no real understanding of what safety felt like until that moment.

I was safe with Damian.

All of me.

Chapter 12

Windsor Elaine Bradley

I called him when I got home. He told me he loved me. I returned that emotion, and in the same breath told him I needed time… time to work without the distraction of his body anywhere within the vicinity of mine.

He understood. He needed the same.

I was glad he felt that way… and, also a little insulted.

I needed to know his soul was as tortured as mine with the mere thought of spending one moment without one another, but I wasn't going to burden him with those thoughts. Honestly, I was kinda relieved when I realized he wasn't going to burden me either.

One word from him and I would have said, 'fuck that soap' and hopped on his dick with no thoughts about the purchase order I needed to fulfill.

I smiled.

We hadn't even made love on our last night together. We sat in the middle of the bed, talking, drinking wine, and eating cheese with buttery crackers and the juiciest grapes I'd ever tasted...

It felt like *that* night.

The night we created a bond neither of us expected.

The night life truly began for me.

Even if I didn't know it then… I knew it now, and I was so excited for the possibility of what was to come. Damian was flying home tomorrow, but I had a million things to do in preparation of fulfilling the hotel's order, plus the twenty orders that trickled into my website over the weekend. Natalie, the hotel clerk, wasn't just gassing me up when she said she was going to tell all her friends about my soap. All the orders came from the Philadelphia area. I put a reminder on a sticky note to send Natalie several bars of soap and a handwritten 'thank you' once all orders had been fulfilled. I'd already ordered supplies and now I just needed to work out the logistics.

My mother had already volunteered to help me, and I knew my sister and niece would help as well. I called Marissa. I immediately regretted it.

She didn't understand why I'd taken such a large order without knowing how I'd fulfill it and wanted to know why I'd flown to Philly without telling her. The part of me that still yearned for our close friendship wanted to tell her everything, but the largest part of me just wanted to cherish my new love without the threat of judgement or criticism, so I held back.

"Can you help me?" I asked hopefully.

"Girl, some of us have jobs," she said with a tone I didn't appreciate. "Maybe that psychic you deal with should have warned you about this great opportunity, so you'd be prepared for it."

"What happened to us?" I asked her. "What's going on with you?"

"Eugene told me what you did," she said flatly.

"What are you talking about?"

"He told me you came onto him at the gallery, and when he rejected you... you left with that man you were dancing with."

"You can't possibly believe that shit!" I yelled into the phone. 'I have screenshots of your man trying to fuck. I cussed him out! I knew this was coming. I knew he would try to flip that shit because he was scared I would tell you."

"Keep your screenshots," she said coldly. "I choose to believe my man."

"You deserve better than him," I said softly.

"No. I deserve better than you."

Marissa hung up, leaving me holding my phone with tears in my eyes. I couldn't understand why Eugene was going through such great lengths to push us apart. I couldn't understand why she would let him.

I called her back. "Has he put his hands on you?" I asked as soon as she answered.

"How dare you!" she said hatefully. "I'm not as stupid as you, Windsor. I'm not the type to let a man beat the shit out of me 'til I have to come crawling back home to my mama."

I hung up without saying goodbye. There was nothing left to say. What could I say? Our friendship was effectively over and there was nothing I could do but pray my suspicions about her relationship weren't true. Her increasing agitation with me had finally turned into unfounded anger. It hurt. It hurt so bad.

I wiped my eyes and tried to compose myself, determined not to let my argument with Marissa put a dark cloud over my accomplishments. I needed to speak to someone who would be genuinely happy for me.

I sighed softly and called LeeLee. As soon as I told her about my meeting with the buyer, she volunteered her services, as long as I promised to feed her and tell her every detail of my time with Damian.

"Come over now," I told her. "I'll make us a pizza."

"I'll bring a bottle of wine," she told me.

She walked in, thirty minutes later, with a bottle of merlot and told me to spill my guts.

"Can I take the pizza out of the oven first?" I asked her. "I'm experimenting on you. I hope you like shrimp."

"On pizza?"

"You'll love it," I assured her. "It's shrimp with avocado and roasted corn."

"I should have bought margarita mix instead," she observed.

"Sis, you know I have a fully stocked bar in the den, right? Make us some margaritas! I'll save the wine for my boyfriend."

"BOYFRIEND? WHAT? I'll be right back. Let me make these drinks."

"Make a pitcher," I said with a smirk before handing her a clear plastic pitcher with a smile painted on the front."

"Are we seriously about to drink margaritas out of the Kool-Aid man?" Her laugh came out like a holler and I couldn't help laughing too.

"Girl, I re-named him Barry and he loves liquor," I told her.

By the time she got back with the pitcher and the margarita salt, I had sliced and plated the pizza.

"Ooohhh, Sis. You've got it bad," she laughed as she slid into her chair.

"What?"

"You haven't even started talking about it and you're already blushing."

"You don't know already?" I asked curiously.

"Sis, I know things… but I don't know everything. I guess I only know… what I'm supposed to know… when I'm supposed to know it." She shrugged. "It's a gift. I don't own it or control it."

"Ooh, girl," I sighed, staring at her with, what I imagined to be, a highly perplexed look on my face. "He was so happy to see me. He was excited, and he was so… open. Girl, he's so emotionally available it's crazy."

"What's crazy about it?"

"It's too good to be true."

"You're scared."

"Will you stop doing that?"

"Doing what?"

"Reading me."

"I promise, I'm not reading you. Anyone with eyes can see you're in love with that man."

"I'm terrified, Sis."

"Why?"

"Because I've never been… loved like that… and it was more than the sex. It was him. It was us. Everything about the past few days was just so… other worldly. My soul wept when we made love. I could feel it… weeping. Have you ever felt your soul weep with joy?"

Her mouth hung open, "I have not."

"It's the most cosmic shit, LeeLee. Like… my chest felt like it was about to burst open and spill my feelings all over that damn bed. Feelings I didn't even know I had. I wrote a fucking poem on the plane. Sis, I don't write."

"Read it to me," she demanded.

I pulled a folded piece of paper out of my pocket, stood up, and started reading like I was on stage at a smokey coffee house.

"Love is a beautiful distraction.
It hangs over my head like the threat of a broken promise.
I want to trust it.
I want to trust him.
I want to spend every day in his lap and every night in his bed.
I want to merge our lives until I'm not sure which one of us I am.
I want him inside of me, around me, surrounding me with guttural vibrations that cause me to sink further into the depths of his love.
I want him deep.
I want him far away.
I want him to allow me to work on my dreams while dreaming of him simultaneously.
I need to miss him.
I don't want to…
Miss him.
I want to kiss him.
Today, tomorrow, tonight
Right
Now
In this very moment
I want him to touch me in ways I could never touch myself.
I want to
Wrap my legs

Around his legs
As he begs
Or is that me?
Begging
Begging him to go away
Begging him to stay
Begging him to kiss me
Begging him to miss me
Begging him to stay…
Away."

LeeLee started snapping her fingers. I took a bow and sat back down.

"Oh my god, Windsor, you are sprung! You wrote that? I didn't know you wrote poetry!"

"Because I don't! I'm trying to tell you… something happened to me. Something… crazy! Where is this shit coming from?"

"It was already in you, Sis. Maybe you just needed to have it… I don't know… fucked out of you."

"That's exactly what he did, LeeLee. He fucked poetry from my brain." I took a long sip of my margarita.

"You should read it to him," she coaxed.

"Nah," I laughed. "He's a real writer."

"Don't do that," she told me.

"Do what?"

"Downplay your talents," she answered. "How can you be confident enough to pick a man out of a crowd and turn him out… but lack confidence when it comes to your hidden talents? Damian got the ball rolling, but you do realize you sealed the deal with the hotel, right? Damian wasn't in the basement cutting soap with you!" She rolled her neck as she said it and I couldn't help but laugh.

She was right. I did have a bad habit of downplaying my talents. It was something I needed to work on.

"LeeLee, I don't know how you did it, but thank you for pushing me into chasing that devil dick," I laughed, changing the subject. "I came back with a man and some money!"

"I know that's right!" LeeLee gave me a high five and then bit into her pizza. "This is good," she told me.

"I'm glad, cuz I wasn't sure how it would turn out," I said before taking another sip of my margarita. "This is the bomb," I said as I licked salt from my lips, it's perfect with this pizza."

"My daddy taught me how to mix drinks. He owns a bar. He keeps trying to get me to work there, but I don't want to be there."

"You'd rather drive strangers around than work for your dad?"

"My dad used to cheat on my mom with women he met at his bar," she told me, "a few of them still work there."

"Ohhhhh…"

"Yeah. Exactly. I don't wanna be in the middle of that shit. They've been divorced for years and they're still asking me about the other one's business. Can you imagine if I worked there? I'd rather drive strangers around than deal with that. Plus, my daddy's friends are dirty old men and they all drink at his bar. But that's boring. Let's talk about you and your boyfriend. Is he coming over to help?"

"I ummmm… told him I didn't want him to come over."

"You what?"

"LeeLee, he's a distraction. A huge distraction." I held my hands out in front of me as a means of measuring just how huge his distraction was.

"Damn," she placed her hand on her heart and choked on her margarita. "I'm intuitive and I know things, but I try not to know that kind of shit about the people I meet," she laughed when she finally caught her breath.

"Well, he has a big heart, and a big dick, and I have a big order to fill. I cannot let him distract me."

"But he could help."

"I don't want his help."

"Okay, now I *am* reading you. You don't wanna need him? You think needing someone is a sign of weakness? You need to meditate."

I pursed my lips and picked at my delicious pizza while LeeLee studied me over the rim of her margarita glass.

"Drunk yoga?" she asked slowly.

"Namaste," I said with a nod.

Chapter 13

Damian Lawrence Anthony

"Please don't hurt me."

Her words haunted me. Followed me throughout my day, dominating my thoughts until I could do nothing but grab a pen and pad and write my feelings down before they overwhelmed me. Confessing my love was easy. When she returned the sentiment, I wanted to tap dance on the ceiling.

Laughter filled the room. We were laughing, tickled by this new love, staring at one another with new eyes as the emotions trapped within our willing bodies began manifesting in the form of words and promises never verbalized.

And then she said it…

"Please don't hurt me."

Her words weren't the only thing that gave me pause. It was the way the laughter left her voice when she said it. The way her eyes filled with tears and the way those tears gushed down her cheeks like a river of cautious regret. Her entire demeanor changed. Her body, once fluid like water, was now as rigid as an icicle hanging from the roof… anticipating the moment it would fall to the ground and shatter into a thousand pieces.

She was happy, but she was also afraid of what our love could potentially mean for her. She was opening more than her body to my eager touch. She was opening her heart, her emotions, her soul… she was vulnerable in a way I could never understand.

The moment the words left her mouth and filled my ears, my conscience was flooded with the realization that love was more than an emotion… it was a responsibility.

I didn't know how to react to her words in the moment, so I did the only thing my instincts would allow. I held her, and as her body lost its rigidity, I heard a small sigh of relief escape her lips. I wanted her to always feel as comforted as she did in my arms, in that moment, in our love.

I don't know why I'm so comfortable with this rapid sequence of events, but I've learned to go with the flow and not spend too much time over analyzing the good things. What did I do to deserve this woman? I don't know, but I'm no longer questioning her presence in my life. I just want to love her for as long as she'll let me, and then five more minutes after that.

Daddy would have loved her. He would have taken one look at Windsor and asked me what kind of deal I made with the devil to be in the presence of all that smooth ebony, darker than chocolate, sweeter than raw sugar... he would have made sure she knew he was available if I ever fucked up.

He'd be joking of course. He loved the hell outta mama, and that was a good thing... cuz she woulda beat his ass if he touched another woman. Mama was all the chocolate my daddy could handle, and he would always point to his silver filling if anyone doubted it.

"You see that? My wife is so sweet she gave me a cavity!"

I missed him. Terribly.

His death was sudden. It was unexpected. It was a wakeup call.

Life is short. Nothing is promised, not even tomorrow... barely today.

I licked my lips and smiled, remembering the last kiss I shared with Windsor before she left. If I closed my eyes, I could still taste her lip gloss. I could still smell the orange-ginger oil she rolled between her breasts as I stood behind her in the bathroom mirror with my arms wrapped around her waist. I could still see the way she closed her eyes and relaxed into me, trusting me to carry her weight and not allow her to fall.

Growing up, I often saw my parents in a similar pose. Daddy would walk up behind Mama and slide his arms around her waist. It didn't matter what she was doing... cooking, cleaning, putting up the groceries... when his arms slid around her, she would close her eyes and lean into him, even if it was only for a moment.

Just knowing he had her back... it was all she needed.

Just knowing... that she knew... well, it was all *he* needed.

I had Windsor's back, and no matter how scared she was... she knew that.

She knew it.

And she trusted it. She trusted me.

I took a lazy sip of wine and leaned back in my chair, watching as my brother, Devin, and his wife, Erika, slow danced in the kitchen as my mama sang along with the Isley Brothers. Mama was baking a sweet potato pie and we were all hanging out in the kitchen as if our presence would make the pie bake faster.

"Come dance with me, baby," Mama held out her hand and I smiled, standing up and pulling her into my arms for a hug before two-stepping with her, Chicago style.

She laughed like a schoolgirl as I danced around her in a smooth circle before grabbing her hand and spinning her. "You've been practicing," she said proudly.

"A little," I laughed, wanting desperately to share my newfound love with her, but afraid she would think I was moving too fast.

"A little, my ass," she told me. "What has you so preoccupied? You're normally the first person to jump up when I turn my music on."

"Nothing, Mama."

"I know you, baby. It's something." She stopped dancing and stared at me questioningly.

What is it with Mamas and their killer instincts? I swear my mama could sense a tear in my eye before a sad thought could even formulate in my mind. She was that aware of her sons, but especially me… the baby. I sat down at the table and she followed, holding out her glass for a wine refill. We sat, watching Devin and Erika for a while, smiling as they seemed oblivious to anyone but each other.

"That's the kind of love I want for my babies," she sighed, happily.

"Is it?" I asked her.

"Yep," she answered wistfully. "You're missing your daddy?"

"Always," I sighed.

"Me too." She put her hand over mine and smiled. "If your daddy was sitting here, he would take one look at you and say, 'boy, you look like a lovesick hound dog!'"

I burst out laughing. "Dang, is it that obvious?"

"Stevie Wonder can see it," Devin called from across the kitchen.

"Shut up," I called back.

"Is it that woman you were all hugged up with in Philly?" Erika grabbed Devin's hand and led him to the table. "Is it the same woman you were dancing with at the gallery opening?" They both sat down and stared at me inquisitively.

How could she possibly know about Philly? The question must have shown on my face because she just started laughing.

"You do know Kobalt posted pictures from the event. Boy, you're all over Instagram with this woman," Erika said as she pulled out her phone. "I'm trying not to be nosey, but you're taking too long to tell me what's going on."

"Let me see her," Mama reached for the phone and then stared at me with a look of astonishment on her face as she turned the screen towards me.

There we were, all hugged up on the red carpet, looking *very* familiar with one another. I couldn't help the crazy grin plastered across my face as I looked at the picture. Windsor was standing next to me and laughing as I whispered something naughty in her ear. My hand was resting on her waist as if it was an accessory for that scandalous red dress she was wearing. We looked like we were made for each other.

"Look! Look at him! That jokah is in love!" Devin teased.

"She *is* gorgeous," Mama said with a knowing gaze. "Your daddy would have been very impressed."

"What about you, Mama?" I asked.

"Baby, I can't tell by looking at a picture," she said laughingly. "She's beautiful… and I can see she makes you happy. I haven't seen you look this happy in a very long time, but you know I've gotta meet her before I give my blessing."

"I know," I said, taking the phone and staring at the picture.

Mama took the phone back. "So, what's her name? who are her people?"

"Oh shit," Erika mumbled. "The last time I heard those questions it started a fight."

We all hollered, remembering the story of Erika accidentally befriending her father's secret love child and then taking her to her mother's house. Miss Gayle tried to scratch that poor child's eyes out.

"Ha ha," Erika chuckled. "I can laugh now but that was traumatizing. Thank God my family worked it out. I think Mama loves Brooklynne more than me now."

"That's because Brooklynne had a baby, and you and this boneheaded son of mine are stingy," Mama said, only half-joking.

It was no secret Mama wanted more grandchildren. She'd even adopted Erika's two-year old niece, AbbiGayle, as her honorary granddaughter, showering her with gifts and kisses every time she saw her. Devin, at 44, and Erika at 42, had made it clear they had no plans on having children. They didn't even want the responsibility of pets.

My little Daniel was her pride and joy. All the McDonald's money she claimed she didn't have when Devin and I were kids… she saved it all for Daniel. I've never heard her tell him, "we've got food at home."

Funny thing about my little sidekick, though… he prefers eating in Mama's restaurant, *Claudine's*. He loves cooking with his granny, and he keeps telling me that he wants to be a "cooker" when he grows up.

He was an unexpected blessing. Now that I was with Windsor, the probability of me having more children was zero. She couldn't have babies. I wondered if that would change my mother's cautious opinion of her.

"The Lord gave me two handsome boys and one of them gave me a gorgeous grandson… but that other one… he's too lazy to make me baby," she admonished Devin, giving him a stern gaze, and then focused on me. "Who is this woman?

What's her name? Is she wife material? Cuz at your age you need to settle down and start thinking about giving Daniel a little brother or sister."

"Mama, don't start that. Daniel is all I need. Plus, he has a little sister at home. I'll let Kelvin and Felicia keep having babies."

"Hmph."

"Anyway, Mama. Her name is Windsor," I said softly. "And before you ask, she doesn't have any kids."

I didn't want to discuss such an intimate subject with my family without Windsor's permission, but I felt like it was necessary to adjust my family's expectations before she found herself under impossible pressure to produce results her body was incapable of.

"How old is she?" Mama asked. "Has she ever been married?"

"Forty," I told her. "And she's never been married."

Mama threw her hands up and stared at me. "Forty? No kids and never been married? What's wrong with her."

"Forty? Where?" Devin took the phone from Mama and whistled. "Damn, she doesn't look forty… thirty maybe…but forty? Have you asked to see her ID?"

I ignored Devin. I was still absorbing what Mama said.

"There must be something wrong with her."

Erika noticed my discomfort and smiled sympathetically. Devin just rolled his eyes. He'd had his fair share of lectures, and was just happy I was the one bearing the brunt of Mama's scrutiny. She'd long ago given up on getting any grandkids out of him.

"Mama, I love her," I said quietly, trying not to let frustration creep into my voice. "But I won't bring her around if you try to make her feel like she's not good enough. She's more than enough."

The room went silent. Even the music suddenly stopped playing as I turned to face my mother. "I love her," I said again. "Besides Daniel, she's the best thing that ever happened to me, and I want to be with her. She told me up front that she couldn't have children. She didn't try to hide it from me, and I'm not going to hide it from you thinking the only way for you to accept her is the promise of another grandchild. It's not happening."

"Son, I just…"

I held up my hand. "Mama, please let me finish. I'm not trying to be disrespectful. I just need you to know that not being able to have children… that hurts her… and when she hurts… I hurt."

Silence, once again, engulfed the room as my mother tried to regain her composure. Erika was staring at me with a sneaky smile on her face, and Devin…

Well, Devin looked proud of me and he was rarely proud of any decision I made regarding my life or my career.

"What does she do?" Erika asked, changing the subject.

The smile returned to my face. "She actually has her own business. She makes artisan soaps."

"Wait," Erika said slowly. "As in, *Windsor Noir*?"

"Yeah, you've heard of it?" I asked excitedly.

"Soap?" Devin asked.

"Yeah," Erika nudged him. "You know… that soap I bought that had you all…" she whispered something in Devin's ear, and it must have jogged his memory because there was no denying the naughty grin on his face.

"That's Windsor?" Erika asked. "I had no idea she was black! I got a bar of her soap in a subscription box and now it's all I use."

"Anybody who can make my wife smell that delicious is cool with me," Devin laughed.

"Okay, I need all the deets," Erika put her face in her hands and stared at me like a kid at story time. "How'd you meet? Was it love at first site? How long have you been dating? And how come we're just now hearing about her? You've been holding out!"

"Yeah, how'd you meet?" Mama asked carefully. "And why *are* we just now hearing about her? I didn't even know you were dating anyone since that last heffa ran around on you. I never liked that damn Priscilla."

The conversation became less strained. Mama put her hand over mine and gave it a gentle pat as I told them about meeting Windsor at Harlem's gallery opening and then parting ways without knowing her last name. I left out the part where she fucked the shit out of me, but from the smile I couldn't wipe off my face, I had a feeling Devin had already figured it out. He told me as much when we stepped onto the back patio for a few tokes of the joint Erika had stashed in her purse for emergencies.

"So, tell me the real story, little brother." Devin stretched out on a chaise lounge and I stretched out on the one next to him as we passed the joint back and forth.

It was something we did often since Daddy died three years ago. Whenever one of us was having a hard time or we just needed to touch base, we would light a fire in the pit, stretch out on Mama's patio furniture and toss a joint back and forth until the roach burned our fingertips. Devin was five years older than me. The gap didn't feel so wide once I turned thirty, but as a kid I felt like we were a lifetime apart.

Devin was accomplished. He ran his own landscaping business, he took care of the books at Mama's soul food restaurant, *Claudine's*, and he was married to a beautiful and accomplished woman who had her own shit before she crossed paths with my brother.

I was the dreamer, the class clown… the kid no one expected to succeed. No one, but Daddy. Daddy always supported my ambitions while mama feared I'd die with nothing but my dreams and a few pieces of lint in my pockets. She loved me, but she didn't completely believe in my ability to provide for myself. She didn't raise me to be a starving artist. Daddy didn't either, but he raised me to follow my heart, and my heart was full of words just waiting to be written. He was my biggest fan. My proudest moment wasn't snagging a publishing deal or even seeing my book in print for the first time. My proudest moment was printing out my first rough draft, running to the copy shop to have it bound and then placing that completed manuscript in my father's hands.

I can still remember the look on his face when he realized I'd finally completed the project I'd been working on for over a year. He read it in its entirety and told me how proud he was, how much he loved it, and gave me constructive criticism on how to make it better.

I took his constructive criticism to heart and worked for another three months, perfecting the manuscript, and then printing it out and running to the copy shop to have it bound.

Daddy died before I could hand it to him.

I stood in the driveway, frozen, with the manuscript still in my hands as medics carried my father out of his house on a stretcher. I saw his feet first, peeking from beneath a sheet, and as my eyes slowly traveled up the length of his tall body, I realized the sheet was covering his face.

The manuscript fell from my hands in slow motion, landing on the ground with a thud that sounded louder to my ears than it probably was.

I remember Devin, slowly walking behind the medics, his arms around my mother's defeated shoulders, holding her close, trying to be strong for her while fighting against the weakness in himself. He locked eyes with me and reached out for me. It wasn't the first time he'd ever shown me affection, but it was the first time he ever held me as if he was afraid to let go.

Held me as if I was important to him… someone he would miss if I one day disappeared from this Earth.

That night, after we finally got Mama to go to bed, we stretched out on the back patio and passed a joint back and forth as we cried together.

It's been three years.
It hurts like yesterday.

Telling Devin about Windsor made me miss my Daddy… because he didn't get to see my dreams come true. I was never going to hear him call me a 'lovesick hound dog' again.

So, as I talked to Devin about Windsor, tears came to my eyes and I found myself choking on my words… words I prayed he could hear in heaven… but wished like hell he could hear on Earth.

Devin reached out and placed his hand on my shoulder. It was a simple gesture, but it was the comfort I needed in the moment.

"I don't tell you this enough, but I *am* proud of you, Damian," he said quietly. "I love you, man. I know that you want Daddy to see the good things happening to you, and please trust me when I tell you that he does. I feel him all the time and I know you do too. He's with us, doing that crazy laugh he used to do when he was really tickled about something. Remember that laugh?"

I had to chuckle despite my tears.

"He never treated me any different," Devin said suddenly. "You couldn't tell that man he wasn't my father. That was my daddy. I don't really remember when he came into my life, I just remember feeling safe with him. You know, my sperm donor didn't want anything to do with me… but he wouldn't let Daddy adopt me? Wouldn't let him give me his last name?"

Devin was three when Mama met Daddy. He'd gone on their first date… at Daddy's insistence, and they had been inseparable since.

"He would take one look at Windsor, and he would know whether or not she was the one," Devin continued. "So, I'm looking at you. I'm looking at the way you stood up to Mama, and the way your face lit up when you saw that picture of y'all together. Now, I don't have Daddy's gift of reading people… but I do know my little brother. You love her. You're not just saying it. So, if you love her… then I love her too. She's one of us now."

"What is in this shit?" I asked, holding the joint out at arm's length and passing it back to Devin. "When did you become so emotionally available?"

He laughed. It was a hearty laugh, almost as robust as our father's.

"I could say the love of a good woman made me this way, but I'd be lying. I had a good woman before I met Erika, but I didn't love her, and I kept trying to force it until nothing fit anymore. I love Erika. I think I may have loved her from the start, but our situations were complicated… and when she was free to love me, she didn't know how. She was scared." He passed the joint back to me and said, "Men did that to her. Men like me."

I pondered what he said and realized how men have a habit of taking and taking from a woman until she has nothing left for herself… and then… when he finds a woman he wants to pour into… she's got her defenses up because she's still healing from the last man who stole from her.

"I don't wanna be like that," I sighed.

"You never have," he told me before extinguishing the joint and staring up at the stars. "So, don't start now."

I closed my eyes and allowed my high to settle into my body. As the herb worked it's magic and tiptoed across my nerve endings, I realized a week without Windsor was a week too long. I needed to touch her… to hold her… to pour into her and allow her to take from me… anything she needed.

Chapter 14

Windsor Elaine Bradley

We promised to always tell one another the truth, but the moment he asked if I needed anything, I said, "no."

I could have used an extra pair of hands helping me cut and organize soaps, taking notes, testing my formulas, and touching me in a way that let me know I was gonna make it through this chaos with my locs still attached to my scalp.

I needed him, but I lied to him and it wasn't even intentional. I was so used to having my own back, I didn't want to tell a man what I needed, only to be disappointed if he didn't come through. At the same time, I had the ridiculous notion that he should already know what I want... what I need... that he shouldn't *have* to ask, and if he did, he should see through my lies and run to my rescue because he wants to and not because I asked him to.

My granny always told me a closed mouth doesn't get fed.

But here I am, mouth closed and hungry as hell.

Hungry for him. His presence, his reassurance, his physical love, because love from a distance doesn't feel as good as love in the same room.

They, whoever *they* are, say, 'absence makes the heart grow fonder,' but absence has made my heart sick, and although the remedy is just a phone call away... I hesitate.

Why do I hesitate? In hesitating, I allow a million idiotic scenarios to traipse through my brain before settling on the notion that Philly may have been too good to be true... that he'd agreed to this separation too easily... that maybe he'd changed his mind about me.

He called me every evening, and every evening he told me he loved and missed me. I always said it back but... what if he was just... saying it? What if he thought it was me who was too good to be true?

89

I mean… wasn't it *my* idea to take this stupid break from one another while I filled the soap order and he worked on his business plan? Wasn't it *my* voice that told him I couldn't speak to him during the day because he was a distraction?

Wasn't he just doing what I asked him to? Even if it wasn't what he wanted, wasn't he just doing what I asked, no, *told* him to do?

I threw a bar of soap across the room and watched as it crashed into the wall before dropping to the floor and leaving a bright purple stain in its wake.

"Girl, what the fuck?" my niece, River, exclaimed, and then, seeing the look on my face, followed up with an apologetic, "Sorry, Auntie. You scared me."

River was helping me cut soap to earn money after school. She normally loved hanging out with her "Aunt Winnie." She'd been my little broke best friend since she was little, but River had never seen this stressed out, sex deprived version of me. If I was driving myself crazy, River was probably *extra* over me and my mood.

I turned my head so she wouldn't see me chuckle at her little cussing faux pas. Once I regained my composure, I leveled my gaze at her and asked, "River Elaine Dixon, who am I?"

"Auntie Winnie," she said with her head down.

"And who am I not?"

She sighed deeply before mumbling, "One of my little friends."

"I ain't no snitch so we'll keep this between us," I said evenly.

"What about you throwing that soap against the wall? Is that between us too?" she asked slyly.

"Yes, smartass. That's between us too." I gave her puffy hair a gentle tug and then stared at her as if I'd never seen her before. I did that a lot. Stare at her. At sixteen years old, she looked so much like me it was scary. Her birth was one of the greatest, yet devastating moments of my life. I loved being in her life and I loved that she looked up to me. She listened to me. She trusted me. The day my sister, Paris, brought River home, I cried, staring down at her in her crib, watching as she seemed to look straight through me.

"She's both of ours," Paris told me. "We'll just keep her at my house."

"You're staring at me again," she said self-consciously. "Why do you do that?"

"Because you're beautiful," I told her. "You're the most beautiful girl in the world."

She stared at me for a moment before shaking her head and saying, "You're such a weirdo."

I rolled my eyes at her.

"So, what's wrong, Auntie? Seriously, you haven't been yourself since you came back from your trip. I mean, you're in here throwing soap. What did that bar of soap ever do to you?"

"Oh, sweetie, I'm just tired," I said laughingly, but I could tell she wasn't fooled by the fake smile I forced into my voice.

River was very intuitive, and although I tried to keep her in a child's place, I often found myself confiding in her, being careful not to share things I felt were too adult for her young ears.

My sister wanted to believe River would always be a baby, but I knew River on a different level. Our souls were connected. River trusted me with her thoughts and feelings as much as I trusted her with mine. I was her safe place. River didn't feel comfortable talking to her mother about certain things.

I was the person River turned to when "because I said so" deserved an explanation my sister wasn't inclined to give.

I explained things to River. Gave her the hows and the whys of life as a young woman navigating a different world than the one her mother and I grew up in. I hid nothing about my past but made sure to divulge some information on a need-to-know basis. It was me that pulled River aside after hearing her complain to her mother about a little boy constantly hitting her and pulling her hair in elementary school.

"Oh, sweetie, that's how you know when a boy likes you," Paris told her.
"That is not what a boy does when he likes you," I said, not caring how Paris felt about the contradiction. "If he does it again, you kick him in the ding-ding."

And then we practiced with a giant stuffed animal until River felt like she was ready for battle. Needless to say, after a swift kick to the groin, that little boy never put his hands on my baby again.

Looking at her now, standing next to me in a pair of overalls and one of my smocks, I had to smile with pride. She was growing up. I still had her by a few inches, but only a few. She was stunning. It amazed me how much I hated myself at her age… how much I hated the way I looked. How could I hate something so beautiful? Looking into her eyes was almost like looking into a mirror attached to a time portal.

"Let's take a break," I told her.

I dusted my hands off on my smock and sat down on the edge of the table, patting the empty space next to me. I looked around the basement. With the help of my family and LeeLee, I was approximately one-hundred bars of soap away from fulfilling my purchase order.

"I'm proud of you, Auntie," River said suddenly. "You're really making it happen."

"I'm trying to, baby," I sighed. "I wish I had done this sooner… before I left home and carried my silly butt to New York."

"You say that a lot," River observed. "But don't you think you'd be a different person if you hadn't left home?"

"Maybe," I told her. "I should have stayed in school… maybe life wouldn't be such a struggle."

"And maybe it would. What if you went to college, got a degree, and then spent your whole life trying to pay back student loans. Life would still be a struggle and you'd probably still end up making soap in the basement… except you wouldn't have a basement because you'd still be living with MawMaw."

She was a mess… and she was wise beyond her years. I couldn't help laughing at the scenario she laid before me.

"If I hadn't left home and become a soap maker, I probably wouldn't have met my boyfriend, huh?" I asked her.

I stifled a giggle as she side eyed me. "Hold up… boyfriend? When did you get a boyfriend?"

"A few weeks ago."

"Wait, what? You haven't even been dating anyone… have you?"

"Nope."

"Then how is he your boyfriend? Are you just messing with me, Auntie?"

"No, I promise," I sighed. "It all happened really fast."

"Obviously." she smiled teasingly, showing off the turquoise bands on her braces. "He must be really special."

I nodded with a smile of my own. "His name is Damian, he's a writer, he's loving and he's kind—"

"Does Mama know? Does MawMaw know?" she interrupted.

"Your Mama doesn't know anything about him. MawMaw knows." I smiled. "And now you know. Wanna see a picture?"

She nodded excitedly and I pulled out my phone, showing her a picture we took on the red carpet. She stared at the picture for a few minutes before sighing deeply.

"Auntie, he's cute… but how do you know he's right?"

"What do you mean?" I asked.

"How do you… know?"

The look on her face told me it was more than a question. She was going to file whatever information I gave in her mental notebook for later use. She not only looked like me, but she also took certain social cues from me, learning how to be free while still being focused on her goals through watching me navigate life. She was constantly watching.

"It's a level of comfort," I said after careful thought. "When I met him… I thought he was cute… I have to admit I lusted after him. I felt fireworks but… not in my heart. River, when you meet a boy… sometimes your body feels things that gives you the illusion of love. It can be very confusing. When it's all said and done, you realize you loved the way he made your body feel… but you hated the way he made you feel as a person. That's not love. You gotta pay attention to your brain… cuz sometimes your kitty can fool your heart. You have to learn the difference."

"When did you know your heart wasn't being fooled?" she asked.

"My soul feels safe with him," I said simply. "He makes me feel good… as a person. He makes me feel important. He makes me feel secure. I can let down my guard and just be myself without having to worry about whether or not I look dumb," I added with a laugh. "I ate spaghetti in front of him and I didn't even feel awkward."

"Oh gosh, please tell me you didn't slurp your noodles."

"Only a little," I assured her.

She stared off into the distance and I watched her pretty face as she dissected the information, storing what she needed and probably discarding the part about the spaghetti.

"Can I ask you something, Auntie?"

"Anything, baby."

"If he's all those things, why hasn't he been here helping us? Why isn't he here when you need him the most? If you love someone… shouldn't you support them? Isn't that why you threw that soap? Are you mad? Am I imagining that?"

It was such a serious question. I was proud of her observations, but it broke my heart to hear her questioning the love I described in comparison to the reality she saw. I was telling her one thing but showing her another.

"I asked him not to disturb me," I admitted. "I told him I needed a break to take care of this order and that I didn't want him to distract me."

The look on her face could only be described as 'what the fuck' and saying it out loud again had me feeling as dumb as it sounded.

"Ummm… I'm sorry, Auntie, but that's just stupid." She hopped off the table and stared at me as if she couldn't quite believe what she was hearing. "I just don't understand what you're doing. Are you crazy or something? I've been in here slaving away making this soap, and you have a whole boyfriend you won't let come over and help? Mannnnn, I call bullshit on that."

"First of all, watch your mouth," I said sternly. "And second of all, you're getting paid remember?"

"I know that, Auntie, but I've been working a lot of extra hours when I could be relaxing. It's been nonstop. I'm tired. What is the point of having a boyfriend if you have to pretend you don't need him? I'm sorry, but that doesn't sound like safety to me."

Damn.

She was only a teenager and schooling me like our roles were reversed. She was calling me out on my bullshit with a curiosity that fascinated and unnerved me at the same time. A literal child could see through the games I was playing with myself. LeeLee was psychic. She didn't count.

"You're right," I finally said.

"About which part?" she asked.

"All of it," I sighed. "It *is* bullshit."

"I just feel like… I don't know… If you're always telling someone you don't need them, they'll feel unappreciated and stop offering to help… I know I would."

I grabbed her hand and pulled her into a tight hug. This kid gave me life. I loved her for reminding me that an independent woman doesn't have to be independent all the time. I was used to being the teacher, not the student, but I loved watching her grow into the woman she would someday become.

"Do you know how much I love you?" I asked her.

"Yep."

"How do you know?"

"Because you always tell me," she said sweetly.

"And don't you ever forget it," I said softly.

River kissed my cheek before running upstairs and turning the television on. As far as she was concerned, her shift was over. In her words, I had a "whole boyfriend" that could be helping. She was done for the day. I couldn't do anything but shake my head and chuckle before going upstairs and joining her on the couch.

Chapter 15

Windsor Elaine Bradley

I wanted to call him.

It was half past two in the morning, and I couldn't sleep for the thoughts racing through my brain.

"That doesn't sound like safety to me."

River's words mocked the independent existence I'd forced myself into since my days as a young model in New York City. I was so determined not to allow a man to take anything from me… I was unable to accept anything Damian wanted to give.

I *needed* him.

The independence I once valued was beginning to feel like solitary confinement. The walls were closing in on me. It was claustrophobic. I was choking on my liberation. Drowning in my freedom. Hungry for the shackles that chained my heart to his.

I didn't even want to make love, I just wanted to touch him. I wanted to feel him on the other side of the bed… hear his shallow breaths in the dark as he slept beside me. I wanted the security of knowing he was there.

I wanted safety without fear.

"I miss him," I texted LeeLee.

"No shit," she texted back. "Call him, dummy."

I dialed his number and listened as the phone rang once, twice, three times. I was just about to hang up when his sleepy voice came over the line.

"Windsor?" he whispered questioningly. I could tell I woke him up, but it was too late to hang up now.

"Can you come over?" I asked hesitantly.

"I'm on my way."

Just like that.

No questions.

No hesitation.

He was on his way.

I didn't think to change out of the oversized t-shirt I was wearing and put on something sexy. I ran downstairs without even glancing in the mirror and opened the front door, standing with my hands pressed against the screen door until I saw the faint glow of headlights slowly easing up my street.

I was standing on the porch by the time he parked and got out of his car, an overnight bag in his left hand as his right hand casually locked his car as he made his way towards me.

I stepped back into the house, holding the door open as he dropped his bag in the foyer and pinned me against the doorframe with his body, his forehead resting against mine, his hands gently encircling my waist.

I lifted my face and stared up at him, taking in the sight of his handsome face. I reached up to touch his newly grown out beard, marveling at how his features had gone from boyishly handsome to '*good lawd*' fine when I wasn't looking.

"I missed you," I whispered cupping his face in my hands and pulling his lips towards mine. Three weeks was a long time to go without physical contact. I hadn't even allowed him to FaceTime me... too afraid seeing his face would have me knocking on his door and ignoring my responsibilities.

"Don't ever shut me out again," he whispered. It wasn't a demand. It was a plea.

The whole time I was obsessing over how his absence was making me feel... I hadn't given a single thought to how our forced separation was making *him* feel. I bit my bottom lip, unsure of what to say to him. What could I say? I felt compelled to tell him the truth.

"I was scared."

"Of me?"

"Of needing you," I admitted. I sighed softly as he backed away from me slightly and pulled me further into the foyer.

He closed the front door and leaned against it, facing me with his arms folded across his chest.

My lord, that beard was making it hard for me to concentrate on the things I needed to say to him. I closed my eyes and balled my hands into fists, cutting into the delicate flesh of my palms with my fingernails.

"Baby, what the hell are you doing?" He started laughing and I suddenly realized how ignorant I must have looked.

"I can't look at you," I whispered, laughing at myself.

"What?"

"It's that damn beard," I told him. I turned my back to him and opened my eyes, "I can't look at you and talk at the same time. That beard makes me…" my voice trailed off. The thought was left dangling in the air.

"This beard makes you what?"

Damian eased up behind me and slid his hands under my t-shirt, resting his palms on my quivering belly. I instinctively leaned into him, my body practically melting into his. If I were wearing panties they would have been drenched.

He put his mouth on my ear and whispered, "Tell me."

His sexy new beard was rubbing against my cheek, both tickling and arousing me at the same time. I could feel the hairs on my arms standing up as he began gently nibbling my earlobe.

"Tell me," he said again, sliding one hand down my torso, cupping my honeypot while my nectar dripped all over his fingers.

"Ooohhh," I moaned, fighting to keep my composure as he began squeezing me with a gentle pulsating motion.

I swiftly turned around to face him, jumping into his arms and wrapping my legs around his waist, kissing him deeply, barely allowing him to catch his breath. His hands brushed against my ass as he unbuckled his pants and pushed them down to his knees.

He slid inside of me and I verbally damned him and that beautiful beard scratching my skin as he buried his face in my neck and gripped me tightly, thrusting up into me with an intensity that could only be fueled by sexual frustration.

"Oooh, I missed you," I whispered breathlessly.

All thoughts of just lying beside him and listening to him breathe were pushed to the back of my mind as he slid me up and down on the part of him I didn't realize I missed until it was inside of me, filling me up with everything he had inside of him.

It was quick. The sensation was too much for either of us to handle as I cried out loudly, digging my feet into his back, trying to pull away but held in place by his strong hands as he hit me harder, faster, until there were tears of pleasure flowing freely down my face.

I gripped him tightly as I felt his body shuddering, a loud moan escaping his lips, as he held me closer, not allowing me to place my feet back on solid ground. He held me, slowly swaying back and forth to a melody only heard in his head. I closed my eyes and laid my head on his shoulder, relaxing in his arms, allowing myself to be cradled with the care I was too stubborn to admit I craved.

"Damian, I love you," I whispered.

"I love you too." He hugged me closer, continued swaying and began singing softly in my ear.

It was the song he sang to me the night we met. A beautiful tune by LTD that spoke of a love we both deserved.

I thought back to that night… the casual way he leaned against the wall as if he didn't give a fuck about that party… the way woman after woman walked past him as if he was blending in with the wallpaper… the way my eyes zeroed in on him like he was the only man in the room… the way he rescued me without me having to verbalize my need to be rescued… the way he looked me in the eyes and told me he saw my confidence before he saw my beauty.

I never imagined I would love him, but there I was… loving him.

I never imagined I would allow myself to need him or any other man, but there I was… needing him.

Needing *him*.

Dick was always nice, but once we disengaged, once he put me down, I wanted Damian to stay. I wanted him with me.

"I need you," I whispered, finally over the distraction of his new beard and his strong hands on my body.

In that moment, in his arms, swaying gently in our own private dance, I gained the strength to tell him everything I felt over the past couple of weeks without him.

"I've needed you every single day," I told him.

"I needed you too, but I didn't want to push you away by insisting we be together when you told me you needed time apart," he sighed.

"I didn't want to get used to depending on you… and then fall apart if you decided you didn't want to be there for me anymore. I didn't want to overwhelm you with… well... me. I can be *a lot*."

"I like *a lot*," he whispered. "I knew you were a lot the moment I met you, Windsor Bradley," he added with a laugh. "Remember what you told me when we were dancing? When I sang to you that night?"

"Ummm, 'I just wanna hear you sing?'" Now it was my turn to laugh.

"After that," he coaxed teasingly.

I rolled my eyes upward as a slow smile spread across my face. "I said, 'if you keep singing like that, I'm gonna have to give you some pussy'."

"I kept singing, didn't I?"

I nodded.

"You wanna know why?"

"Because you wanted some pussy," I said matter-of-factly.

"I mean, yeah, I wanted some pussy. I'm not gonna lie," he chuckled. "But I wanted you. I just wanted to be in your presence, even if it was just for that night.

Your boldness made me feel bold. Your confidence was infectious. You weren't scared of me. You told me what you wanted, and what did I do?"

"You gave it to me," I said softly.

"I didn't even love you yet," he reminded me. "At least I didn't know I did... so, keep that same energy, baby. Don't be scared of this... of *us*. Tell me what you want, and if it's in my power to give it to you... it's yours."

I raised my head and looked him in his eyes.

"What do you want, Windsor?" he asked me.

"Right now?"

"Right now."

"I want you to help me make these last one hundred bars of soap," I said evenly.

"Done," he laughed. "And then?"

"And then I want you to stay," I told him.

"For how long?"

"Forever," I could feel my confidence returning and I had no intention of letting it, or him get away from me again.

"Forever is a long time," he told me.

"Is it too long?" I asked softly.

"It's not long enough," he said after a few thoughtful moments. "I can do forever, Windsor, but I can't do that without putting a ring on your finger."

"That's crazy." I started laughing but stopped short when I realized Damian wasn't joking.

He was staring at me intently and I couldn't look away as he slowly lowered me to my feet. I shivered as my bare feet rested on the cold tile in my foyer. I suddenly felt naked standing in front of him. I was cold but I made no move towards him, and he made no move to reach out and hold me. He kept staring at me and I couldn't tell if he was trying to find the words to continue the crazy direction our conversation was taking or trying to figure out how to take it all back.

"Baby, I'm nowhere near a rich man, but I'm doing my best to get there. I've been chasing this dream for years and it's finally within my grasp. I've been doing okay by myself, but with you, I feel unstoppable. You make me feel like I can do anything." His voice faltered as he reached out to grab my hand. "All that I have to offer you is my love, Windsor. My love and my pride, and my devotion and everything that I'll ever have from now until forever," he said intensely.

"But... we've only known each other for-"

"How long did Adam and Eve know one another?" he interrupted.

"What?" I asked loudly.

"Okay, okay, I took it too far," he said hurriedly. "But baby, I'm just a man. I'm just a man trying to get you to understand that it doesn't matter how long we've known each other. It doesn't matter how we met. None of that matters. I love you! God made Eve and he gave her to Adam—"

"And she made him eat that apple and got them kicked out of paradise," I laughed without meaning to.

Damian smiled as he pulled me closer to him. "He wanted that damn apple almost as much as I want you. I can't get kicked out of paradise, baby. Paradise is wherever you are."

My knees faltered just a little. He noticed and gripped my elbows, steadying me before placing a loving kiss on my forehead.

"Windsor, will you-"

I put a finger to his lips, not allowing him to finish his sentence. It was happening too fast. This wasn't right. Not here. Not now. Not like this…

"Not without a ring," I said softly.

He stared down at me and smiled. He nodded his understanding and kissed my finger. I slid my arms around him and rested my head on his chest, swaying in the silence as he began singing again. I closed my eyes and lost myself in his arms, in his voice, in the words sliding from between his lips, and decided I was in the safest place on Earth.

Chapter 16

Damian Anthony Lawrence

I reached out for her but found myself gripping a fluffy pillow instead of the handful of supple ass I was hoping for. I opened one eye and groaned in disappointment when I realized Windsor was no longer sleeping peacefully beside me. I glanced at my watch and couldn't believe it was only seven. Windsor's early morning call had me hastily packing a bag and jumping on the highway with no thought to speed limits or any other traffic laws. Had I been pulled over, I'd have simply shown the officer a picture of Windsor. There was no way he or she wouldn't understand why I was in such a hurry. And if they didn't understand? Well, I'd have paid any fine just to see the look on her face when I pulled into the driveway and practically skipped up the walkway. She was waiting for me. Not looking out of the window, periodically checking for my arrival, Windsor was standing in the open doorway with her hands pressed against the screen like an eager child who'd been promised a piece of her favorite candy. I prayed she would always consider my presence a treat.

I stretched and reminisced on our early morning lovemaking. It was sweet and salty. Sugar and sweat, her orgasmic tears teased my taste buds as I kissed her with all the frustration of a man who hadn't touched his woman in almost three weeks.

Sleep hadn't come easy. I couldn't stop staring at her. Couldn't stop touching her, kissing her, holding her, intertwining my arms and legs with hers until we resembled a chocolate covered pretzel. I couldn't get enough of her and I finally fell asleep at four o'clock, clutching her like she was my long-lost security blanket.

I sat up and took in my surroundings, for the first time looking around Windsor's bedroom and allowing myself to relax into the fantasy world she'd created there. I was lounging in an English Tudor styled, four poster king-sized bed with beautiful blush and gold tapestry gathered and tied with a bow at each corner. It was a bed fit for a queen. It belonged in a royal bedchamber. I expected nothing less from a woman who was named after a castle.

There was a chaise lounge in the corner by the window. It was covered in the same beautiful tapestry that hung from the bed. I got out of bed and slowly walked towards it, curious about the open book I spied peeking beneath a fuzzy throw blanket.

It was my book. I hadn't given her a book. I didn't want her to think I was expecting her to read it out of loyalty to me, and I didn't want to stress myself out over whether she liked or disliked it.

She had my book.

She purposely bought my book and was intentionally reading it with no pressure from me. It touched me in a way that made me, once again, ask God why he'd chosen me for someone as lovely as her.

I didn't want to sound ungrateful. I didn't want to feel like I didn't deserve her, but damn. There are people who buy lottery tickets every week and never win. I scratched her surface and hit the jackpot on the first try.

I took a deep breath and did a slow 360. My eyes scanned her bedroom, taking it all in, feeling amazed at the spirit of belonging I felt standing in the middle of her sanctuary.

This morning she said she wanted me to stay forever. What did she really mean? Because her requesting my presence forever immediately had me wanting to ask her to marry me.

The words were on my tongue before I realized, and her gentle finger to my lips brought me back to reality.

"Not without a ring," she'd joked with a hint of a smile on her face.

Could it be that she thought about it too? Even in the short time we've been together?

"Awwwww, man, you woke up." She sounded disappointed.

I turned to find Windsor standing in the doorway with a breakfast tray in her hands and a cute pout on her juicy lips.

"I was wondering why you were up so early," I said as I happily returned to bed. "What do we have here?"

"Don't get too excited," she laughed as she placed the tray in front of me and then climbed into bed next to me. "These are frozen waffles, but I plated them perfectly."

And she had. Strawberries and bananas were sliced and fanned out around the waffles with a little ceramic cup full of sweet syrup. It didn't look like the average frozen waffles I'd been served in the past.

"Aren't you eating?" I asked.

"This is for both of us." she laid her head on my shoulder and picked a strawberry slice out of our plate.

"What if I don't like sharing?" I asked jokingly.

"You like sharing," she told me. "You shared the night we met."

"As I recall, I fed you the night we met."

"I earned it." She snuggled closer and opened her mouth as I cut the waffles.

I smiled and gave her the first forkful before taking a few bites for myself. My eyes darted around the room, looking for the remote control before realizing there was no television in Windsor's room. I was so used to watching television while I ate at home, it seemed a little strange to be enjoying breakfast without the morning news blaring, whether I was paying attention to it or not.

"Where's the television?" I asked her.

"Downstairs in the den," she told me.

"All the way downstairs?"

"What do you need a television for? You have a plate full of frozen waffles and a beautiful woman to entertain you," she said. "Besides, bedrooms are for sex and sleeping. When I'm in here, it's because I want to fully relax."

"It's a beautiful room," I told her. "Very tranquil."

"It's not too girly for you?" she asked me.

I shook my head. "I like it. It's comfortable."

I placed the, now empty, tray of food on the floor next to the bed and pulled her into my arms. As she rested her head on my chest, I sensed there was something she wanted to say but didn't quite know how.

"What's on your mind?" I asked, smoothing her fine edges with my fingertips.

"What do you mean?" she answered with a question.

"Something felt off just now," I told her.

"Oh, come on. We're having a beautiful morning. Let's not complicate it with feelings and emotions," she laughed and then added thoughtfully, "I don't always want to talk about my feelings because I don't want to ruin the moment."

"So, I was right. Something is off."

"Something's always off, baby." Windsor rolled over, turning her back to me and snuggled deeper under the covers, "I'm gonna try to get a little more sleep before I start working on that soap order. We only have about a hundred bars to go."

I could have let it go. Maybe I should have, but I didn't want to leave it like this... with her thinking sharing her feelings was ruining the moment.

I tapped her on the shoulder and when she didn't respond, I pulled her into me, sliding my arms around her and placing my cheek on hers.

"I love strong, powerful, bold as fuck, bossy Windsor," I told her, "it's who you are. Who you've become, but it's okay to be scared or sad or unsure or hell, pissed off if that's what you're feeling at any given moment. You don't have to constantly fight to keep your composure with me. In Philly, when you asked me not to hurt you, I made a vow that I never would. I need you to trust me enough to prove that to you."

"I just feel like… I don't know. We're having a good morning but… sometimes things trigger me, and I have to control my reactions."

"You don't have to control shit with me, baby. What triggered you? I need to know so I can make sure to be more aware."

"It's stupid," she sighed. "The whole TV in the bedroom thing. It just brought up some bad memories."

"Tell me."

"I suffer from clinical depression. A television in my room would make it easier for me to just stay in here and hide from the world. It's crazy. I can be happy, and it will just… BAM… hit me out of nowhere. I used to be on medication, but it made me sick, so now I use coping mechanisms. I meditate. I do my deep breathing, she explained. "I make soap," she added with a little laugh. "I garden, I sit on my back patio, I eat an edible or smoke a little weed… anything to keep me out of this bed. I am always consciously aware of my emotions."

"How do you feel now?" I asked her.

"I'm happy, Damian. But that doesn't mean that depression won't try to creep up on me. It's a disease. A disease I'm beating by taking the necessary precautions. If I wanna watch TV… I have to walk my ass downstairs and sit on the couch. When I'm in my bedroom… I'm asleep… or reading. I don't even play on my phone anymore cuz TikTok will have my ass up until the wee hours of the morning."

"That shit is the devil, ain't it?" I laughed. I'd watched my fair share of TikTok videos. I knew how easy it was to not realize you've been watching for hours.

Still, something else was going on. I wanted to know, but I didn't want to push her. I rolled over until I was facing her. I stared into her face, afraid of what she wasn't telling me… afraid of whether or not I'd be able to handle it if she did. She opened her mouth to speak but closed it several times. It was obvious she didn't know how to say what needed to be said.

"Do you think you'll wake up one day and want more kids?" she asked.

"No," I told her.

"How can you be so sure? Daniel is only 4."

"I'm sure," I reiterated.

She didn't look sure. She sighed loudly and then looked at me intently. "I love you."

"I love you too."

I did. I *loved* her. I loved her so much that whatever secret she was keeping… I knew I'd still love her, no matter what it was. When she was ready to tell me… I'd be ready to listen.

"I almost asked you to marry me last night," I said suddenly.

"I know," she said, staring at me, her eyes a little watery.

"You stopped me."

"I saved you," she told me.

"I don't need saving."

I pulled her closer until her head was resting on my chest, her warm breath tickling my flesh as I lay there, afraid to let go of her. She fell asleep. I felt my heart swelling as I lay there just listening to her breathe. Every time she stirred, I held her tighter, pulled her closer, kissed her forehead, smoothed her hair… anything to let her know that I was still there… and I wasn't going anywhere.

Chapter 17

Damian Lawrence Anthony

I awakened to the sound of multiple voices laughing at a joke I couldn't hear. I recognized Windsor's voice speaking in low tones, but couldn't make out the rest of the voices, giggling like schoolgirls.

I hopped out of Windsor's bed and opened two closet doors before finding the entry into her spacious master bathroom. An old-fashioned claw tub sat in front of a beautiful bay window and I stood there for a moment, imagining Windsor soaking in that tub, immersed in bubbles as candles flickered all around her.

There was a walk-in shower on the other side of the bathroom, and a separate door that contained the toilet I needed badly first thing in the morning. It wasn't until I stood at the sink washing my hands, that I realized she laid out a big fluffy drying towel and a washcloth for me. My overnight bag was nestled in a corner and I breathed a sigh of relief. I most certainly didn't want to have to tip-toe downstairs in a towel to retrieve it.

I quickly showered, dressed, and then looked at myself in the mirror. I stared at my beard. I was still getting used to it. I'd planned on shaving it off, but Windsor's reaction had me considering keeping it permanently. It was finally past the prickly, itchy new growth stage. I turned my head to the side a few times, admiring my reflection. Daddy had a beard like this. It was thick, and full and perfectly trimmed. I used to go to the barbershop with him and watch as Mr. Brooks, his old school barber, would wash, steam, and trim his beard early every Saturday morning. It was a ritual the boys of the family had. Up early to go get donuts and then haircuts. The barbershop tradition survived, although less frequently, as Devin and I eased into adulthood. It was our first experience with self-care and not a day goes by that I don't remember standing on a stepstool in the bathroom mirror as Daddy taught me how to brush my waves and tie a satin do-rag around my head before I went to bed at night.

"Brush with your waves, not against them," he would say as he fit my little hands around his big wave brush until I was old enough to have one of my own.

The older I got, the more I looked like him and I knew my mama would faint when she finally saw me with the beard. I smiled broadly, bit my bottom lip, and then stroked my beard while giving myself a 'come hither' gaze in the mirror. I burst out laughing at my own stereotypically 'lite skinned' poses before giving myself a final once over. I was kinda feeling myself with the beard. My swagger was different. Women noticed me now, more than ever, but their subtle looks and sometimes bold advances were in vain. I was taken and I didn't mind telling them so.

I was walking out of the bedroom when I found myself face to face with a much younger version of Windsor. She stared at me openly, curiously, as if she were sizing me up and deciding whether I was worthy of being in her space. I was taken aback, unsure of what to say. Her presence was shocking.

"I know," she said as if she could read my mind. "I look just like Auntie. Everybody says it."

"Yeah, you could be—"

"Her daughter. I know," she interrupted impatiently. "You look better with a beard," she added thoughtfully. Her tone told me she wasn't impressed, merely being observant.

"Thanks?" I answered. "And you are?"

"I'm River," she said slowly. "And you're Mr. Anthony."

I nodded, "You can call me Damian."

"I'm not allowed to call adults by their first names." She seemed insulted; I would even suggest such a heinous thing.

"Can you tell me where your Auntie is?" I asked.

"Can is the ability, Mr. Anthony. The question is, *will* I tell you where my Auntie is…"

Ohhhh, she was a smart ass. A Sixteen-year-old smart ass who had inherited more than her looks from her Aunt. She was still a kid, but I decided the best course of action was to show no mercy. I could be a smart ass too.

"Are you always this pleasant?" I asked her.

"Nope. I'm usually very mean," she told me. "I'm not sold on you yet."

"Well, you just met me."

"So did Aunt Winnie." River narrowed her eyes at me. "Why weren't you here when we were struggling to make all that soap?"

"Windsor said she didn't need any help."

107

"Well, she did. *We* did," River said accusingly. "She doesn't always tell people what she needs. You have to *know*."

"I know that now… and I apologize," I said sincerely. "You're right. I shoulda been here. It won't happen again."

"It better not! What are your intentions?"

"What do you mean?"

"What's your end game, Mr. Anthony?" she said it slowly, and in an annoyed voice, as if I were a pesky toddler asking if she had games on her phone.

I stifled a chuckle. "I wanna marry your Auntie," I told her.

"Do you have a ring?"

"Well, not yet. I'm—"

River rolled her eyes, held up her hand and said, "Get your business straight."

She walked away as if she didn't have time to hear my excuses. I could do nothing but chuckle, out loud this time. She not only looked like Windsor… she acted like her too.

"Yes, ma'am!" I laughed, marveling at her audacity while admiring her ability to own her thoughts at the same time.

"Auntie's in the kitchen," she called over her shoulder before disappearing into a room down the hall. "Just follow the smell of coffee."

I shook my head as I made my way downstairs. Using my nose as a guide, I followed the smell of coffee into a spacious kitchen where four women were sitting at a table laughing and sharing a plate of pastries.

"Oh, hey, babe," Windsor grinned the moment she saw me.

"Good morning, or should I say, afternoon?" I said, smiling at the ladies sitting at the table. I pulled Windsor into my arms for a quick kiss and then laughed in surprise as my eyes spied a familiar face.

"LeeLee!" I exclaimed happily. My grin was huge.

LeeLee stood up and gave me a big hug that I returned with enthusiasm. She was the reason I was standing in Windsor's kitchen. She was the person who brought us back together after our unconventional beginning. I owed LeeLee a debt of gratitude that could never be repaid.

"Damian, this is my mom, and my sister, Paris," Windsor said warmly.

"Which is which?" I asked.

Seriously.

The three of them looked more like sisters than mother and daughters.

"Oh, you just scored major points with me," Windsor's mother stood up and gave me a big hug, "I'm Patricia, but all my friends call me, Pat."

"You can call her, Miss Pat," Paris said, rolling her eyes before offering me her hand to shake.

"You must be River's mother," I said with a laugh.

"Oh, Lord, you've met our little smart ass," Miss Pat laughed. "She spends wayyyy too much time with her Auntie Winnie. Please tell me she was nice to you?"

"I think she was probably as nice as a teenaged girl who slaved away making soap with her Auntie while I was missing in action, can be," I answered jokingly. "She definitely got it honest," I added, winking at Paris who, to my surprise, blushed a little.

"She went there?" Windsor asked.

"Ohhhh yeah," I grabbed a pastry and bit into it. A gush of strawberries and cream cheese filled my mouth and the sudden explosion of flavor startled me in a good way. "Oh my god," I mumbled with my mouth full.

"Good huh?" Miss Pat said proudly. "Paris made them."

"Wow," I said to Paris. "You need to sell these!"

"I do, I have a little bakery down on Greenwood," she told me.

"Wait a minute, *Paris de Tulsa?* That's you?" I asked.

Her smile said it all. I passed up *Paris de Tulsa* several times because I thought it was a part of the gentrification of Black Wallstreet. I was honest and told her that. She understood, stating that, unfortunately, many blacks thought she was white owned.

"Well, I was a marketing major. Let's work together and change that," I told her, "I can put together a marketing plan that would have black folks lined up to get one of these strawberry cream cheese things."

"Really?" she asked me.

"Yeah, I do all the marketing for my mother's restaurant, *Claudine's*."

"Your mother owns *Claudine's*?" LeeLee, Paris, Miss Pat, and Windsor yelled in unison.

I started laughing. "Yep. My brother does the books, I do the marketing, mama and a couple of my aunties do the cooking and a few of my cousins are servers. It's a true family run business."

"I love Claudine's," Miss Pat told me. "Me and the girls eat there all the time, but it's usually carry-out. We like to take it up to *The Gathering Place* and have a picnic when the weather is nice, or sit in my kitchen and eat and gossip about our week."

"Well, you'll have to come as my guest on tasting night... all of you. Once a year, Mama and my aunties try out potential limited-edition menu items on the staff and our other family members. It's a good time. We do karaoke and play spades and dominoes. It's like a family reunion up in there."

I couldn't believe how at ease I felt with Windsor's mom and sister. I pulled up a chair and we all sat there talking and laughing together as if we'd known one another for years. Even sullen River came downstairs and sat on the counter, listening to our conversation while writing in a notebook. Every now and then she'd hear something she couldn't pretend to ignore and burst out laughing.

It was like sitting at a table surrounded by my own family. I looked over at LeeLee and smiled. I could tell Miss Pat had adopted her as one of her own. LeeLee had a look of contentment on her face as she looked around the table. There was a story there and I had the sudden thought that I needed to write it down.

LeeLee looked over at me and smiled, nodding as if she knew exactly what I was thinking. It should have unnerved me, but it didn't. LeeLee's gifts brought Windsor and I together. I embraced it and wanted to know more about her and how she realized her extraordinary sense of perception and spirituality.

My mind wandered off as I began weaving a fictional tale in my mind about a woman who drove a cab and unintentionally read the minds of her passengers. One night a passenger hopped into her car and the cab driver immediately knew her passenger had just murdered his wife and planned on killing her too.

I pushed back from the table and everyone jumped.

"I'm sorry, I just had an idea! I gotta grab my laptop. You ladies just keep talking, I gotta write this out before I lose the thought," I said hurriedly as I quickly made my way out of the kitchen.

"Writers, boy I tell ya!" I heard River scoff.

Everyone laughed, including me.

I went into Windsor's bedroom, grabbed my laptop, sat in her beautifully upholstered settee near the window and began typing.

When I looked up from my laptop again, the sun had gone down, and the laughter downstairs had ceased. Windsor was sleeping soundly in the bed across the room. I looked at my watch. It was late. I must have been so engrossed in my writing that I didn't notice her come in.

I imagine she probably stared at me from the doorway, taking in the sight of me lounging so comfortably by her window and decided not to disturb me, not even for a kiss good night. Or perhaps, she had called out to me and I was so preoccupied by my laptop, I hadn't answered. Maybe she'd shrugged, a little dejected that my writing could take such precedence over her, and had gone to sleep feeling neglected.

That last thought made me feel sad. My writing has always been a time-consuming passion, and more than a few relationships have fallen by the wayside in my attempts to write a best-seller. My money was sometimes a little funny, and while my most basic needs were always met, my son came first. The last woman in my life, Priscilla, didn't like that. She wanted more.

So, did I.

But 'more' to me meant something beyond the material. Something beyond money. It meant having someone who understood my need for time. Time with my son. Time to research. Time to write. Time to reflect. Time to love on her, but not always in the time she needed it.

I never wanted Windsor to feel like I was choosing my words over her heart. I'd burn every page, stomp on flash drives, break every pen and pencil in my house if it meant I could wake up every morning and roll over into her warm body.

I'd give it up for her.

She would never ask me to.

I closed my laptop and slid out of my clothes before sliding into bed with her. She was naked. I pulled her body close to mine until her warm buttocks were nestled snugly in the spoon of my crotch. Her long locs were carefully braided and stuffed under a long satin bonnet, exposing the back of her neck. I buried my nose in her exposed skin, inhaling slowly, taking in the scent of the orange ginger oil she often dabbed on the back of her neck, her wrists, and the valley between her breasts.

I inhaled again, pulling her closer, sliding one hand down the length of her body until her honey pot lay nestled in my palm. I squeezed gently, holding it in my hand, pulsating against her until I felt her sensual juices seeping through my fingers.

She stirred, moaning softly in her sleep, legs parting ever so slightly. I watched her sleeping face as her mind lingered somewhere between deep sleep and lucid dreaming. Her breathing quickened as I slid my fingers inside of her, caressing her until the walls of her love swelled, gripping my fingers as if she didn't want to let me go, nearly trapping me inside of her.

I kept stroking her, gently at first, and then harder, faster, the whole time watching her face as it contorted with expressions of both pleasure and confusion, waiting for the moment her eyes would fly open and she would step into this reality with me.

"Damian," she whispered.

She reached for me, eyes still closed, back arched, legs opened wider, lips parted, a river of orgasmic juices pushed past my fingers and spilled into my palm, baptizing my hand in her divine sweetness.

I kissed her, maneuvering my body until I was resting between her legs, ready to push past her swollen walls and fill her up with the part of me that needed to show her that I would never neglect her, would always be available to her, would never leave her wondering how or what I felt about her.

She wrapped her legs around my waist, guiding me inside of her and locking me in place as my gentle rhythm became more intense. She pushed back against me, meeting every thrust with wild abandon. I was the mystery lover in her lucid dream. Her fantasy and her reality.

She was my everything.

And as my body shuddered, pouring my seed into a womb that couldn't receive it, I realized I was truly giving up everything for love.

For her.

Was she asking me to, or had I volunteered?

She opened her eyes and stared into mine, love and lust reflected in her pupils as I leaned in to kiss her.

I volunteered.

Chapter 18

Windsor Elaine Bradley

I almost told him. I almost opened my mouth and spilled my heaviest secret. It was nobody's business, and although I knew I'd have to confront it one day... I didn't want to lay it on him the first time he woke up in my bed.

Still... he knew I was hiding something. He didn't press me for answers I wasn't ready to give, and for that, I was appreciative, but my reluctance to tell him my whole truth was forcing me to take a step back and look at myself. It was forcing me to look at *us*.

I barely knew this man.

But I *knew* this man.

I knew him in more than just the biblical sense.

I knew his soul, even if I didn't know every detail of his personal history. He knew my soul despite not knowing every detail of my personal history. I didn't want to ruin it with too many details about things I couldn't change. Things I didn't want to think about. Things I pushed past every day as I tried to forget.

I loved him. Every new thing I learned about him made me love him more. I didn't want to lose him.

I couldn't believe how quickly I fell for him. He's not the first relationship I've had since Ian, but he's the first man I've allowed to penetrate my surface and dive headfirst into *me*... not just my body.

I loved the way he looked at me, the way he held me, the way he supported me, loved me... the way he accepted every part of me... the good and the bad. The ugly and the beautiful. The unknown.

Allowing Damian, a glimpse into some of my weaknesses didn't make me feel weak. It made me feel stronger, and in that strength, I found a happy medium between the Windsor who always had to be in control and the Windsor who was willing to stand back and allow someone else to take the lead… and not just anyone else.

Damian.

It had to be Damian.

Standing in front of him now, his arms around my waist, his hands on top of mine, mimicking my actions as I cut soap into tiny bars while old school slow jams played in the background, was one of the most sensual experiences of my entire life.

I felt like Demi Moore in *Ghost*, except this scene wouldn't end with Damian and I making love covered in shea butter and essential oils. It would end with Damian helping me box the remaining bars of soap and shipping them to Philadelphia.... that shit was sexy as hell to me.

This sale was going to enable me to buy supplies strictly from my profits without dipping into my savings. With any luck, *Windsor Noire* would become a solid source of income. My dream was to move my little soap factory out of my basement and into a small warehouse, but I didn't want to lose the intimacy of hand cutting my soaps. It was a ritual I learned to rely on for my own sanity. It was a Xanax and a Zoloft with a side of marijuana. It was a natural antidepressant, and in my heart, I knew allowing a machine to cut my soaps would tear away at my soul, removing the little piece of me I put into every bar.

"This is relaxing," Damian said, gently nibbling at my earlobe.

"Sir, that's not what we're doing here," I laughed, shifting my neck in a feeble attempt to escape the tingles he was sending down my spine. That shift caused my neck to be exposed in a way that was obviously irresistible, because he bit me, gently, like a vampire buttering up a virgin for that life changing nip.

"See, you're trying to get something started we don't have time to finish." I slid out of his arms and crossed the room quickly, putting space and boxes of soap between us.

"Maybe I should go upstairs and grab my laptop… do a little writing while you print out your shipping labels," he laughed.

"No," I said, a little too quickly.

I needed him to learn to prioritize his time and not run to his laptop whenever a new thought or idea hit him. I needed *our* time to be *our* time. Not time in between his inspirational thoughts.

He spent the entire afternoon and night before writing.

He didn't notice when I came into the bedroom to tell him lunch was ready.

He didn't notice when I came into the bedroom to tell him dinner was ready.

He didn't even notice when I got into bed without kissing him goodnight.

I wasn't mad at him, but I was disappointed.

Maybe I was getting a taste of my own medicine. I mean, I had told him to stay away so I could finish my work, and was that really any different than what I was lowkey complaining about now?

Still… I had to nip that behavior in the bud. I admitted I needed him, so he needed to be here with me… mind *and* body.

I told him that.

He nodded in agreement.

"What do you need me to do?" he asked sincerely.

I put my reading glasses on and sat down at my computer.

"I need you to grab these labels as I print them and put them on the boxes," I told him. "And then I need you to help me carry them to the door so the post office can pick them up."

As I printed the last five shipping labels, I glanced around the basement and smiled at all the boxes being picked up by the post office in the morning. I did it. With the help of my family and my new friend LeeLee, it was done… an entire week ahead of schedule. Once I printed all the labels and Damian placed them securely on the coordinating boxes, I logged into my invoicing account and sent the final invoice for the wholesale order.

I was proud of myself. Proud of *us*, but if this led to more large orders, I was going to need more help. I couldn't do this by myself, and I wanted to preserve the methods that pulled me out of an identity crisis and taught me to pursue a career that made me happy.

It was a beautiful problem to have.

I watched as Damian placed the last label, and then carried the last box to the designated waiting area. Not only did I have the large hotel order, but I also hadn't halted production on my customer's orders. A local celebrity had bought a few bars of soap and loved them. Now I also had orders pouring in from the unexpected, yet welcome, free advertising her love of my products brought.

That was also a beautiful problem to have.

I stared at Damian, marveling at the way his basketball shorts brushed against all the right parts as he moved shirtless through the basement. His slim, yet toned body was glistening with sweat as he made sure all the boxes he moved were stable and secure. If an intellectual man was a turn on, an intellectual man working until sweat poured from his body was like placing a volcano between my legs and coaxing it to erupt.

Damn.

He was both.

Intellectual and hard working.

My erogenous senses were tingling, and while I didn't want to feel like our relationship was built on sex, our relationship was literally birthed from sex. I couldn't deny the way my body reacted when I was around him.

It was that fucking beard.

That beautifully lined up, perfectly oiled, grown man beard that had me wanting to jump into his arms and let him make love to me against the boxes we just packed.

Bold Windsor pushed away from my desk and approached him, taking off my smock as I closed the distance between us. I was half asleep when he made love to me last night, but I was fully awake now and I wanted to feel him inside of me again.

I didn't know how long the feeling of always wanting to be physically connected to him would last, but I wanted to take advantage of every minute of it.

This is what new love feels like.

Fucking and loving and working and playing, and then fighting and fucking and loving and working and playing until you settle into a rhythm that either leads to monotony and comfort or monotony and restlessness.

I couldn't imagine feeling restless with Damian in my life, but something in my spirit was worried he would eventually become… restless. He would eventually want… more.

More than me.

More than I can give him.

It's a sobering thought, but not sobering enough for me to stop pouring into him as enthusiastically as he was pouring into me. I wanted him for as long as he was willing to let me have him, and although I was afraid of what heartbreak possibly lay ahead, I was more afraid of not being loved by him in this moment.

I took his hand in mine and kissed the tip of each finger.

"Thank you for helping me, baby. How can I ever repay you?

I stared up at him with a look I hoped conveyed innocence.

"I can think of a few ways," he stared down at me and smiled.

"Tell me."

He pulled me into his sweaty arms and showed me.

Chapter 19

Damian Lawrence Anthony

"Daddy!"

The force in which he threw his little body into my arms nearly toppled me over. I held him close, inhaling his scent. The new baby smell was slowly transitioning into a mixture of outside, peanut butter, and the dash of cologne he insisted his stepfather, Kelvin, spray on him every morning.

FaceTime was cool… but there was nothing like seeing him in person and holding his tiny body in my arms. I hugged him a little tighter. That four-hour drive was worth it just to see the look of joy on his face when he saw me standing in the front yard.

"How's my main man?" I asked, holding him out at arm's length, marveling at the resemblance between us. Trying not to frown at the little Jacob Sanders, Dallas Cowboys jersey he was wearing.

Kelvin did that shit on purpose. He knew I was a Chiefs fan. I chuckled at his audacity.

"Daddy, your beard is scratchy," Daniel giggled before giving me eskimo kisses and then hugging my neck again. "Daddy, are you sleeping in my room?" he whispered into my ear.

"Don't I always sleep in your room?" I whispered back.

Daniel nodded happily and then waved at Felicia.

"Mommy, look! It's Daddy!"

"I see, baby! Are you so happy?"

"I'm SO happy!"

I loved how happy he was to see me. When Felicia announced she was moving to Dallas with her new husband and my baby… I was furious. More than that, I was hurt. I understood Kelvin had a job offer he couldn't turn down, but the thought of my baby living in another state devastated me.

I saw him whenever I wanted… which was all the time when he was in Tulsa. Unless his mother had plans for him, I was free to scoop him up for Daddy and Daniel time three or four times a week.

When they moved, my primary thought was… would Daniel forget me? He was two years old. Would he suddenly look at Kelvin as his Daddy and see me as just a man who made a four-hour drive to see him every other weekend… in good weather? In bad weather I flew standby as much as possible, but I couldn't always get a flight out.

I FaceTimed Daniel every day, even if it was only five minutes. I read him stories, made funny faces, told him how much I loved him as he kissed the phone, leaving spit and food residue all over his mama's screen.

Two years later… I still wasn't used to this new normal, but I accepted it, realizing my anger was rooted in pain, not any malice on the part of Kelvin and Felicia.

Shit, I was in the process of looking for a job in the Dallas area when I met Windsor. Did halting that process make me a bad father or just a fool in love?

I blinked a few times and stared at Felecia. She was standing on the front porch watching us with a big smile on her face.

I walked onto the porch, still holding Daniel in my arms and gave her a big hug. "Hey, Leesh," I said, kissing her on the cheek. "You look beautiful, as always," I added, still impressed by the sight of this woman who had given me my greatest gift.

Her closely cropped, blonde hair was tapered into a curly mini afro. It complimented her oval face and high cheekbones. Her brown skin, free of makeup, looked as smooth as silk. There was once a time when we spoke every day… when we told one another everything. Our transition from friends to lovers, back to friends, and then co-parents had been seamless. We were both convinced our ill-fated romance was just the universe's way of giving us a kid neither of us knew we wanted. We were tied to one another forever.

"I see you're still out here thirst trappin' with that beard," she said, reaching out and putting her palm on my cheek. "It looks good. I bet somebody's daughter is all over you," she added with a laugh.

If only she knew.

She led me into the house. The smell of Kelvin's famous slow cooker ribs caressed my nostrils, and I couldn't help the excited smile that took over my face. I would never tell my mama, but Kelvin's slow cooker ribs were a smidge better than hers. He usually served greens and cornbread with them. As I walked into the kitchen, I was thrilled to see a pan of cornbread on the counter and a pot of greens sitting on the stove.

"Look Papi, Daddy's here!" Daniel yelled in his high-pitched voice.

Papi. We don't know why Daniel calls Kelvin that, but it works. He knows I'm his daddy, but he also knows that Kelvin is his bonus father. I like Kelvin. I like the way he takes care of Felecia and Daniel, and he isn't jealous of our friendship. I think the friendship Kelvin and I formed with one another was a surprise to us both. We had a lot in common and it just made things easier.

"Heyyyy! What's going on, man? As you can see... I used you as an excuse to make these ribs." He gave me a quick bro hug and then handed me a cold beer.

"My man!" I exclaimed as I took a long sip.

Daniel scrambled to get down and ran into the den where I could hear Winnie the Pooh playing on the big screen.

"He's getting so big," I said in astonishment.

"Growing like a weed." Kelvin agreed.

"So, what's up with that bullshit jersey you got my son wearing? I know you did that shit on purpose! Sanders ain't even in the league no more."

Kelvin's exaggerated laugh confirmed my suspicions. I felt a tug on my jeans and looked down to see Maleah, Kelvin, and Felicia's two-year old, holding her arms up, a sign she wanted to be picked up!

I sure hoped she didn't hear me say, 'bullshit.'

"BB!" She yelled, jumping up and down until I scooped her up in my arms and showered her with kisses.

No one knows why she calls me BB, but that little cutie could call me whatever she wanted. She had me wrapped around her finger as if she were my own. I never showed up empty handed. If I bought something for Daniel, I made sure to pick up something for Maleah as well.

"Maleahhhh," I said, dancing around the kitchen with her, "BB is gonna buy you a Kansas City Chiefs cheerleading outfit! You wanna be a cheerleader?"

"I will K-I-L-L you!" Kelvin threatened jokingly.

He motioned for me to sit down at the kitchen table. Felecia wandered in and took the seat directly across from me. Kelvin immediately placed a small mason jar full of orange juice in front of her. Knowing Kelvin, it was freshly squeezed. He didn't play around when it came to the health of his family. He'd gotten me into juicing and had even gifted me a juicer for my 39th birthday.

"Mmmmm, you put ginger in this?" Felecia asked after taking, what looked like, a long satisfying sip.

"Yep. That will help with that swelling in your knee," he said lovingly.

I loved to see it. I loved to see her being loved the way she deserved to be loved. Loved seeing her taken care of.

I bounced Maleah on my knee and stared at Kelvin and Felicia.

"I met someone." I blurted it out without thinking.

They both stared at me in astonishment.

"Ima need another beer for this. You want one?" Kelvin laughed.

Without waiting for an answer, he placed another Stella in front of me and a sippy cup in front of Maleah.

"Is it the woman I saw pictures of you with a few months ago?" Felecia asked.

"You saw those?" I asked. "Why didn't you say anything?"

"I figured you'd tell me when and if there was something to tell." She shrugged.

"There's something to tell," I told her.

"Do tell…" She put her elbows on the table and stared at me with her chin in her hands.

"I hate it when you do that," I told her.

"I know. Tell me about this woman," she said with a smile. "How does she feel about you being here?"

"What do you mean?"

"You're here almost every other weekend unless you have a publicity engagement. Does she have an issue with it?"

"An issue with me seeing my son?" I asked her. "No. She thinks it's great. She's happy for me. She has her own thing going. She's probably grateful for the break," I added with a little laugh.

"She knows how close we are? Not all women can handle that."

"She knows, and she has no issue with it. She encourages it. Says it's better for Daniel that we don't have any drama."

"Kids?"

"No kids. Never been married. Forty, and before you ask, there's nothing wrong with her."

Felecia rolled her eyes and glanced over at Kelvin as if she was waiting for him to jump in on this interrogation.

"What's her name?" Kelvin asked carefully.

Okay. They were gonna play good cop, bad cop with me. I decided to go along with it.

"Her name is Windsor."

"You love her," Kelvin said, staring at me. He glanced over at Felecia.

"Oh my God. You want to introduce her to Daniel," she said with a stunned expression on her face.

I nodded.

"Wow," she said simply. "Does Mama Dot know? Has she met her yet?

"I mean, she knows about her. She just hasn't met her yet," I confessed. "I wanted to talk to you first."

It was reminiscent of a conversation Felecia and I had three years ago. She'd met the man she wanted to spend her life with, and she wanted to introduce him to Daniel. When Felecia and I split, we both agreed to shield Daniel from the ups and downs of our dating lives. There were to be no casual acquaintance introductions. The last thing either of us wanted was for our son to be confused.

At that time, I told Felecia she could introduce Daniel to Kelvin, but I needed to meet him before he met my son. It wasn't that I didn't trust Felecia's judgement. I didn't trust anyone with my child… or his mother. I wasn't in love with her, but I would always love her. I didn't want her spending time with anyone who would fuck her over and harm my child in the process.

"So… it's serious?" Felecia asked.

"It's very serious," I answered, looking her squarely in the eye.

"How serious?"

"She's the one, Leesh."

A hush engulfed the room. The only noise was the sound of Maleah sitting in my lap, slurping from her sippy cup.

"You've asked Mama Dot for the ring?" Felecia asked, wide-eyed.

"Not yet."

"But you plan to?"

I nodded. "You know she won't give me that ring unless she approves," I admitted. "

"What does she do? What did you say her name was?" Kelvin asked curiously.

"Windsor," I repeated with a smile. "She has her own business, she's loving, she's kind—"

"What if your mama says no? How long have you been dating?" Felecia interrupted.

"We've been together since November."

"Are you serious? That's barely three months!"

"Mommy mad?" Maleah asked, staring at me with a tiny-toothed smile.

"Mommy is *not* mad, come here," Felicia held out her hands and I passed Maleah across the table to her.

"*I'm mad*," she mouthed at me as she held Maleah in her arms. "Three months?" she asked out loud.

"Felecia, I know it sounds crazy, but I need you to trust me the way I trusted you when you told me about Kelvin," I said calmly. "She's the one. When I think about you and me… the way we were when we were together…" I stared deep into her eyes. "Felecia, when I met Kelvin, the first thing I noticed was the way you looked at him. I thought to myself, '*Damn. She never ever looked at me like that.*' You looked at him like he was the most perfect person in the world. That's how Windsor looks at me. No one has ever looked at me like that, loved me like that. The first time I noticed I was like, '*Wow. So, THIS is how it feels to be loved completely?*' I can't let her go. I love her in a way I can't even articulate."

"Damn, Damian," Kelvin said when it didn't look like Felicia was going to say anything. "It's like that?"

"Uh uh… that poetic S-H-I-T doesn't work on me," Felicia snapped. "I was with Kelvin for a full six months before I brought him up to you."

"And I trusted your judgement, didn't I?" I asked her. "How long were you together before you knew Kelvin was 'the one'?"

"Come on, man. I had Felicia at, "*hey, shawty!*"" Kelvin laughed.

"Shut up, Kelvin!" Felicia said, ignoring his attempt to lighten the mood. "It's different with women. We don't think with our Pu—" she stopped short of saying 'pussy' with a toddler sitting in her lap drinking from a sippy cup.

"Maleah, let's go see what Bubby is doing." Kelvin stood up and took the baby. He kissed Felicia's cheek before leaving the kitchen. He threw me a sympathetic look before disappearing from view.

Felicia sighed loudly and took a swig of Kelvin's hastily abandoned beer.

"Damian, I trust you. I always have, you know that," she finally said. "But what could you possibly know about a woman you've only been dating for three months?"

"I know that I love her, Felicia. I've loved her from the moment we connected. Whether it's three days or three months or three years… she's the one. I'm almost forty. I don't see a point in dragging this out. I know that I want this."

"And I want it *for* you. That's all I've ever wanted for you," she said as she leveled her gaze on me. "Damian, I want you to be happy, but…"

"But what, Leesh?"

"It's too soon. You don't think it's too soon? Three months and you're already trying to wife her? Are you crazy?"

"I'm not going to beg," I said abruptly. "I'll respect your wishes. I won't introduce her to Daniel. Forget I said anything. You're absolutely right. Me living any kind of life outside of this cozy little family we've created is just crazy. What the F-U-C-K was I thinking?"

She looked stunned as I stood up and said, "You know what's crazy? You trust me with our son's life… hell, you even trust me with Maleah's life… but you don't trust me with my own?"

I was pissed, but there was no way I was leaving... not with my son playing in his room upstairs. I came here for him, but I knew I needed to calm my nerves before I said something to his mother I couldn't take back.

I walked out onto the patio and took a few deep breaths before walking out into the back yard and sitting on the swing set I helped build.

I thought about the day Felicia told me she was seeing Kelvin. I didn't want another man around my son but what could I do? Felicia and I weren't together. I couldn't realistically expect her to stay single until Daniel was eighteen. Still... the thought of another man in my son's life made me feel threatened.

I trusted her, though. I knew she wouldn't have told me she was seeing someone if it wasn't serious. I knew she didn't have to tell me shit. She could do what she wanted... same as me... but she respected me enough to tell me what was going on and ask... *permission* is the wrong word... she asked for my *blessing*, which I gave with no visible hesitation.

"Why haven't you introduced her to Mama Dot?"

I didn't even notice Felicia sitting on the swing next to mine until she spoke. I turned to look at her.

"Because I wanted to keep her to myself," I admitted. "Plus... after Priscilla..."

"I still can't believe you introduced Priscilla to your mama."

"Mama hated her immediately. That heffa had bad energy. That's why I never even considered bringing her around Daniel... or you. Her cheating ass probably would have tried to fuck Kelvin."

"I would have beat her ass in the name of Jesus," Felicia chuckled.

I couldn't help laughing.

She sighed softly.

"On our first date, Kelvin drove me out to the country, and we had a picnic in the back of his old pick-up truck. He remembered me mentioning I'd never seen a shooting star. It was just something I said in passing. It wasn't a big deal, but Kelvin researched and discovered there was going to be a meteor shower that night. Damian, we sat in the bed of his truck and just... stared up at the sky while the stars fell around us."

"That's when you knew."

"That's when I knew."

We were silent. I could hear the tickle monster attacking Daniel and Maleah inside the house. We both smiled.

"Sometimes you just know, Leesh."

"You know that I loved you, right?" she turned to me and said softly.

"I loved you too," I told her. "Still do."

"But..."

"We didn't have a connection… not a real one. It was more like…"

"A convenience," she finished for me.

"Yeah." I turned to her. "We were never *in* love. We had great times together, but we never completely connected romantically."

"When I found out I was pregnant with Daniel… I was pissed," she chuckled."

"You never told me that," I whispered. "It makes sense, though. I mean, we'd been broken up for two months. When you told me… you sounded worried… but not upset."

"Because I didn't want you to see my panic. Your response shocked me. I knew you were a good man, but I wasn't expecting you to propose on the spot."

"Thank God you said, 'no'. We would have been miserable trying to force it. We disappointed a lot of people when we broke up."

She started laughing.

"We couldn't worry about what anyone else thought. We knew it wasn't right."

"This is right, Leesh," I whispered. "She's right. I know it sounds crazy. Everything about this relationship is crazy, from the way we met to the day I told her I loved her. She gives me courage. She gives me love. She's my peace. I've never had that."

"I was never your peace, punk?" Felecia side-eyed me.

"You were a calming presence in my life," I said with a smile.

"Everything about us was calm, wasn't it?" Felecia reminisced. "Like… there was no excitement. We just went through the motions doing what we thought people expected of us."

"Look at you now. Married to a great man. 2 kids…"

"Do you think you'll have another one?" she asked.

I shook my head. "Daniel is enough for me."

"What about her? Does she have kids?"

"She can't," I sighed.

"And you're okay with that?"

"I love her."

"That's not the question. Do you want more kids?"

"I've never really considered it," I said truthfully. "You know my situation. I'm working full-time and trying to work my dreams in my free time. I just got the rights back to *Three First Names*. I'm publishing it myself… but that takes time and money. Even if I wanted more kids… I can't afford them… mentally or financially. Daniel is my everything. He's all I can handle."

"One day you'll be able to quit that damn job and write full time."

"From your mouth to God's ears," I chuckled.

"She loves you?" Felecia asked, quietly steering the conversation back to Windsor.

"Yes."

"And you trust her?"

"I do."

"I trust you Damian. If Mama Dot gives you that ring... I'll meet Windsor and... if I like her... she can meet Daniel."

"That's fair," I told her.

"Let's go eat. I know you want to spend some time with your little mini-me."

I hopped out of my swing and offered her my arm. "Shall we?"

"We shall."

Chapter 20

Damian Anthony Lawrence

I walked into my mama's kitchen and sat down at the table, waiting for her to notice me. Her back was turned as she sang along with The Dramatics and rolled out the crust for her famous peach cobbler. I watched as she sprinkled cinnamon and sugar onto the crust before she gingerly placed it on her top-secret peach mixture.

The recipe, one passed down through generations, was a staple at our family's soul food restaurant. She made this cobbler so much in the restaurant kitchen, it was rare to see her making one at home. She hadn't done much baking at home since Daddy died. Not the cobbler, anyway. It was his favorite.

Funny, I never thought to ask her why. I just assumed it was because she realized he wasn't there to sneak into the kitchen as the pie was cooling and steal a piping hot spoonful. No matter how many times he burned his tongue, he was determined to get that first bite, if only to see my mama pretend to be angry and then laugh at his antics.

I laughed at the memory, causing mama to quickly turn around. She gasped when she saw me.

"Damian Anthony?" she said, hesitantly. "Boy, you look just like your daddy with that beard! It's hard to get used to it."

"Do you want me to shave it off?" I asked.

"No. I love it. It just… wow. It always takes my breath away. You know he was so proud to have a grandbaby named after him. I'm so glad he got to spend time with him before…"

"Me too, Mama," I said, smiling at her.

"And how is my baby?" she asked, switching gears. "Did you talk to him today?"

"Yes. He's excited to spend the summer cooking with his Granny," I told her.

"And how is Miss Maleah?"

"As cute as ever," I laughed. "When I was there a couple of weeks ago, she followed me everywhere."

"You know, I'm proud of you and Felicia... Kelvin too. If every parent could handle things the way you three have... there would be less damaged children in this world."

"Thank you, Mama."

She leaned against her flour covered counter and stared at me with her arms folded across her chest. I watched her as she watched me, taking in the sight of everything I loved about my mama. Her arms were made for hugging and I could tell she needed a hug but was afraid to touch me.

I don't know how I know that.

How do I know that?

Maybe it's the hint of sadness in her eyes as she looks at me, looking like him, but not really being who she really wanted to see sitting in that chair as she made peach cobbler. She shook her head and smiled at me.

"You look just like him. It's like looking into a time machine and meeting your daddy for the first time. You know, it was your brother who met Daniel first. That little rascal ran right up to him, threw his little arms around Daniel's legs, and called him 'daddy.' I was so embarrassed," she said, laughing at the memory.

"What happened next?"

I loved this story and the animated way Mama told it.

"Well," she wiped her hands on her apron and winked at me. "Let me put this cobbler in the oven."

She gently picked up the long pan and placed it in the oven. She set the timer and then walked over to the fridge. "You want something to drink? I've got wine, milk, orange juice, water, ummmmm ooh, here it is. I have almond milk; I keep forgetting you don't drink cow's milk."

"Water," I told her.

"Well, I'm gonna have me a glass of wine," she said, grabbing a wine glass out of the cabinet and pulling a bottle of merlot from the wine cooler.

"Get two glasses," I told her. "I think I want some wine too."

Mama handed me a glass of wine and took a long satisfying sip before looking at me and laughing, "Where was I? Oh, so Devin runs right up to Daniel and starts hugging that man's legs like his little life depended on it. I watched, in horror, as that strange man picked up my baby and hugged him back. I was running by then, and I kind of snatched Devin away from him and said, "I'm sorry, he's never done

127

that before, I'll get him out of your way so you can finish doing what you're doing."

"Was he fine?"

"Ohhhh, that man was so fine I could hardly look at him. I was babbling and stuttering, and that man looked down at me and said, '*You have the most beautiful eyes I've ever seen.*' Chile, I almost melted into a little puddle of nothingness. I think he saw me stumble because he grabbed Devin and held him again. I looked at that man holding my baby as if it was *his* baby and my heart told me he was the one. Honestly, he fell in love with Devin before he fell in love with me. Shit, Devin had him at 'daddy'." She laughed again and put her hand over mine. "That peach cobbler is for Windsor, but she has to eat it here." She tapped the kitchen table with her index finger. "Right here… in my kitchen… at my table."

"Right now?"

"Yes. You two have been together long enough, don't you think? That conference was in November. It's February. It's time to stop hiding away with her and start introducing her to your family."

I stared at her in annoyance, and she tilted her head as if she were daring me to say something. My mama was famous for making last minute plans and then expecting everyone to just drop everything to appease her wishes.

She motioned towards my phone and I rolled my eyes before picking it up and called Windsor.

"Put it on speaker," Mama directed.

"Seriously?"

"Put. It. On. Speaker," she said aggressively through clenched teeth.

"Hey, baby. I was just thinking about you." Windsor's voice still made me smile, even while under duress.

I opened my mouth to speak, but to my horror, Mama took over the call. If Windsor was shocked or embarrassed, she hid it well as my Mama all but demanded she come over immediately for cobbler and ice cream.

"I don't know, Mrs. Anthony, you're talking like you have the best peach cobbler in town or something. You're asking… no, *telling* me to drop everything and come to your house. I think you just want some tea on your son," Windsor responded jokingly when Mama finally allowed her to speak.

"We can have tea too." Mama was laughing as she hung up the phone, turned to me and said, "I like her, she's a little crazy like me."

She instructed me to get her ice cream maker from the highest cabinet. The old metal ice cream maker had been passed down through the generations, and Mama only used it to make her special vanilla ice cream on special occasions. Mama hadn't even met Windsor yet, and she was pulling out her prized ice cream maker.

"Mama, don't ask her about…" I stopped short of saying it and Mama sighed softly.

"I won't mention babies," she sighed, holding the ice cream maker in her hands, and inspecting it carefully. "You know, this ice cream maker is meant for you," she said thoughtfully. "It goes to the first child to have a child. That's how it's always been. Great Granny passed it down to Granny. Granny passed it down to my mama. Mama passed it down to me and… I'm passing it to you. One day, when you become a grandfather, you can pass it to Daniel."

"I know Daria was hoping none of us had kids so it would be passed down to her by default," I said with a laugh.

Daria was my favorite cousin. She was getting married next month, and she was shocked when I told her I had a 'plus one'. Daria and I are the same age, practically twins, and we were inseparable growing up. We still speak at least once a week and she's dying to meet Windsor.

"Look in the cabinet and get me some rock salt," Mama said, a little more pep in her voice. "And rinse this ice cream maker. I'm gonna go get dressed. I can't have your girlfriend looking better than me in my own house."

Chapter 21

Windsor Elaine Bradley

I stared at myself in the rearview mirror, making sure my face looked okay. I wanted to look good, but I didn't want to look like I was trying… so I kept my makeup simple. Just a little tinted moisturizer, a bronze highlighter on my cheeks and down the center of my nose, and my favorite lipstick, a deep red that too many melanin haters thought black women shouldn't wear. It was the first thing Damian noticed when he met me on the sidewalk in front of his mother's house.

"Spin for me," he said, smiling as I twirled one good time, showing off my flowy black skirt and my even simpler, but elegant, black top.

There was a little ice on the ground, so instead of wearing heels, I chose a pair of black ballet flats that made my tall frame look even shorter standing next to Damian. I liked it. I could tell he liked it too, giving me a 'barely there' kiss on my lips and telling me he didn't want to mess up my pretty lipstick before his mother saw it.

"Your mama has a lot of cars," I said suspiciously.

I was under the impression it would just be Damian, his mother, and me. It looked like a few more people had been invited to the peach cobbler social. I looked up at Damian and tried not to be swayed by his pretty smile. He didn't tell me it was going to be a party.

"Who drives the truck?"

"My brother, Devin, and he's not here. He parked it here yesterday before he and Erika went out of town."

"So, it's just us?" I asked slowly. "No pop-up party where the new girlfriend gets grilled by every member of the family?"

"No, baby. It's just me, you, and mama. I promise."

"If I walk in here and there are a bunch of people, I'm leaving," I warned him.

"No, you're not," he said smugly, as if he knew I'd stay just to make him happy. He was right, but I wasn't going to tell him that.

"Oh. That's a big ass truck," I changed the subject and focused my attention on a big black truck sitting in the driveway.

"Yes, it is. It was my dad's. My brother drives it during the summer. I think I told you he owns a lawn care business."

"What does he do in the winter?" I asked.

"He keeps the books at the restaurant, remember? And he does taxes and shit, carpentry, he's a jack of all trades like my father."

"And you?"

"I know my way around a hammer," he subtly placed my hand on his belt as we both impulsively looked down at his crotch.

I looked away quickly, my nervous giggles morphing into loud laughter. It was effortless, the way he made my jitters disappear, leaving me to wonder if I was ever actually nervous in the first place.

"I'd better take you inside before I decide to mess up your lipstick," he said with a sexy wink.

"Maybe I'll mess it up myself later," I teased.

"Oh yeah? How?"

"Oh, I don't know. Maybe I'll kiss your hammer."

He hooked his thumbs in my belt loops and swiftly pulled me towards him. He didn't kiss me. Just stood still with his pelvis so close to mine, I could feel what my words triggered in his groin. He rested his chin on the top of my head and sighed loudly.

"You see what you do to me?" he whispered.

"And you think this is helping you?" I mumbled into his neck, doing everything in my power to keep from giving it a gentle lick followed by a kiss that would leave a big red lip print for the world, including his mama, to see. He'd bathed with the soap I made especially for him and the faint aroma of Egyptian musk was driving me crazy. If we weren't standing in front of his mother's house, I'd have already pushed him up against my car and had as much of my way with him as I could in public.

"This isn't helping, but I can't let you go," he told me.

"What if I told you there's a lady spying on us through the living room blinds," I whispered. The blinds opened slightly as two fingers tried to open them further without being noticed.

I could feel his chin slightly rotating on the top of my head as he turned his head to look at his mother's window.

"She is so damn nosey," he mumbled.

"Well, you better think about something unsexy before she sees more than she bargained for," I warned as we both looked down at the result of our sexy banter.

"Is there anything in your car I could pretend to be getting while you knock on the door by yourself?"

"Actually, there is. I made your mom a basket of soap and lotion samples. It's in the front seat on the passenger side."

"Okay," he said, taking my car keys and giving me a playful swat on the butt. "I'll get the soaps and cool myself off while you sweet talk my mama."

"Try not to watch me walk away," I said as I slowly walked away from him and made my way up the sidewalk.

Damian's mother opened the door before I had a chance to ring the bell. She was gorgeous. Her flawless skin glowed under a light dusting of makeup, and her jet-black hair, slightly graying at the edges, was pulled back into a braided bun. She smiled as I stepped onto the porch and greeted me with a big hug. It was a 'mama hug'. I liked it. I liked her immediately. Her vibe was welcoming and not suspicious in any way.

"I'm happy to finally meet the young lady that keeps a smile on my baby's face," she said warmly. "Come on in and keep me company in the kitchen."

I stifled a giggle as I spied her permanently bent mini blinds. She obviously spent a lot of time spying on the neighbors, and she'd probably gotten a little less than an eyeful as watched her son and I clowning around on the sidewalk.

"Thank you for inviting me over, Mrs. Anthony." I said as I glanced around her comfortable living room. There was a fire going in the fireplace, and she still had her Christmas tree up. It was almost Valentine's Day. I chuckled. At least she decorated. I'd been so busy with soap orders I hadn't had a chance to put my tree up at all. I was more than a little disappointed with myself. River and I usually decorated my house together, and I'd missed out on that precious time with her.

"Thank you for dropping everything and coming over," she said with a laugh. "Some people get all kinds of pissed off when you make last minute plans."

"Well, I have to admit… I'm 'some people'," I told her. "But the minute you said, 'peach cobbler', I was sold.

"Ohhhhh, so all I gotta do is feed you to get my way," she said as she led me into her spacious kitchen and motioned for me to sit down.

"Pretty much," I said truthfully.

The smell of peaches and cinnamon was overwhelming. I closed my eyes and inhaled slowly, loving the way the delicious aroma tickled my nose and slid down my throat, lingering in my mouth and causing my tastebuds to dance with excitement. I took off my jacket and draped it over the back of my chair before sitting down. I recognized the old school music playing in the background and started humming along as she got three bowls from her dinnerware cabinet and set one down in front of me. There was an oblong glass baking dish in the middle of the table, and I watched in anticipation as she slowly lifted the foil, revealing the most beautiful, from scratch, peach cobbler I'd ever seen.

"Ay dios mios," I whispered in awe.

"What is that? Spanish?" she asked me. "What does it mean?"

"It means, 'oh my god'," I whispered.

I'd had Mrs. Anthony's peach cobbler several times in her restaurant, but this was different. I was sitting in her kitchen watching her pull the foil off a cobbler she'd made just for me. This was special.

"You speak Spanish?"

"No, I just know a few phrases. I can ask where the bathroom is and a few other things." The slightest of smiles graced my face as I remembered how I learned how to say 'oh my god' in Spanish, but neither Damian nor his mother needed to know about the sexy masseuse that blew my back out in Cancun several years ago. I almost brought him home with me.

"Who knows Spanish?" Damian walked in and placed the basket on the table before sitting down next to me.

"What took you so long?" I asked nonchalantly.

He looked at me and smiled before handing me the car keys. "I cleaned out your car," he told me. "I have a feeling this should be a weekly thing. I found receipts from three years ago!"

I was embarrassed. My car was a hot mess. I tried to keep it clean, but for some reason, it always ended up looking like a second home/trash can. I couldn't believe he'd cleaned it out for me. No man had ever taken it upon himself to clean my car. It was a sweet gesture.

"Thank you," I said, putting my hand over his.

"You're welcome," he smiled and then turned his attention to the cobbler. "Y'all ain't dipped in yet? Come on, Mama. What's the hold up?"

"I was waiting for the ice cream to be ready," she said as she placed an old tin container on the table. My jaw dropped. She made me peach cobbler AND ice cream? Homemade ice cream?

"You did all of this for me?" I asked her.

"I wanted to make you feel at home." She handed me the big spoon and said, "You get to go first."

She didn't have to tell me twice! I picked a sticky corner I had my eye on and filled my bowl with cobbler. I took a small bite and closed my eyes. Sex didn't even taste this good.

"Oh my gosh. How can this taste even better than your restaurant?" I asked, nodding eagerly as she placed a big scoop of vanilla ice cream in my bowl.

She sat down across from me at the table and laughed. "I'm glad you like it. At the restaurant we make the cobber in large batches. When you make a small batch, it has a little more flavor. She noticed Damian about to dip into the cobbler and said, "You go eat your cobbler in the cave. I'm sure there's some movie or a game on. I wanna talk to Windsor alone."

"Yes, Ma'am." Damian got a huge helping of pie and ice cream, and then left me alone with his mother without a backwards glance.

"What's the cave?" I asked.

"My husband expanded the den and turned it into his own personal sports bar. He called it '*The Cave*'. Whenever there was a big game on, especially the Super Bowl, he'd invite his friends over and they would make it a party. I think he would have liked you," she told me. "You look like the kind of girl that would sit and watch the game while the rest of the ladies assembled in the kitchen to play cards and gossip."

She nailed it. I was usually one of the only women interested in the game at a Super Bowl party before I started boycotting the NFL.

"I brought you a gift." I handed her the basket and she smiled.

"Damian has been bragging about your soap! Thank you, I can't wait to try it! How is that going for you... financially?"

She said it so casually, I had to smile with a mouth full of cobbler and ice cream. So, this was how she was going to play it. She was going to fill me up with that delicious cobbler and homemade ice cream, and then subtly interrogate me as I ate.

"That was subtle," I observed, the words passing through my lips the moment they ran through my mind.

"Well, I'm just asking questions that need answers." Mrs. Anthony smiled and pushed the cobbler towards me. I served myself another spoonful. Taking my time as I put it in my bowl and then motioned towards the ice cream. This was obviously going to be a two-scoop conversation.

"Well," I said, matching the sweetness in her voice. "You can ask me anything." I smiled. "I'm making it... financially," I said carefully.

"Did you really quit your job to start making soap?"

I nodded. "My mama was not pleased," I reminisced. "But I felt like I was suffocating at that job. It wasn't where I belonged, and I'd had enough of being in a place where my soul felt uneasy." I smiled at her. "But... to answer your question, I'm trying really hard not to dip into my savings to pay my bills. I paid cash for my car, and I plan on driving this one until the wheels fall off. I own my house and my bills are being paid either early or on time every month."

"You're forty, right?" she asked.

I nodded.

"I hate to get in your business, but how did you manage to pay cash for a car? All of that from making soap?"

"I used to model. I had money saved up from that, and my mother decided she needed to take control of it. She's an accountant. I was resentful of her for kind of bullying me into that, but... now I'm glad. She knows what she's doing. She handles all my finances, and we have a "business meeting" every week to discuss where the money is going. You see, my mama didn't agree with me quitting my job to sell soap... but she believed in me enough to crunch the numbers and tell me it wasn't impossible."

"So, you're a woman who listens to her mother." She nodded thoughtfully. "I like that."

"Things happened quickly with you and my boy." She leveled her gaze at me. "What is it about him that makes you think you're in love?"

Her question didn't catch me off guard, but her wording totally took me by surprise.

"I don't *think* anything, Mrs. Anthony." I looked her in the eye as I spoke. "I love Damian. I've never loved anyone the way I love him, and I've *thought* I was in love a couple of times."

"And what about his finances? My son is a dreamer. He always keeps a job and freelances here and there, but what will you do if you decide you need more than he can give? Women these days want a man who has already made it... not one still working towards his dream and paying child support."

It was a valid question. She wanted to know if I was going to be able to handle his struggle if there was no reward. I didn't miss the subtle hint about his little boy.

"His dream is my dream," I said honestly. "We're two people trying hard to make a future for ourselves. I would never leave him. We complete one another. Where I falter, he excels, and where he falters, I excel. We balance one another out."

I pushed my cobbler away and rested my elbows on the table with my chin in my hands.

"Mrs. Anthony, I love your son," I said quietly. "I don't need a rich man. I've done that. Some men will tell you they love you and their actions say anything *but* love... Damian loves me. He tells me, he shows me, he makes me feel love in a way I've never felt it." I could feel my eyes watering.

She stared at me for a moment before saying, "What about Daniel? Can you handle the time he spends with his baby? Can you handle the friendship he has with Felicia and her husband?"

"I haven't met Daniel yet, but I know all about his relationship with Felicia and I have no problem with it. I think it's good for parents to be friends. It makes it easier for the child. Daniel seems like an incredibly happy little boy."

"He's brilliant," Mrs. Anthony said with a proud smile on her face. "That's my baby. I waited a long time for a grandbaby." She paused before saying, "I think he would like you. He's a sweet little boy who loves everybody."

I smiled. I hoped he liked me. I knew it could destroy Damian and I if he didn't.

"I have never seen my son so in love, Windsor. I'm sorry for the interrogation but I have to make sure you're right," she told me.

She started to say something else and then stopped suddenly, looking down at her bowl. I sighed. In my heart, I knew she was going to ask about children. It had to be a major concern for her. What mother of adults doesn't think about how wonderful it would be to have multiple grandchildren running around and getting into everything?

"Mrs. Anthony, I need to be honest with you," I sighed. "I know Damian told you not to ask me about babies, but I know it must upset you that he chose me over someone who can give you more grandchildren."

"I need to be honest with you too," she sighed. "I was prepared to not like you. I didn't want to like you, but the moment I saw the two of you together, the moment I hugged you, I just knew you were the woman for my son, even without babies. You make him happy, and I will never stand in the way of his happiness."

I nodded, afraid to speak, not wanting her to hear the tears in my voice. I could tell she understood. Her eyes softened and she smiled.

"I like you," she told me. "And you can call me 'Miss Dot' for now."

"Miss Dot," I rolled it around on my tongue for a moment. I understood the importance of her allowing me to transition from calling her 'Mrs. Anthony' to 'Miss Dot'. I wasn't going to take it for granted.

"Is Dot short for Dorothy?" I asked. "My Granny's name is Dorothy. She passed away about 10 years ago."

"Yep." She smiled sympathetically. "My husband called me, 'Dottie.' I loved the way it sounded when he called my name. He would say, '*Dottie, get in here and get some of this lovin'*.'"

We both laughed. She told me Damian's daddy would have liked me. He sounded like a great man, and I knew I would always keep those words close to my heart.

We sat and talked for literal hours. She asked me about my family. She asked about my time in New York and my modeling career. I didn't gloss over anything, but I also didn't go into great detail. When I told her why I left, tears came to her eyes.

"I've been there," she said softly. "That's why I left Devin's biological father."
We sat in silence for a moment.

"You know," she mused. "I haven't met a woman yet... who hasn't been abused in some way... be it sexually or mentally... physically... emotionally... some of us are able to pick up the pieces and live good lives, either by ourselves or with a man who deserves us... but some of us are stuck and that makes me so sad."

I thought back to all the females in my family. My father was absent most of my life and I could remember hearing my mother cry in the middle of the night while he berated her and broke her down. My sister had been sexually assaulted in college by someone she considered a friend. It astounded me that so many women had gone through what we endured... and many of them have never discussed it with anyone.

"You are a beautiful woman, Windsor," she said lovingly. "And it's not just that chocolate skin or that beautiful smile... it's in here." She placed her hand over her heart. "You're beautiful inside and I hope you know that."

"I know," I said honestly. "But it took me a long time to see it."

"I'm glad you did." She smiled. "I usually make a big dinner on the first Sunday of the month. I'd love it if you would come next week. You can meet Devin and Erika. Erika's sister, Brooklynne, and her husband, Harlem usually come too. They have the cutest little girl."

"I would love to come," I said excitedly.

I left her house with a long hug, a large to-go container of peach cobbler, a container of ice cream I needed to get into the freezer immediately, and a plate of greens, cornbread, sweet potatoes, and black-eyed peas. Damian walked me to my car and hugged me tightly before opening the door for me and watching me slide into the driver's seat. He took my food and carefully put it in the back seat.

"Call me as soon as you get home," he said as he stared down at me.

"If you come with me, I won't have to call you," I told him.

"If I come with you, I'll never want to leave," he licked his lips. It was a beautifully random habit of his.

I reached out to touch him, and he grasped my hand tightly.

"Then don't," I said softly. "Stay with me."

It wasn't a spontaneous suggestion, or a passion filled exclamation I would regret later. I'd been thinking about waking up next to Damian and realized I wanted to see him on the other side of my bed every morning.

"Things are moving so fast with us, but it doesn't feel fast," he crouched down in my open car door and put his face close to mine. "I don't want to make any assumptions, baby. You know you can have anything you want, but I need to know that what you're saying, and what I'm hearing, are the same thing."

"What did you hear?" I placed my hands on his cheeks and looked into his eyes. I leaned in to kiss him.

"Do you want me to move in with you?" he asked in the moment before our lips touched.

"Do you want to?" I mumbled against his lips.

"I don't know if it's even appropriate for us to be having this conversation right now. It's only been a few months. People would think we're crazy."

"Do you think it's crazy?" I asked him.

"I think it's insane," he kissed me again. "But everything about us is insane. I'm crazy in love with you."

"I'm crazy in love with you too," I said softly, hoping I hadn't ruined our dynamic by suggesting he move in with me. What the hell was I thinking?

I wanted to take it back. I wanted to take it all back. Every time I woke up in the middle of the night and rolled over into Damian, I wondered how much longer I could endure the nights I slept alone. Every time I woke up to his sleeping face in the morning, I wondered how I'd ever lived without him.

Had I ruined everything by moving too fast?

Of course, that thought was ridiculous. Everything between us had happened too fast, from having sex to falling in love to deciding that we 'go together'... every aspect of our relationship was based on moving too fast.

"Maybe we should talk about it before jumping into it based on emotions," he suggested.

It made sense, but I couldn't help the pout that formed on my lips... which shocked me because I'm not a pouter. This dude was changing me from a strong independent woman to an emotionally spoiled independent woman and I kinda liked it.

"Don't pout," he said with mock sternness.

I increased the severity of my pout, the whole time looking him directly in his eyes, and gently stroked his beard.

"I know we aren't scheduled to spend the night together, but you need to stay with me tonight," he told me.

"Why would I do that when it's not on the schedule?" I asked him.

We'd recently decided to only spend two nights together per week so that I could use the rest of that time to fulfill orders and he could finish his book and work out the logistics of starting his own publishing company.

"I'm going to pour red wine on your pussy and lick it off," he said leaning in to kiss the pout off my lips.

I loved it when he put a little authority in his voice every now and then.

"Do you wanna drive?" I asked, handing him my keys.

"Yep, I'll be right back. I need to let mama know I'm leaving my car here tonight."

I got out of the car and walked around to the passenger seat. I was eagerly anticipating the shenanigans that awaited me back at his place, but still cringing a little about my premature suggestion that he move in with me.

I hadn't lived with anyone in years, yet I had no issue with welcoming Damian into my space. I knew his lease would be up in a little over a month. He could literally live with me, rent free, and chip in on the bills. He could finally quit that job he hated and write full time. He could save his money and start his publishing company.

I could wake up next to him every morning and kiss him, morning breath and all… if he wanted to.

I really wanted him to want to.

Chapter 22

Damian Anthony Lawrence

I slid into the driver's seat of Windsor's car and did my usual ritual of adjusting the mirror and sliding the seat back until my long arms and legs could be accommodated. I was pulling away from the curb when Windsor nonchalantly placed her lacy panties on the steering wheel.

I smiled inwardly and slipped the panties into my pocket. Windsor had already taken over the Bluetooth, and as the sensual sounds of Jhenè Aiko surrounded us, my left hand tightly gripped the steering wheel. My right hand gripped the flowy fabric of her long skirt, bunching it up into a ball as I slowly slid my hand between her legs.

I had her panties in my pocket, but I still felt an element of surprise when my hand connected with her naked flesh. She shifted in her seat and parted her legs.

I bit my lip as I held her in my hand. Her moisture dripped onto my palm and bathed my fingers in her essence. I was desperate to taste her. I slid my hand away from her, letting go of her just long enough to lick each finger, one by one.

I wished we were in my first car, a blue, 1979 Buick Regal with cloth bench seats. If we were in *that* car, I'd have already grabbed her, slid her next to me, and worked her pussy until she came all over the seats Those seats were hell to clean, but it would have been worth it just to hear her scream that scream she screams when she falls into an orgasmic abyss. I do my best to make her cum every time I put my hands on her, but there are times when she cums so hard, my ears are filled with the most carnal screams I've ever heard.

I loved that fucking scream, loved seeing her eyes roll to the back as her body convulsed.

I was going to throw her into that abyss tonight.

I put my hand on her naked thigh. My fingers were close enough to graze her southern lips, and far enough away to cause her to squirm in anticipation. I caressed her gently, sliding my fingers up and down on the insides of her lips, grazing her clit with my knuckle at every pass.

"Girl, you feel good," I mumbled as I slid a finger inside of her.

Her legs opened wider, my pace increased, she moaned softly, placing her hand over mine as if she was afraid I'd stop touching her.

"Take off your bra," I told her.

"What?"

"Take that shit off," I said calmly, keeping my eyes on the road as my dick painfully strained against my zipper.

I licked my lips and smiled as I heard her scrambling to take her arms out of her bra without taking her blouse off. She dropped her bra in my lap, and I balled it up in my hand, bringing it to my nose and inhaling slowly, savoring the smell of her orange ginger perfume oil before tossing it into the back seat.

She grabbed my hand and tried to place it between her thighs again, but I resisted, instead I slipped my hand under her shirt and cupped her left breast in my hand.

She gasped as I held her pebble hard nipple between my thumb and forefinger, gently squeezing. I glanced over at her, marveling at how beautiful she looked with her locs spilling into her lap and her skirt bunched up around her thighs. Both her hands, balled up into little fists, were jammed in between her thighs as she tried to calm the surge of sexual energy that had built up and gathered in her pretty little loins.

"Touch it," I said, putting a little authority in my voice.

She placed her hand on my thigh, but I shook my head. "No. Not me. I want you to touch yourself."

I hit a button and slowly reclined her seat so she could spread her legs a little wider.

"Touch it," I whispered.

She slid a hand under her skirt, and I covered her hand with mine, helping her, guiding her in all the ways I wanted her to pleasure herself.

"You want me to pull over?" I asked her.

"What about that red wine?" she asked.

"Oh, you gon' get all that when we get to the house. I'm asking if you want me to pull over right now."

I put just enough pressure on one of her fingers to cause it to slide inside of her. Her breath caught in her throat as I slid my own finger in after it. Her moans got louder as we fingered her together.

141

"Pull over," she managed to choke out.

I pulled into a grocery store parking lot and looked around. The store was closed and there were only a few cars in the parking lot. I found a parking spot on a dark side of the building and backed in.

"You gon' let me watch?" I asked. I pushed her skirt up to her waist and then reclined her seat until she was lying flat on her back.

It was dark in the car, but the glow from the stereo flooded the front seat with just enough light for me to see her pussy glistening in the shadows.

And just like that, I was a conductor, and she was the only woman in my orchestra, playing her sexual instrument while I directed her with precision.

I leaned back against the door and stroked my beard while her fingers slithered up and down, around and in between her lips. I turned the stereo down, preferring the sound of her moans over the music. I leaned over the gear shift, giving myself a better view of the private show she was putting on just for me.

"Oooohhh, just like that," I whispered as her hand started moving in a circular motion. "Yeah, go faster," I said excitedly as her moans became soft whimpers.

"How does it feel, baby," I asked her.

"It feels good, baby," she stuttered.

"You're doing so good." I licked my lips and pushed three fingers inside of her. "Don't stop," I whispered as she started to move her hand away from mine, "keep going."

She was extremely wet and the harder and faster I pounded her with my fingers, the faster her hands worked, until I heard her breathing intensify, quickening and becoming more labored as she moved closer and closer to the edge of climax.

She grabbed handfuls of her skirt and started gyrating against my hand, lifting her hips to meet my fingers as they plunged inside of her over and over again.

And then she was screaming… that piercing, yet guttural scream that let me know I was giving it to her so good there was no way she could control herself. I kept stroking as her liquid passion pushed past my fingers and created a sexual puddle in the leather seat.

She grabbed my hand with both of hers and held it tightly, restricting my movement as she breathlessly whispered, "*ay dios mios.*"

I loved it when I made her speak Spanish.

I carefully pulled my fingers from between her extremely swollen walls and realized her body probably wasn't up for any more sex. The red wine bath would have to wait, and unfortunately, so would I.

"I should have taken you home," I said with a strained laugh.

"Not necessarily." She sat up and put her hand on my zipper. "Let me show you what this mouth do."

I reclined my seat, closed my eyes, and said, "show me."

Chapter 23

Windsor Elaine Bradley

It was easy.

Like a Sunday morning.

It was awakening to the sun shining brightly through the blinds, but it's too cold to go outside, so instead, you take a long shower together, rub one another down with shea butter and just… be… together. Inside, with nowhere to go and no desire to look for alternate entertainment. Content to simply sit cross legged on his couch while he lays with his head in your lap as you watch old episodes of Gunsmoke and share a single glass of wine.

Occasionally you stroke his beard, and he looks up at you and puckers up for a kiss before turning back towards the television, placing a lingering kiss on your knee as he snuggles deeper into your lap.

Deeper into you.

Deeper into *me*.

His beard tickled my thigh and I blushed at the memory of him pouring cold red wine between my thighs last night, soothing my swollen kitty with his tongue until I was hoarse from screaming into his pillow.

It was easy.

Easy to be spontaneous with him.

Easy to pull the car over and do things with him that would make a super freak blush.

Easy to pretend the rest of the world didn't exist.

Easy to pretend no one could walk up and could see us as we sat in a dark car in a dark corner and fingered, fondled and sucked as if we didn't have two perfectly good beds between us.

I was still sore from those shenanigans, but it didn't stop me from requesting my wine bath the moment we walked into his house.

It was too easy.

Too easy to pretend I didn't have orders to fill, and he didn't have pages to write, and marketing campaigns to work on for multiple clients, including me, and his mama, and my sister… but it was '*us*' time. We'd spontaneously changed our schedule. This beautiful Sunday was our self-designated day off and nothing could come between us and our time alone.

So, I pushed every responsibility out of my mind and sat there, cross legged on his couch, with his head in my lap, gently stroking his beard while we watched television.

"Remember that night I came over and almost asked you to marry me?" Damian asked so casually it almost didn't register.

He rolled over and looked up at me. I stared down at him; a bit thrown off by the question.

"Yeahhh," I answered slowly.

"My lease is up in forty-five days," he told me.

He twisted one of my locs around his finger. It was something he did when he was near me and in deep thought. I twirled a loc around my finger as well. Now I was in deep thought too.

"Are you going to renew it?" I asked.

"That depends," he answered.

"On what?"

"That night," he reminded me. "Do you remember what you said when you shushed me?"

Why was he talking about a conversation that happened two months ago in the heat of passion? I remembered exactly what I said that night, but I didn't want to answer. Last night he'd basically shut me down when I sort of suggested moving in together. I didn't want to revisit that, and I *definitely* didn't want to revisit his spontaneous 'almost' proposal. I didn't want to get into any conversation that could suddenly make this easy Sunday morning hard.

"Do you?" he pressed.

"Yes, but I don't know what that has to do with whether or not you're going to renew your lease," I said just as Matt Dillon reappeared on the television screen. "Your show is back on," I told Damian.

Damian picked up the remote and turned the television off.

"Tell me what you said." He picked up another loc and started twisting it with the one he already had in his hand.

The tug to my scalp felt good and I wanted to reverse positions, him sitting on the couch while I placed my head in his lap and let him play in my hair. I wiggled around until I found my sweet spot and then relaxed as he massaged my scalp. My eyes closed and I smiled with contentment.

Ahh, Sunday morning.

It was back to being easy.

"Windsor," he said loudly.

I opened my eyes and sighed loudly, "I said, not without a ring."

"Did you mean it?" he asked me.

"I don't understand the question," I said truthfully.

Was he asking me if I'd thought about marriage? Was he trying to see if the only thing keeping me from marrying him was a ring? Was he trying to feel me out to see if I only said that to get him to shut up and fuck me that night?

"Damian, I don't know what you're asking me," I was frustrated and trying hard to keep my voice even.

It must have shown in my eyes because Damian tapped the top of my head gently, his signal for me to sit up.

"Stand up," he told me.

I stood up and looked down at him. He patted his lap and I sat down, curling my legs up on the couch and resting my head on his shoulder. He turned the television back on and began watching another episode of Gunsmoke. I was slowly falling asleep when he whispered into my ear,

"What if I had a ring?"

"What if you did?" I answered his question with a question.

He kissed the tip of my nose and started laughing, "You are the most exasperating woman I've ever dealt with in my entire life!"

"Really?" I laughed back. "Your entire life? The whole thing? All thirty-nine, almost forty years?"

"In its entirety," he chuckled. "You weren't lying when you told me you were '*a lot*'."

"As I recall...you said you liked '*a lot*'," I reminded him.

"I love '*a lot*'," he said kissing me softly. "But go look in the mirror, you've got something in your nose."

Oh my god. How embarrassing. I stood up and briskly walked into the bathroom with my hand over my nose. I stood there for over thirty seconds, staring up my nose trying to see what he saw. It wasn't until I decided he was full of shit that I leveled my face with the mirror and sighed loudly.

"You play too much!" I yelled.

I could hear him laughing loudly all the way in the other room. I was just about to turn and walk back into the living room when something shiny caught my attention. Whatever it was, it was in my hair. I looked closer and then wrapped my hand around a section of locs Damian had braided while my head was in his lap. I pulled the locs around to my face, but whatever it was... was braided too far up for me to see. I was gonna have to unbraid my hair to get it out.

I stood in the mirror, quickly unbraided my hair and, as the shiny thing slid down my locs and landed in the palm of my hand, I screamed.

Damian casually strolled into the bathroom and leaned against the sink as I stood there with a stupid grin on my face, repeatedly staring from my hand to his face.

"What's wrong?" he asked me.

"It's a… it's a ring," I said staring down at it.

It *was* a ring, and it wasn't just *any* ring. It was the ring I saw his mother wearing last night. It was definitely whatever two months' salary looked like over thirty years ago. Rose gold, with an emerald cut diamond with several smaller diamonds surrounding it and spreading out onto the band.

"What? A ring?" He took the ring out of my hand and stared at me, but I could barely see him because my eyes were full of tears.

"You play too much," I said, half laughing, half crying as he wiped my eyes with his thumbs.

"What," he said, giving me a soft peck on my lips. "If..." He kissed me again. "There was..." He gave me another kiss. "A ring?" This kiss lingered and my whole face started to tingle with excitement.

"I would let you do more than *'almost'* propose," I whispered, once again blinded by tears.

Damian grabbed the faded decorative hand towel hanging on his towel rack and gently wiped my face before holding my left hand in his.

He took a deep breath and said, "Windsor, I had an entire speech in my head and now I can't remember anything I wanted to say."

He paused and I realized the wells of his eyes were moist. Now it was my turn to take the towel and wipe his tears away.

"When I went back into the house last night, it wasn't to tell mama I was leaving my car," he revealed. "It was to tell her I was ready for the ring."

"What did she say?" I asked breathlessly.

He turned the ring over in his palm and smiled. "She had already taken it off and cleaned it. She knew." He looked at me intently. "She told me she was glad we found one another. She gave me her blessing."

"She did?" I asked him.

"My daddy proposed to her with this ring. She wouldn't have given it to me if she had any doubts about you."

I was stunned. This was a big deal. My legs felt wobbly. I walked into his arms, took his face in my hands, and gently rested my forehead on his.

"Please hurry up and ask me," I whispered. "Because I don't know what kind of speech you had in your head, but I don't know if there's anything else you could say to make me feel more special."

"Are you gonna let me finish though? Cuz when I asked you to be my girlfriend you answered before I could finish asking the question."

"I promise not to interrupt," I chuckled.

His eyelashes were tickling mine and I could feel our fresh tears mingling and then falling between us like little raindrops, splashing my bare feet.

"Windsor Elaine Bradley, will you marry me?" he asked.

"Yes," I said as soon as the word 'me' left his lips.

I lifted my face and gazed up at him. This wasn't a joke. It wasn't a dream. He was really proposing to me. I was really saying, 'yes'. I felt like I was seeing him for the first time all over again.

Damian was standing in front of me, tears sliding down his cheeks, loving me in a way I'd never been loved. He was *more* than loving me. He was accepting me. He was accepting my past, he was showing up and showing out in my present, and he wanted to be a permanent part of my future. He wanted it to be *our* future. It was a feeling like no other, and as he slid the ring onto my finger, I felt like I was being hugged from the inside. It was like a soul hug. Like my heart had wrapped itself around my lungs and squeezed. It took my breath away. It gave me life.

I stared at the ring, loving the way it twinkled on my finger, and then looked at the man who put it there. I grabbed him by his boxers and pulled him closer to me, somehow managing to maneuver my body around his.

I don't know if he picked me up or if I jumped, but the next thing I knew, I was sitting on the vanity with my legs wrapped around his waist and my arms wrapped around his neck.

He kissed me. It was a different kind of kiss. It was a 'still starving when you've already eaten' kind of kiss. It was frenzy in a moment of calm, a state of being that was both chaos and peace at the same time.

My nether regions pulsated with the mere thought of engaged sex, but I was still sore from the night before. I was unsure if my mind was as willing to risk it all as my body obviously was.

"I want you so bad," I breathed heavily into his ear. "But I'm still sore from last night."

"I'll be gentle," he whispered as he lifted me up and carried me into the bedroom.

True to his word, Damian treated every inch of my body like it was black porcelain, fine China you only put on the table when you have company coming over. He feasted on me, licking me here, sucking me there, smelling me, mumbling against my flesh as if he were tasting the flavors of a brand-new girlfriend... a fiancée.

My passionate cries were already filling the room as he carefully slid inside of me. My walls welcomed him. Hugged him and cried for him, whispered his name every time he pushed a little further, stroked a little faster, plunged a little deeper, until I was overflowing, full of his love and bursting with orgasmic joy.

Later, he walked to the kitchen, nothing covering his nakedness but our sweat, and came back with a mini charcuterie board, a bottle of red wine, and two glasses.

We sat in the bed, naked... feeding one another, talking, laughing... It was just like the night we met.

We were strangers then.

Strangers who *knew* one another before we got to *know* one another. Strangers who had gone from slow winding in an art gallery to slow grinding on a bed with no intention of ever seeing one another again.

"Twenty questions," he mumbled with a mouth full of gouda.

"Yes or no questions," I offered.

"Did you see this coming?" he asked me.

"No. Did you?"

"Yes."

"You did?" I asked him. "When? When did you know?"

"I knew the moment you snuck into that writer's conference," he told me. "I thought to myself, *'now there's a woman who would win the 'for the dick' challenge with no problem. I must make her my wife!'*"

"I flew to Philly for the dick," I rapped. "Lied for the dick, cried for the dick, almost died for the dick- "

He spit laughed, and as he turned his head, a spray of red wine dotted the pillowcases. "Almost DIED for the dick?" he asked me.

"I mean, there was a lot of turbulence on the plane. I second guessed my decision a couple of times." I popped an olive into my mouth and then smiled at him.

"I know we joke about it, but did the dick really bring you to Philly?"

"*You* brought me to Philly," I said truthfully. "Admittedly, with a little push from LeeLee. I was just gon' text you and wait for you to text me back."

"I would have texted you back, but… I think our story would have ended differently if it happened that way."

"Me too," I agreed. "This story is much better."

"It's a strange story… It's a beautiful story… but it's *our* story. Maybe I'll write it down one day," he said thoughtfully.

"Well, change my name," I told him as I bit into a buttery cracker. "Cuz I don't want nobody thinking I'm a ho."

Chapter 24

Damian Lawrence Anthony

It was loud, the strong smell of bleach and paint mingling with the chemical smell of whatever was in the carpet cleaner. I stood in the middle of my empty living room and inhaled the memories cleaning products could never cover.

I'd been renting this house from Devin for the past ten years. He had several rental properties around town. He always said I was his best tenant. My rent was always paid on time, my lawn was always mowed, and I often invited my family over for dinner.

"Damn, boy! You put yo foot in this!" I can still hear daddy saying with a mouth full of shrimp alfredo. It was the first of many meals I cooked for my family in my little house.

"Yeah, I gotta hand it to you, young'un. You get down in the kitchen," Devin added with a fist bump.

"You still get excited over shit like that?"

Priscilla's voice still nonchalantly entered my thoughts every now and then. The way she dismissed me when I told her I told her I made the Dean's Honor Roll while studying for my master's degree. The way she competed with me and seemed to relish in every failure while dismissing every accomplishment. Our relationship was a black hole of despair. When we finally broke up, Erika came over and smudged the entire house with sage.

"We gotta get that evil bitch's energy up out of here!"

Windsor's laugh. She was laughing the first time her feet crossed the threshold. I can't remember what I'd said, but it had tickled her funny bone and when the laughter stopped, she asked, *"Where is your bedroom?"*

If I concentrated, I could still hear her moans bouncing off the walls.

I could still hear her scream when she realized I braided an engagement ring in her hair.

I could still hear myself asking her to marry me.

I could still hear her saying, '*yes*'.

"You sure about this?" Devin walked into the living room and looked around slowly. "This is a huge step, little brother."

"Do you think you'll have a hard time renting it out?" I asked him.

"Nah, I'm going to sell it. I already have a potential buyer. It won't be on the market long." He looked around the room with pride. "This was my first property." He smiled. "You were my first tenant."

"It's a good house," I told him. "I kinda hate to leave, but I can't live like a bachelor forever, right?"

"Nope, you can't," he agreed. "I can't believe you're finally getting married."

"It's time."

"She's definitely a keeper. I'm proud of you, Damian. She seems devoted to you."

"She is, man. It's a different kind of feeling when someone believes in you."

"I know that's right," Devin nodded in agreement. "I have something for you… actually, it's from Daddy."

"What?"

I watched as he pulled an envelope out of his pocket and held it out in front of me. I was afraid to touch it. I reached out for it with shaky hands. I opened it slowly, unsure of what to expect. Was it a letter?

It was a deposit slip.

It was a deposit slip for my bank account.

I blinked several times when I saw the amount.

$72,000.

I stared at Devin with a puzzled expression on my face. "Man, what the fuck?"

"Daddy wanted you to have this the day you found your soulmate and moved out of this little house. He wanted Windsor for you so badly. He always knew you and Felecia were better as friends, even when she had the baby."

"$72,000 though? This is so random. I don't understand."

"Not really. Daddy bought this house outright. He paid cash for it, and then he paid me to remodel it. He gave it to me with one stipulation. He said, '*rent it to your brother… but put the money in a savings account. The day he moves out will probably be the day he finds a wife. Give him the money back. You keep the interest and the house.*"

I stared at the check in my hands with tears in my eyes. My Daddy was always thinking about us. Always taking care of us. Even when we didn't know it. That check represented 10 years of rent payments… all on time no matter what I was going through. I looked over at Devin who was smiling broadly at me.

"Start your publishing company, little brother," he said proudly.

I felt like I was going to collapse. Devin caught me, just as I faltered and held me as I tried to reign in my rogue emotions.

I was stunned. Too stunned to speak. Too stunned to cry. Too stunned to do anything but stare at the deposit slip in my hand, with a crazy grin on my face.

And then I was surrounded. Surrounded by my family. Mama, Devin, and Erika were surrounding me with love and support, praying for me. Telling me how proud they were of me. Telling me how proud my Daddy would be to see me so happy.

And then I heard his voice.

"Damian, you and that lil chocolate gal sho' look good together. I see you've got a sweet tooth, just like ya Daddy. Always been proud of ya, boy! Neva gon' stop!"

Not only did I hear him… I felt him… whoosh through me like a cool breeze, soothing me from the inside out. I felt joy and immediately recognized it wasn't mine… it was his. He was full of joy. He was surrounding us with his joy. Surrounding us with his love.

"He's here," I whispered to no one in particular.

"I feel him," Mama whispered back.

"Like a cool breeze," Devin said quietly.

"Like a hug… flirty, but not really?"

We all looked at Erika and burst out laughing. It was exactly like he would have greeted her in life. Pretending to take her from Devin until he laughingly exclaimed my mama was the only chocolate he could handle.

I laughed until I cried.

And then we were all crying as the happy emotions in the moment settled in our hearts. I found myself in the middle of a group hug. The last one I'd ever experience in this space.

"Thank you, Daddy," I chuckled through my tears.

"I'm starving. Let's get this stuff over to your new place," Erika said, wiping her eyes as she broke the family embrace.

"Yes, lets," Mama sniffled. "I'm eager to sit down and break bread with Windsor's family. I can't believe I'm about to meet your future in-laws."

"Will we be able to…" Damian smoked an imaginary joint and I fell out laughing.

"Not tonight. Her niece is spending the weekend with us. You're gonna freak out when you see her. She's the spitting image of Windsor. I've never seen anything like it," I told them.

Ebony Farashuu

I looked around my old living room one last time before smiling and leading my family out the door.

Chapter 25

Damian Lawrence Anthony

River looked me up and down as I walked into the house carrying a stack of boxes. Without asking if I needed any help, she grabbed the one on top and asked, "where to?"

"The office," I said following her as we made our way to my new office.

It was originally a small library, but Windsor was using it for storage before I moved in. It was plain. There were three beige walls just waiting to be decorated and one wall that was nothing but a built-in bookcase. I was in love with it.

Moving in with Windsor was like a culture shock. Although I'd been spending at least one night a week at her place, it was hard to believe it was now '*our*' place. I'd been renting my one-bedroom bachelor pad from my brother for the past ten years. I was going from living in a giant man-cave to residing in a respectable home with multiple rooms and decorative pillows.

I loved it.

River put the box on my desk and then sat in my chair, spinning around as if she were on a small merry-go-round.

"I see you got your business straight." She stopped spinning and focused her teenage gaze on me. "That was pretty smooth, tying the ring in her hair." She acknowledged it in a way that let me know she was impressed without sounding like she was impressed.

"Well, I'm a smooth kinda brotha," I told her.

"I guess," she started spinning again.

She looked so much like Windsor.

Mama actually pulled me aside and asked me if I was sure River wasn't Windsor's baby. She stared from Windsor to River the entire night. She even pulled River aside for a conversation. I was shocked to see River laughing and

155

giggling like a little girl. She even hugged my mama before she left. River hadn't even hugged me yet.

River had a certain disdain for me that wasn't hateful, just… cautious. She didn't fully trust me with her Auntie. I had a feeling she didn't trust anyone with her. She was close to Windsor and I was cutting in on the time they used to spend together.

"Is this gonna be your man-cave?" she asked.

"Yep."

"How are you gonna decorate?" she asked.

"I don't know. I haven't thought about it," I told her. "I'm gonna fill those shelves with books and stuff, but I'm not sure what to do about the rest, you got any ideas?"

She looked around thoughtfully. "You should put a flat screen TV on that wall," she pointed to the wall to emphasize her point. "You should get a nice couch or some gaming chairs, do you play video games? Cuz you could set your system up and play games when you aren't writing your books."

"Or maybe you think you could come in here and play?" I asked laughingly. "You have an entire bedroom upstairs. Don't you have your own TV and games?"

She shook her head, "Auntie won't let me have a TV in my room."

"Well, I don't really play video games, but maybe you could help me decorate. Give me some more ideas."

"Maybe," she sighed. Then she perked up. "I can help you decorate your little boy's room."

I looked at her in surprise. "I'd like that," I said sincerely. "Are you okay with him having the room next to yours? I know that used to be your playroom when you were younger."

"I don't mind. I think it'll be cool to have him around. I can babysit, but you have to pay me."

"What do you charge?" I asked.

"I mean… I could give you the family discount. How does $10 per hour sound?" she asked.

"Sounds pretty cheap to me. Are you sure?"

"Is he bad?"

"No, he's actually a really good boy. I'm not just saying that."

"Okay. Then $10 is fine." She smiled. "Dinner was fun. Your mom is really nice. She said I could call her Granny Dot. She's going to teach me how to make ice cream."

Lord, my Mama had officially adopted another honorary grandchild. I chuckled inwardly. She didn't let just anyone touch that ice cream maker.

I started unpacking one of my boxes and River immediately zeroed in on a snow globe my mom bought me when I was a little boy. There was a little black child in a red snowsuit standing in the middle of the globe with his little arms outstretched as snow fell around him.

"Oh my god, The Snowy Day!" River suddenly sounded much younger than her sixteen years.

I watched as she shook the globe and smiled. "That was my favorite book as a little boy," I told her. "Mama bought me that thing when I was six or seven."

"It's lowkey, still my favorite book," she said, carefully placing the globe back on my desk. "Aunt Winnie used to read it to me whenever I slept over. She even bought me a red snowsuit with a little pointed hood." She started laughing. "I thought I was the sh- the bomb."

I chuckled at how quickly she edited her statement when she remembered she was talking to an adult.

"I had one too," I told her. "I thought I was the *shit*," I added with a laugh.

She couldn't help laughing with me.

"What do I call you?" she asked suddenly, "I mean... you're just shacking up with Aunt Winnie, so you're not really my uncle yet. But now that you live here... Mr. Anthony sounds kind of... I don't know."

"Honestly, I hate it when you call me, 'Mr. Anthony," I told her.

"I know," she said casually. "but I might keep calling you that until you marry my auntie." She studied me closely. "Do you have white people in your family?"

"What?"

"White people you know, folks that don't have any melanin?"

"I know what white people are," I chuckled. "You think I have white people in my family because I'm kinda brown?"

"I mean, you're much lighter than us," she mumbled and then asked, "Have you ever done a DNA test? They have these kits where you send them some spit and they tell you what you are. Like, I might be part of an African royal family and not even know it."

I was officially confused. I told her so.

"I need one of those kits," she told me. "I want to know where our people came from. All my friends are doing it."

So, this was why River was suddenly following me around and helping me with my boxes. She wanted me to buy her an ancestry kit. It was out of the question. I told her so.

"If you get it for me, I'll stop calling you 'Mr. Anthony," she promised.

"River, I want us to get along. I want you to like me, I really do. I want you to feel like I'm part of the family and someone you can trust, but I'm not buying you that kit. That's something you need to ask your parents."

She sighed heavily and stared at me, disappointment written all over her face, "I'm gonna ask Auntie."

"Please, don't do that," I said softly.

Her look of disappointment slowly morphed into a look of surprise, and I desperately wanted to end this conversation and pretend it never happened. River wasn't being messy or disrespectful with her request. She was truly curious about her ancestry and just wanted to be a part of the conversation her friends were having. I knew she had a habit of running to Windsor when her parents said, '*no*,' and I didn't want this to be another one of those times.

"I don't dislike you," she said after a few minutes of silence.

I was shocked.

"My answer is still no," I told her.

"I know." She picked up the snow globe again and shook it gently. "It's not that I don't like you. I'm scared."

I looked up suddenly, taken aback by this sudden confession.

"Scared of what?"

"Scared of the 'what-ifs'," she said quietly. "What if you hurt Aunt Winnie?"

"River, I would never hurt your Auntie," I said gently. "Why would you think that?"

"I read your book." She leaned back in the chair. "You dedicated it to your dad and your little boy… and then you mentioned your future children. You said you wanted to raise them the same way he raised you."

"Oh, sweetie—"

"My Auntie can't have babies," River interrupted, sadness in her voice. "I remember when she had to have her surgery. She cried every day."

I sat on the edge of my desk and decided to just listen to what River was saying without interjecting with my reassuring comments. She needed to be heard and I needed to let her speak her peace.

"Auntie loves you," she told me. "I've never seen her this happy. If you leave her, she'll be devastated."

She stopped talking and I took that opportunity to speak my own peace.

"I love Windsor, River, I wouldn't be here if I didn't. Sometimes life makes you trade something you *thought* you wanted, for something you already have and want to keep. Does it suck that I'll never know what my baby would look like with Windsor? Yes. But I have a son. I don't need more children to be happy. I just need Windsor."

"Do you promise?" she asked.

"Pinky promise," I answered, holding out my pinky.

She hooked her pinky onto mine and we both tugged gently. She smiled and I couldn't help smiling back at her. If I had a daughter, I'd want her to be as fierce and as protective of Windsor as River. She was a good kid just looking out for the woman we both loved.

"You really read my book?" I asked her.

"Yeah… it was good," she told me. "I want to be a writer too, but my mama wants me to go to college and get a degree to fall back on. Maybe I'll let you read my stories one day."

"I would really like that," I said enthusiastically.

River stood up abruptly and headed for the door. "I'm going to trust you, Uncle Damian," she said over her shoulder as she left the office.

I heard a soft chuckle and looked up to see Windsor leaning in the doorway. "Wow." She shook her head in amusement and then walked into my office. "Did she just call you *Uncle Damian?*"

"She did," I could hardly believe it myself.

I decided not to share our entire conversation. Instead, I sat down in my office chair and motioned for Windsor to join me.

"You don't mind her sleeping over on your first night officially living here?" she asked, sitting down in my lap, and wrapping her arms around my neck.

Paris had accompanied her husband on a work trip... to Hawaii, and River was staying with us until they got back. She could have just as easily stayed with her MawMaw, but River preferred to stay with Windsor, and honestly, I felt like this was a good time for River and me to get used to being around each other.

"She can stay over whenever she likes," I told her.

"Well, we'll have a romantic dinner in a few days," she reassured me. "Paris and Troy will be back on Sunday. Can you wait that long to get some of this lovin?"

"We ain't gotta wait." I lowered my voice, "I can be quiet if you can be quiet."

"Ooh, a challenge," she giggled.

"Have you thought of what kind of wedding you want?" I asked her.

"Actually… I have," she told me. "I want something small and intimate. Just our family and close friends. Is that okay?"

Okay? It was more than okay. When I proposed I hadn't given too much thought to wedding planning because I didn't want to think about the cost involved. A small wedding was perfect.

"Do you have a date in mind?" I asked.

"Not really, are you in a hurry?"

"Hell yeah, I'm in a hurry," I said earnestly. We were already living together. I wanted to make it official.

"How soon do you want to?" she asked.

"Tomorrow."

"Boy, stop playing." She kissed the top of my forehead and then stood up. "Do you have more boxes?"

"Nope. This is it," I told her.

She smiled.

"Welcome home, baby," she said softly before blowing me a kiss and leaving me alone in the office.

Chapter 26

Windsor Elaine Bradley

"Auntie, have you ever done one of those kits where you spit into a tube and find out what part of Africa you're from?" River's question came out of nowhere, and the presentation was completely out of character for her.

I stared at her over the rim of my reading glasses and made her repeat it.

"Auntie, you know. The kit where you find your ancestors…"

"We're black, that's all you need to know." I dismissed her question and went back to filling out shipping labels for my monthly subscription boxes.

"Ugh, why won't anyone let me get a kit?" she sulked.

"Well, who else have you asked?"

"MawMaw, Mama, Daddy…" River ran through the list of names as if all of those 'no' answers would suddenly inspire me to say, 'yes'."

I trusted my sister's judgement and never went behind her back to give River anything she wasn't allowed to have. The last thing I ever wanted to do was undermine my sister's authority. If I wanted River to have something, I had a rational conversation with my sister about it. Sometimes we agreed, sometimes we didn't… but Paris' word was always the final word.

Always.

This time was no different.

A DNA test? Ancestors? Since when did River care about her ancestors? My family vowed to never take a DNA test when those ancestry kits started popping up all over television.

"River, why are you so worried about your DNA?" I pushed away from my desk and narrowed my eyes at her.

"All the kids at school are talking about their DNA results. Charity found out she's related to Benjamin Franklin. Mr. Miller is the whitest white dude I know, and he found out he's like thirteen percent Nigerian.

"And what do you think you'll find out about us? Trust me, baby. Those ancestry tests are nothing but a way for the government to get your DNA and clone you… and I can't imagine the horror of two of you walking around."

River threw her hands up in exasperation and stomped all the way upstairs. I breathed a huge sigh of relief, happy to end the conversation.

River had been with us for three days, helping us paint and decorate Daniel's room… picking out toys she thought he'd like. She was already planning trips to the neighborhood park when he came to stay with us for the summer. It made me smile despite her uncharacteristic tantrum.

I looked around my workspace and sighed heavily. The hotel had just placed another huge order and I was now getting requests for other wholesale orders. I was busy. Busier than I'd ever been, but instead of being elated… I was stressed.

Between the overwhelming order and River's curiosity about her DNA, I just wanted a glass of wine and some alone time on my back porch.

Paris and Troy picked up their child a few hours later and, for the first time ever… I was happy to see River go.

I poured myself a big glass of red wine and curled up in the bed swing on my back porch. I knew I needed to talk to Paris about the DNA thing, but I didn't want to deal with it until I had a chance to calm my nerves.

I took a small sip of my wine. I could hear Damian calling my name, but I didn't bother answering. He'd eventually poke his head out the back door and ask if I wanted some company. I'd say, 'yes' even though the current answer was 'no', because as much as I wanted to be alone with my feelings… I didn't want to be by myself.

I closed my eyes and inhaled deeply. My next-door neighbor had his chiminea going. He always lit it when he smoked weed. One day I was going to have to tell him it wasn't masking anything. It literally smelled like weed and whatever wood he decided to burn in his chiminea on any given night.

I took another sip of my wine, this time gulping it down before refilling my glass.

I really needed to call Paris, but I knew she would end up just like me… damn near catatonic on the back porch. I called her husband, Troy.

"Troy, has River been bugging you about getting one of those ancestry kits?" I asked him.

"Yes, did she ask you too? I swear I thought I nipped that in the bud," he told me.

"Yep," I confirmed.

"Shit. She's in her room right now complaining about us on TikTok. I heard her saying her family doesn't want her to know about her ancestors."

"Because we don't," I whispered harshly.

"We can't keep this from her forever, Sis. She's Sixteen," Troy said sadly. "You know I love that little girl with everything in me… but I'm scared."

"Me too," I told him. "Where is Paris?"

"She's sitting on the back porch drinking a glass of wine. She doesn't want to talk about it."

"Yeah. I get it. I'll talk to you later," I said softly.

"I love you, sis," Troy told me.

"I love you too," I said before hanging up and staring off into space.

"Who are you out here lovin?" Damian stepped out onto the back porch with a bowl of grapes.

I smiled and made room for him inside my blanket.

"Should I be jealous?" he asked.

"That was just Troy," I sighed. "Something's going on with River."

"Ok. I was gonna talk to you about that, but I wanted to wait until she left. She asked me to buy her a DNA kit."

His announcement took me by surprise, and I could feel my wine sliding down my throat in a huge lump.

"When?"

"It came up while we were unpacking my office," he told me.

"Jesus." I took another swig of wine and rolled my eyes. "What did you tell her?"

"I told her, 'no,' but she's really worked up about it," he told me. "I think it would be cool. All her friends are doing it. She feels left out."

"She'll be fine," I said dismissively, desperately wanting to change the subject. I didn't care what we discussed, as long as it didn't concern River and her quest for a DNA test.

"Leroy has his chiminea going," I inhaled deeply and stood up. "I think I still have a few pre-rolls left, you wanna smoke?" I tried to walk away, but his hand on my arm stopped me in my tracks.

"I think we need to talk," he said simply. "And neither one of us needs to be high right now."

But I did. I needed something to calm my nerves, and the wine was barely putting a dent in my anxiety. My mind was racing, and I couldn't focus enough to meditate.

"About what?" I asked.

He stood up and put his hand on the small of my back, gently pushing me forward until we were standing in front of the kitchen table. He pulled out a chair for me, and I reluctantly sat down. Damian took the chair directly across from me and held both my hands in his. I wanted to look away from him but couldn't seem to drag my eyes away from his burning gaze.

"Twenty questions," he whispered.

"I don't feel like playing this game," I whispered back.

"Twenty. Questions," he said softly but firmly.

I didn't answer him, but he moved forward with his little game anyway.

"Is there something you need to tell me?" he asked.

"What?"

"You know what I'm talking about, Windsor."

I did know. I knew exactly what he was talking about. He wanted me to dive deep into my shame, ball it up and throw it to him like a game of hot potato. He wanted to dredge up a past he pretended to be okay with not knowing every detail.

"Damian, I don't want to talk about that," my voice was shaking. My eyes were pleading.

"Is he River's father?"

"He who? Troy?"

"No. Not Troy."

"You're acting crazy."

"It's a yes or no question, Windsor... and it doesn't take all this."

I refused to answer him, not while he was staring at me with an accusation in his eyes. I wanted so much to be angry with him, but I couldn't. I tried to pull my hands away from his, but he swiftly slid his grasp from my hands to my arms, holding me firmly in place.

He knew me too well.

My eyes filled with tears and I looked away from him.

"She's like your little clone," Damian said softly. "Which isn't unusual because I have cousins who look like twins and they have two different sets of parents. Paris is your sister so... there's definitely a chance her child would look just like you, but... they give her everything she wants, Windsor. She's a good kid. So why is this DNA test such an issue? Is there a secret in her DNA? Is Paris not her mother? Is Troy not her father? Is it both? Why were you out there whispering with Troy?"

"Let me go," I whispered. I turned to look at him, leveling my gaze at him, trying my best to regain control over my emotions.

"No," he told me. He paused as if he needed to think about what he was going to say next. "You lied to me, Windsor."

He was hurt. I could see it in his eyes. I could hear it in his voice.

"I need to hear you say it," he told me.

I looked down at his hands holding onto my arms and burst into tears.

"Say it," he said, louder than he intended, but enough to make me even more anxious.

His volume caused me to flinch. Every memory of my time in New York came flooding back to me at once, filling my brain with a panic I swore I'd never ever feel again. I snatched my arms and stood up so hard my chair crashed to the floor as Damian looked up at me in surprise.

I ran upstairs with Damian following closely behind me as I ran into the master bedroom and slammed the door, locking it behind me. Panic enveloped me. I felt like I was choking as the stress of the situation squeezed every bit of oxygen from my lungs. I ran into the bathroom, creating a double barrier between us as I closed and locked that door too.

I stood in the middle of the bathroom, walking around in circles, wringing my hands, wishing I had the courage to climb out of the second story window. Tears blurred my vision as I stared at the bathroom door, bracing myself for the moment it would come crashing in on me.

The last time I locked myself in a room...

I sat down on the floor and wrapped my arms around my knees, pulling them close to my chest as I slowly rocked back and forth, trapped inside of my mind as scenario after scenario played, reminding me of a time I desperately wanted to forget.

I'd never experienced Damian's anger Yes, we had small disagreements, but there was always laughter that led to compromise and then, we returned back to our normal routine as if there had never been a disturbance. This was different. Seeing the anger in his eyes... hearing that same anger in his voice... it was too much for me. It reminded me of a time when I walked on eggshells to make sure I didn't ruffle the peacock feathers of a man who was looking for a reason... any reason to hit me.

I could faintly hear Damian calling my name from the hallway. He alternated between calling my name and knocking. The knocking would stop for a few minutes and then start up again as he begged me to open the door, begged me to let him in.

Eventually, I heard him fumbling with the door, using a small emergency key to open it. His footsteps paused in front of the bathroom door. I held my breath.

"Windsor?" he called softly.

I held myself tighter, unsure if I was unable or unwilling to answer him.

"Baby, please let me in," he pleaded.

But I just sat there, afraid. Not of Damian, but afraid of the truth, and how it would forever alter our relationship. I was afraid of the possibility of losing his trust… losing his love.

Damian stopped knocking. He stopped calling my name and I watched as the shadow beneath the door darkened as he sat down on the other side. I could hear him leaning his back against the door and I slowly crawled until I was sitting as close to him as I could get with a thick piece of wood between us.

"Please talk to me," he whispered.

"I'm scared," I whispered back.

"Of me?"

"I was… for a moment," I admitted. It was hard to process my unexpected reaction to him raising his voice, but only I truly understood where my emotional cracks originated.

"I'm sorry," he whispered. "I shouldn't have reacted that way."

"Well, if it makes you feel any better… I would totally yell at you if I found out you had a secret baby you'd been hiding in plain sight." I tried to force laughter into my voice, but the cracks revealed my pain.

"Will you open the door?" he asked.

I reached up and unlocked the door before opening it just wide enough to see his hand resting on the floor. He reached inside and held my hand without asking me to open the door any further. It touched me that he somehow knew it would be easier for me to tell this story if I didn't have to look at him.

"She's yours," he said softly.

"Yes."

There. I said it. It was out in the open. I lied to him, but technically… was it a lie? River was my biological child, but Paris and Troy adopted her. They were her parents. I was the cool Auntie, even as the shame of my decision to give her up weighed heavily on my heart.

"When you yelled at me… it reminded me of *him*." I could feel him squeezing my hand as I spoke... giving me the courage to keep talking, to keep telling him my truth. "He used to tell me how beautiful I was, how special I was… and then, out of the blue, he started telling me how worthless I was. I remember I used to try so hard to be perfect for him and he would always find something wrong with me. One day I spoke up for myself and he hit me. When I look back… I realize he was waiting for me to show a little strength so he could put me back in my place. Damian, I know you would never intentionally hurt me… but, in that moment, when I felt like all these memories were being forced out of me… I was terrified."

"Baby, I'm sorry," he apologized again but I softly shushed him.

"I don't like talking about it. I don't like saying his name. I don't like… remembering the things he did to me, Damian. That last night with him…" I took a deep breath. "I was trying to leave him… but he came home early. He saw me standing there with my suitcases and…" My voice failed me.

"You don't have to tell me," he whispered.

"You need to know." I shook my head, knowing I needed to tell him the entire truth about my past so he could fully understand my present.

"He started hitting me and when I finally fought back… he grabbed a knife and…"

I could barely hear myself as the memories swirled through my mind and projected into my vision. It was as if I was watching a horror movie, but instead of being a spectator, I was being forced to live through the terror.

I could still feel the knife against my throat as Ian loomed above me, forcing himself inside of me as the knife held me in place. I didn't know I'd been cut until he pushed off of me and went into the bathroom. I could hear him singing in the shower as I lay there bleeding.

"I don't even know how I got out of there," I told Damian, "I just remember grabbing my bags and praying my neighbor would answer the door. I didn't even get dressed. I didn't have time. All I could think about was getting to a place where he couldn't touch me again."

I didn't even know my neighbor's name but the moment he saw me, standing half naked and bleeding in his doorway, he grabbed me and yelled for his wife to bring him a blanket.

"I don't remember anything after that," I sighed. "I woke up in the hospital a few days later. My bags were in a corner and Mama was sitting next to my bed crying. My neighbor found her number in my phone and called her."

"He got away with it," Damian said softly.

"His father was a Benin Diplomat so, yeah. He got away with it. Diplomatic immunity by birth." I shook my head. "He lost a lot of clients in the US. No one wanted to work with him after everything hit the news." I chuckled wryly. "It's ironic though. Some of the clients who refused to work with him, actually had their makeup artists cover my bruises on a regular basis. I guess it only mattered when it could hurt their brand."

He gently pushed the bathroom door open, and I moved out of the way as he took a seat on the floor next to me. He slid his arm around my waist and hugged me close to him. I instinctively laid my head on his shoulder and allowed my tears to fall freely.

"River was conceived that night," I told him. "When I found out… it was like being assaulted all over again. I didn't want her. I didn't even tell anyone. I just wanted to get rid of her quietly and try to put myself back together."

"What changed your mind?" Damian asked.

A wave of guilt washed over me, and I pulled away from him. "I had no choice," I said simply. "It was out of my control. By the time I realized I was pregnant…"

"It was too late," he finished for me.

"Yeah," I sighed.

I picked at a loose thread on my yoga pants and took several deep breaths as I tried to regain my composure. This was the part of the story I never wanted River to know. I never wanted her to know I only had her because I couldn't get rid of her.

"I wanted to kill myself," I whispered. "It wasn't the first time. I actually tried once… when I was with… *him.*"

Even while in the safety of Damian's arms, I couldn't bring myself to utter his name.

"I swallowed a bunch of pills one night. When I woke up, all I had was a damn headache. I thought… maybe I deserved to live in pain for the way I shut my family out of my life."

"Did you try while you were pregnant?"

I nodded sadly. "I was already depressed, but hiding the pregnancy got to be too much. I was in a lot of pain. My heart was broken, my spirit was broken. I thought the only way to escape the pain was to not exist."

I closed my eyes and lost myself in the memory.

I sat on the kitchen floor and pressed a knife to my wrist. It was the sharpest knife in mama's kitchen. Part of a set she bought after watching a late-night infomercial. I carefully placed the blade against the delicate skin of my wrist and made a quick but deliberate slicing motion.

"The damn knife wouldn't cut me," I chuckled. "This fucking knife could cut a tin can and then delicately slice a tomato, but it only scratched me. No blood on either wrist just… these horrible welts that hurt like hell."

"Why won't you let me die?" I stared up at the ceiling and yelled at the top of my lungs.

"You don't belong up here with me," I heard my granny say, clear as day. "Put that knife down."

"Now, mind you, my Granny died when I was sixteen so hearing her voice in my head scared the shit out of me." I paused thoughtfully. "I never told anyone about my Granny speaking to me from the great beyond. Do you think I'm crazy?"

"No, baby," he told me. "I know you heard what you heard, and it saved your life."

"She told me to stop trying to figure shit out on my own. She told me to protect myself and my baby at all costs. She told me that one day I would love my baby with all of my heart."

I could still feel the chills that settled over my body as Granny spoke to me that day. It changed the course of my life.

"I called a family meeting that night. They were shocked because I hadn't spoken very much since I came home. Everyone just… kind of tip-toed around me because of what I'd been through."

Mama grabbed my hands, crying openly as she saw the raised welts on my wrists. "Baby, why?" she kept asking as she hugged and kissed me repeatedly.

Paris sat next to me, holding, and kissing my hands, assuring me I could come to her with anything. That when I was ready to talk about what happened to me, she was there to listen.

"It's still happening," I wept openly, years of stress and abuse and mental anguish cascading down my cheeks, "I can't get away from him!"

"That muthafucka bet not set foot in Tulsa," a booming voice said loudly. "I got something for him if he shows his face around here! Has he been calling you again?" Troy asked angrily.

I shook my head. Troy owned a security company and had mama's house being monitored 24/7 for my protection.

"I'm pregnant," I said flatly.

The entire kitchen went silent. Even the clock seemed to stop ticking as my words hung in the air between us.

"Babies are a blessing," Paris finally whispered into the silence.

"Not this one," I whispered back.

"It's not the baby's fault," Paris started.

"I know that," I snapped. "Don't you think I know that? Don't you understand? I can't have that man's baby!"

"Well, I can't even have my husband's baby!" Paris yelled. She got up and ran from the room before I could react. Troy shook his head and went after her.

Mama and I sat in silence for a few minutes.

"You've been gone a long time, baby," she finally said. "I know you were going through your shit, but Paris has shit too. We all do. Four years, Windsor. You didn't come home for four years and at least three of those years we heard nothing from you."

"I'm sorry," I whispered.

"No, I'm sorry. I should have known what was happening!"

"How could you have known?"

"I knew the routine. Older man, young girl, all of a sudden, you're fighting with your mama over this man because she says he's no good... but you stay. Your contact with friends and family becomes sporadic and eventually you just kind of disappear. I lived that, Windsor. I lived that and I should have known!"

"Mama, no! It's not your fault!" I hugged her fiercely, suddenly realizing how traumatic it must have been to see me laying in a hospital bed. The cuts and the bruises and the black eyes... I was her baby.

"Mama, I'm scared," I whispered.

"I know, baby," she stroked my hair. "But you aren't alone. You have me. You have Paris and Troy. I promise you'll love your baby when you hold it in your arms."

"Mama, I can't keep this baby. He'll come after me if he finds out. He'll come after me and the baby. He'll come for the baby... just to hurt me."

"So, you want to give it up? Is that the only reason? If that man wasn't in the picture... would you want your baby?"

"I don't even want myself right now," I cried. "I have nothing to give a child. I'm not okay, Mama! Mentally, I'm a wreck. I'm emotionally unstable, I'm depressed, I'm not the kind of parent a child deserves. My child would suffer. I don't want that."

"If you still feel this way when your baby is born... Paris and I... we'll adopt it," I hadn't even noticed Troy standing in the doorway. "Windsor, please think about it. Please don't give your baby to strangers when you have us."

"And have the baby running around reminding me of how it got here? No. No way," I told him.

"Windsor, you have to do this for Paris. If you don't want this baby... Paris does. We've been trying for years and... she can't..."

I put my head down. Instantly ashamed of my earlier declarations. I told Paris my baby wasn't a blessing... when a baby was all she ever wanted.

"Do you ever regret giving her up?" Damian asked softly.

"Every single day," I choked out. "When she was born, they put her in my arms and all I could do was cry. She was so beautiful, Damian. I loved her in a way I never expected. I wanted to keep her. I did keep her... for two whole weeks. I breastfed her. She was my baby no matter who her father was... but her father... her biological father... he's crazy. If he knew about her there was no way he would let us live in peace. He would have fought for custody just to spite me. He would have forced visitation just to hurt me. My baby would have grown up watching him beat some other woman the way he beat me... the way I watched my daddy beat my mama! I didn't want that for her. The only way to keep her from him was to give her to Paris and Troy. At least it kept me in her life."

For a moment I thought I saw a brief look of disappointment take over his face. It broke my heart. No one could understand unless they had been in my position. He couldn't possibly know what it felt like to be abused that way.

"You think I did the wrong thing."

"Baby, no! I think you did what you had to do," he said, pulling me into his arms and hugging me tightly. "You did what you had to do. It just pisses me off that it was necessary. You shouldn't have had to give up your child out of fear. I'm so sorry, baby. I'm so sorry that happened to you."

Damian's phone rang in the distance, but he ignored it, holding me closer while I cried softly.

"I'm so sorry I lied to you," I whispered. "I didn't want you to think I was a horrible person."

"Never," he whispered.

"His name is Ian," I said softly. "Ian Boco."

Saying his name out loud... telling Damian exactly who hurt me... it freed me, but not completely. I closed my eyes, and for the first time, I was able to relax a little, stop fighting against the demons in my past for a moment. I could walk into my future with Damian, almost free from the secrets that haunted me. He now knew everything there was to know and he wasn't running away from me. He was pulling me closer.

"He'll never hurt you again," Damian told me. "and we will never mention his name again."

"Promise?"

"I promise," he assured me. "Never again."

I wanted to believe him... but there was still a small empty space in my heart I didn't think anything, but a miracle, could heal.

Chapter 27

Damian Lawrence Anthony

Windsor's revelation didn't change the way I loved her… but I knew it had somehow changed the way she loved herself all those years ago.

Deep down, I think I knew. The moment I saw River, I knew, but didn't trust myself to know… so I accepted Windsor's version of the story. I accepted that River was Windsor's niece despite the nagging feeling in my brain.

Mama knew. She knew immediately. Pulled me aside and said, *"You and Windsor need to have a conversation."*

I was ashamed of the conversation I had with Windsor. Ashamed of the way I'd raised my voice. Ashamed of the fear in her eyes when she looked at me.

It broke my heart.

I'd spent all this time thinking she was over it when, in reality… how the fuck do you get over something like that? Can you? Ever?

I held her close as she cried, wishing there was something… anything I could do to make it better. There was nothing. All I had were the arms that held her and the ears that listened as she poured out her heart to me.

"When they told me I needed a hysterectomy… I thought I was being punished. You see… I wanted to make it up to myself. I wanted to have another baby. I had them save some of my eggs… just in case, but I didn't think I'd ever find someone who would want to have a baby with me… that way… and I was too unstable to try to do it on my own. By the time I got my shit together I was too old to try."

"You're not too old," I told her. "We're not too old."

She started laughing despite her tears, and I wasn't sure if she was hysterical or genuinely amused by my declaration.

"Look, you've got eggs. I've got sperm. It's worth a try."

She shook her head. "I love you for wanting to do that for me, Damian. But loving one another isn't a good enough reason to go through that process. I love you and you love me, but we haven't been *us* long enough to bring a baby into the equation. And surrogacy… that's an expensive path. Neither of us have it like that, and even if we did…"

"I have the money from my Daddy," I said suddenly. "We can—"

"No," she said quickly. "No," she said again, in a gentler tone. "I love you so much, Damian, but no. I won't let you do that. I've made peace with not having more children, but if that's what you want, I wouldn't blame you for leaving right now and never looking back. You deserve everything life has to offer."

"*You're* everything, Windsor."

"Am I?"

"Yes," I told her.

"I know I act like I have my shit together, but deep down I still have cracks from where I glued myself back together. It took me years to realize I only wanted another baby because I was trying to replace River. Another baby isn't going to suddenly erase the past and make everything okay."

It was a huge thing for anyone to admit, but where she saw cracks, I saw character. Where she saw flaws, I saw a masterpiece… an abstract piece of modern art that made you look at it from all angles without ever truly understanding it… just knowing you want it hanging on your wall. Her truth didn't change that. If anything, it made me love her even more.

"She needs to know," I whispered into her hair.

"I know," she whispered back. "We have time."

I prayed she was right.

Chapter 28

Windsor Elaine Bradley

We sat on the back porch, passing a joint back and forth as our chiminea battled with my neighbors, as the smell of two different types of wood and two different strains of marijuana wafted through the air.

"Y'all ain't fooling nobody, Winnie," my neighbor, Leroy called over the fence.

"You ain't neva fooled nobody, Leroy," I called back with a laugh.

Damian's phone rang. He silenced it.

"You can answer it," I told him.

"No, it's probably a spam call. It's been calling all day," he told me.

I leaned into him and relaxed. It had been over a week since our conversation. A week since he learned my full truth, and he was still here, chilling with me on my back porch as our bed swing swayed in the breeze.

I passed him the joint and exhaled softly. The legalization of medical marijuana in my state was one of the greatest things ever. Now, instead of swallowing antidepressants that altered my mental status and made me feel like a zombie… I smoked a joint every now and then, or ate an edible.

"Did they leave a voicemail?" I asked him.

"I don't know."

"Boy, give me your phone," I sat up and held out my hand.

He dropped his phone into my hand, and I tapped his code in before opening his voicemails. He had 7 voicemails from an Atlanta area code and a hundred missed calls from the same number.

I put the phone on speaker and pressed play,

"Hi, this call is for Damian Anthony. My name is Janita Diggins, and I'm calling on behalf of *Conversations with Sandra K. Poole*. Ms. Poole read your book, *Three First Names,* and would like to set up a meeting with you. She'd like your novel to be the next selection for her International book club."

"What the fuck?" Damian stared at me in disbelief. "No way. No fucking way she'd be calling after five if this was legit."

"Well, she already called a hundred times. Maybe she thought she had a better chance of reaching you after business hours! Call her back, dammit!" I yelled excitedly.

"I don't know, Windsor," he hesitated.

"Oh, hell." I tapped redial and tried to steady my voice as Janita Diggins' voice came over the line. "Miss Diggins? This is Windsor with Damian Anthony's office. Please standby for Mr. Anthony," I said before shoving the phone in his face.

"Say hello," I said through clenched teeth.

He stood up as he answered, pacing back and forth in front of the bed swing as his voice became calmer and calmer. I stared at him with pride. I was watching Damian transform before my eyes. He'd gone from a bundle of nerves to a sophisticated author with a book about to be featured on Sandra's Literary Picks.

He hung up the phone and stared at me with a silly grin on his face.

"Baby, she's featuring my book in June."

"Oh my God… the Juneteenth show?" I asked excitedly.

He nodded in disbelief. "They're coming here to film the human-interest part of the story… and then they'll fly us out to Atlanta to film the actual book discussion in June."

"Wait… Sandra K. Poole is coming HERE? TO OUR HOUSE? You're going to be on the show?"

"I can't believe this! I'm going to be on *Conversations with Sandra K. Poole,*" he said triumphantly. "She's going to announce me as the June pick in April… .and then she's going to have a contest where five book clubs send in a video saying why they deserve a personal appearance from me and Sandra." His voice cracked. "She'll announce the winning book clubs on the Juneteenth show and then we will leave immediately to meet with them in their hometowns."

Damian stopped talking abruptly and sat down on the porch bed. He buried his face in his hands. It wasn't until I slid my arms around him, I realized… he was crying.

Chapter 29

Damian Lawrence Anthony

I sat.

Disconnected from my body.

Shoulders slumped.

Face in hands.

Mind… still.

Still like... the wind before a tornadic storm.

And then, my thoughts were jumbled.

Swirling around my mind and altering my sensibilities.

Speechless.

Unable to express the words caught in my throat.

I could only cry, and as Windsor wrapped her arms around me… I could only cry harder.

Every word I wanted to say… every thought passing through my mind… every emotion my heart wanted to convey… all spilled forth as a river of unstoppable tears.

"Daddy, I did it. That thing you always said I'd do. You believed in my dream. You weren't just humoring me, you told me I would make it. You told me Sandra K. Poole would be calling me one day. You manifested this through your words and your actions… and you aren't here to share it with me."

A hurricane, fueled by my dueling emotions, ripped through my joy, and left me momentarily broken.

Windsor held me.

Just… held me.

No words.

Just… held me.

"He should be here," I finally managed to choke out.

And then her breath was in my ear... softly sprinkling love and warmth throughout my entire body. Her touch energized me. Her words healed me.

"He is here," she whispered. "He's always been here. He's in every cardinal that tiptoes across the patio when you look out the kitchen window. He's in that sudden gust of wind that sends chills through your body on a sunny day."

She hugged me tighter and said, "he's in YOU, Damian. You hear his voice sometimes... guiding you... telling you things that only he could know... praising you... chastising you... that's not your imagination."

I pulled away from her, staring at her through my tears.

"He's proud of you," she said softly. "Always been proud of ya, boy. Neva gon' stop."

"How do you know that?" I asked her, my voice a little steadier. "How?"

"That he's proud of you?"

"No, the other thing...you said, 'always been proud of ya, boy. Neva gon' stop'. Why did you say that?"

If I sounded as insanely intense as I felt, she didn't falter. She just shrugged her shoulders and said, "I don't know... it just kind of... dropped into my head."

"He used to say that to me all the time when I was a little boy," I chuckled.

"See? Told ya he was here." She wiped my tears with the bottom of her t-shirt and smiled at me. "Are you gonna call your mama?"

"No, I can't, and... even if I could, I just want to... I don't know..."

I didn't know.

I was thrilled about this wonderful thing that could catapult my career and set Windsor and I on the path to financial security, but... I wasn't ready for anyone else to know. Something inside of me wanted this moment to be ... sacred. A thing we shared that the world didn't have access to... not yet. Plus, Janita asked me not to discuss it with anyone and I didn't want to ruin things by running my mouth.

I studied Windsor.

She looked... serene. All the stress from the past week had magically disappeared from her eyes. It was as if she pushed her worries to the side to fully embrace my sudden emotional outburst. She absorbed my pain and replaced it with joy.

I kissed her.

I slid my hands through her locs and cupped the back of her head, firmly locking her into place, and kissed her like the first time... only this time, there was no frenzy, no frantic sexual chemistry threatening to consume me if I didn't slide inside of her soon. There was no hurry.

We slowly fell backwards onto the bed swing, facing one another as I kissed her, periodically pulling back to hold her face in my hands and just… stare at her.

An occasional burst of hearty laughter filled the air as Leroy and whoever he had sitting around his chiminea passed an aromatic joint back and forth. The neighbor's dog whimpered, begging to be let back inside, and I lay there, holding Windsor as if the background noise was the greatest love song ever played.

"Sometimes I hate saying 'I love you' because it doesn't feel like enough,' I told her.

"Same," she whispered.

"How do you feel right now?" I asked her. "How would you describe this moment."

"I feel energized," she stroked my beard and kissed me gently. "I feel like my energy feeds off yours… not like a… parasite, but more like… we share the same energy. We fuel one another. When my battery is low… all you have to do is touch me and suddenly I'm at full capacity."

"And when I'm low you pour into me." I closed my eyes, relaxing in the sensation of her short fingernails raking through my beard, gently scratching the flesh underneath. "Just like you're pouring into me right now."

I'd never experienced so many highs and lows in a single moment. I was glad Windsor was there to hold me through it. I wasn't sure what that would have felt like alone.

She slid her hands underneath my shirt, and as she placed her palms on my chest, the world stopped. There was no rambunctious laughter, no whimpering dog, no crickets, no airplanes traveling overhead, no cars honking in the distance… only her smile casting an iridescent glow in the little bubble we created.

The swing gently swayed back and forth as I rolled her over onto her back and found my way inside her little pajama shorts.

I threw a blanket over us and gently slipped inside of her, swallowing her contented sighs with kisses.

Her kisses taste like honeysuckle. Tiny bursts of sweetness that tease and tantalize my senses. No matter how many I devour, it's never enough.

I made love to her slowly, oblivious to our surroundings, not worried about what the neighbors would think if they happened to peek through their upstairs blinds.

We were invisible inside our bubble.

Nothing existed outside of it.

We would deal with the rest of the world tomorrow.

Chapter 30

Windsor Elaine Bradley

I couldn't believe Sandra K. Poole was sitting on my patio drinking sweet tea and I couldn't tell anyone. The non-disclosure agreement was very specific. The book club pick was top secret. The only people who knew *Three First Names* had been chosen were me, and Damian and, of course, Ms. Poole and her crew.

It was killing Damian to keep this secret from his family, but we were planning a surprise viewing at our house on the night the show premiered.

"Why aren't you dressed?" Janita, Ms. Poole's assistant asked hurriedly. I could tell she wasn't southern by the way she pronounced her words, and her quick and precise delivery. Definitely west coast, maybe Cali.

"Dressed?"

I thought I looked cute in my jeans, cute heels, and Black Wallstreet T-shirt. I'd even thrown a fitted blazer over it. It was cute and casual without the appearance of trying too hard to look cute and casual. My locs were pulled away from my face and hung down my back in a high ponytail, and my lip gloss was super shiny.

"I thought I was just in the little scenes we already filmed?" I told her.

They'd already filmed Damian and I walking hand and hand through the garden, clowning around in the kitchen, answering the door together... little snippets of our relationship as part of his story. I hadn't planned on or expected to be filmed any further.

"Hold on," she tapped her headphones and whispered to whoever was on the other end of the line, "what else was his fiancée supposed to be wearing? She's only in the opening sequence, and why would she be changing clothes if this is just supposed to show them lounging around the house?"

There was a long, drawn-out explanation on the other end. I could tell by the way Janita was rolling her eyes and doing a 'wrap it up' motion with her free hand.

"Oh my gosh, these motherfuckers…" she mumbled and then, realizing she'd accidentally verbalized her thoughts, immediately apologized.

She was definitely a Cali girl, but she'd obviously grown up somewhere in the valley, because I had never heard a black woman pronounce her "arrahs" so properly as she cursed. This went beyond code switching. The whole thing made me laugh.

"It's more than okay. So, what did those muthafuckas do?"

She cracked a smile and then laughed, "Well, don't worry about getting dressed up. He wasn't thinking straight, but Ms. Poole wants to speak to you too."

"On camera? I would really rather not… this is Damian's thing. I'm just supporting him," I told her.

"Hmmmm...." she mused before taking a handkerchief out of her pocket and dabbing at the corner of my left eye. "You had a smudge. Don't worry, I didn't blow my nose with that. Ms. Poole will meet you on the patio in a few minutes." She walked away and then called over her shoulder, "Stay here, I'll come and get you."

"What the?" I mumbled, too stunned to respond.

"Don't feel defeated," the producer's assistant, Kandyss told me. "She has a way of getting folks to agree to do shit they never actually agreed to. Ron wanted you in a sexy dress with your hair down, but Janita didn't think it made sense because, as you said, you're relaxing at home. He agreed without knowing it too."

I glanced over at the producer, Ron, who winked flirtatiously at me. He tried it. Kandyss gave me a knowing 'sista girl' look and then went back to writing on her clipboard. I couldn't help laughing a little.

I was intrigued by the thought of speaking to Sandra K. Poole. I wasn't camera shy, but I was wary of what kind of attention being on her show, even in the smallest sense, could bring to me. Any attention I got could show up on Ian's radar. It wasn't like he couldn't find me if he wanted to. I wasn't hiding from him personally, but I knew he would pursue River to spite me if he had the smallest inkling of her existence. Just to be safe, I had removed all pictures of River from sight before the crew came over to set up.

I'd given River the day off with explicit instructions not to come over. I made up some story about planning a romantic day with Damian full of kissing and hugging. Once she finished her over exaggerated gagging, she asked if it counted as PTO or an eight-hour company holiday.

I still had to laugh at that. She was definitely being raised by Paris and Troy because the hustle was strong with that one.

"Ms. Poole is ready for you." Janita grabbed my hand and pulled me through the kitchen and out onto our back patio.

Damian was sitting comfortably on the wicker couch while Sandra K. Poole was sitting cater-corner in one of my plush wicker chairs. That chair matched nothing else on the patio, but it was the first piece of furniture Damian and I bought together. A spectacular item we found, at a garage sale, in one of the more affluent parts of town.

Damian smiled broadly as I approached and patted the empty space next to him on the couch. I immediately found myself surrounded by people making sure I was mic'd up properly and sitting at the correct angle. It brought back memories of my modeling days and I had to smile. It wasn't all bad.

"Thank you for joining us Windsor," Sandra extended her hand and I had to mentally slap myself to keep from fangirling. "I know we met briefly when I arrived, but Damian spoke so highly of you I had to get to know you a little better."

"Well, it's nice to meet you," I gushed. "You're even more beautiful in person."

It was true. She was impeccably dressed in a black pantsuit with a pair or red heels to give it a pop of color. Her silvery gray hair was styled in chin length locs, a controversial move for a black woman in television. Her hair was the topic of conversation for weeks when she started her loc journey live on television and didn't hide the process as her hair went through the many stages of growth. She'd been extremely transparent with her journey, giving many black women the confidence to rock their starter locs without buying into the myth of the 'ugly stage'. She taught us that locs were beautiful in all stages.

"Your hair is beautiful," I told her. "I admire your journey. I could have used that kind of encouragement when I started mine fifteen years ago. I got so much criticism."

Janita chose that moment to tip-toe into the frame and pull my ponytail from behind me until it hung over my shoulder and covered the right side of my blazer.

"Beautiful," Sandra said, nodding her approval. "That was not an easy thing to do, letting it all hang out like that on television, but I felt like I owed it to all the black women being told they need long straight hair to be beautiful. You're beautiful no matter how you wear your hair."

"Oh, it's a definite lesson of self-confidence," I agreed. "I learned how to tie scarves like a pro," I added with a laugh.

"I heard that," she raised her hand for a high-five and as I slapped my hand against hers, I damn near melted into that wicker couch.

I just slapped high-five with Sandra K. Poole. I was not worthy. None of us were.

"Oh, are we ready?" Sandra glanced up at the producer and then nodded towards me. 'You'll be fine," she whispered reassuringly, and as they counted down from five to one, I found myself staring into the camera and praying I wasn't making a huge mistake.

Chapter 31

Damian Lawrence Anthony

Two weeks after Sandra Poole's visit and I was still floating on air. The segment we filmed was going to run on April 22nd… that gave us a little over three weeks to plan a surprise party for our families and closest friends… with a twist. With the help of Ms. Poole, I'd dropped one helluva bomb on Windsor during our interview. I couldn't wait to see everyone's faces when they found out they were not only witnessing my big break... but they were also going to be witnessing a backyard wedding… in real time.

I was sitting in my office, sorting through party RSVPs when I recognized Felecia's familiar slanted cursive. She'd included a handwritten note thanking me for inviting her and Kelvin to our party and telling me she was excited to see Windsor and I again. I smiled. Their first meeting had been easy. It was as if they had known one another for years, and as Windsor sat on the couch, patiently laughing as both Daniel and Maleah climbed her like a jungle gym, there was no doubt in Felecia's mind that Windsor was, indeed, the one for me.

It warmed my heart that my son and my 2nd family would be there to see Windsor and I say, 'I do', even if they had no idea it was going to happen. I jumped up and did a little happy dance. I stopped short when I saw River standing in the doorway, staring at me with a… look on her face.

"Hey, Rivvy," I said, easing into the nickname I'd given her when she started calling me 'Uncle Damian.' She usually smiled when I said it, but today her look was somber… almost sad.

Without responding, she walked into my office and sat in the armchair in front of my desk. It was how we had conversations. She would sit in that chair, and I would sit behind my desk as we talked about her day, or her desire to get a driver's license, or the latest episode of one of our favorite anime shows. Other times, we would sit and play video games in front of the flat screen she convinced me to put in my office.

Like Windsor, I was a sucker for River. She pretty much got what she wanted, but it was easy to spoil her. Despite her aloofness and smart mouth when we met, River was really the sweetest sixteen-year-old I'd ever met. She was loving, caring, and smart as a whip… but she was a young sixteen, despite her maturity.

Seeing her look sad made me feel sad. I never wanted to see tears fall from her pretty brown eyes. I watched as she picked up my Snowy Day snow globe and shook it a few times before placing it back on my desk and watching as the snow and glitter swirled around the toddler in the red snowsuit.

"Uncle Damian, I did something really bad," she whispered, her eyes still on the snow globe, tears beginning to stream down her cheeks.

"Rivvy, what happened?" I instantly jumped into 'daddy' mode. I quickly walked around my desk and crouched down in front of her chair. That's when I noticed the balled-up piece of paper in her hand.

"Can I see that, sweetie?" I asked gently.

She shook her head vigorously, still staring at the globe, refusing to look at me.

"Rivvy? Please," I said gently prying her fingers from around the paper. She didn't fight me. Merely relaxed her hand as I gently pulled the paper from her limp fingers.

I literally felt my heart fall into my stomach when I saw the words, 'Ancestry DNA' at the top of the page.

SHIT! I almost yelled out loud.

My mind was reeling. This couldn't be happening. No! No. No. No. No. No. NO!

What had she done?"

I stared at her profile as she continued staring at the globe and my heart broke for her. I looked down at the paper. It was a family tree. It listed distant cousins on her maternal side… and on the other side of the tree… it listed distant relatives, a grandmother… and a father.

Ian Boco.

My mind momentarily flashed back to the things Windsor told me a few weeks ago. Once again, it took everything in me not to scream my frustrations at the top of my lungs.

"My parents have been married for over twenty years," she finally spoke, her voice hushed, like she was afraid someone would overhear us. "I'm only sixteen. Mama cheated on my Daddy? Do you think he knows? Is that why they didn't want me to do the DNA test?"

She looked to me for the answers and all I could do was shake my head.

"Where did you get the kit?" I asked her.

"I saved up and bought it on Amazon," she admitted. "I just wanted to know what part of Africa we're from... It's Benin. But that's not us... it's him... that Ian person."

She started crying then, soft little sobs that told me she was trying very hard to stay in control of her emotions. I put my arms around her, and she broke down.

I heard the front door open and Windsor's footsteps coming down the hall, speeding up when she heard River crying.

"What happened?" she stared wide eyed at me as I held a crying River in my arms.

I handed her the DNA results and said, "Call Troy and Paris... Your mom too. We need to have a family meeting."

Windsor glanced down at the paper in her hand and her face immediately went gray. She wobbled on her feet slightly and I prayed she didn't pass out.

"Windsor?" I said hesitantly, watching as she grabbed the door frame and steadied herself.

"I'm good."

"You sure?"

She shook her head and walked away on unsteady legs.

Chapter 32

Windsor Elaine Bradley

I stared at the crumpled sheet of paper in my hands and my world suddenly stopped spinning on its axis, causing me to stumble. I couldn't allow River to see me upset, not when she was so upset and confused. Her Uncle Damian was comforting her. I needed to pull myself together.

I wiped my eyes and grabbed my phone. I tried to compose myself, but the sound of my mother's voice broke me down.

"Mama?" I said tearfully, the moment she answered the phone.

"What happened?" she yelled in a panic.

"Mama, please come over. Call Troy and Paris. They need to get over here now! River snuck and got that DNA test. She knows Ian is…" I couldn't even bring myself to utter those last words.

Ian wasn't her father. He would *never* be her father. Troy was her daddy. Handpicked by me, and he adored River. His daughter.

He adored... my… daughter.

I buried my face in my hands. I knew this day would come, but I hadn't expected it to come so soon. I thought we had more time. We planned to tell her when she was eighteen… when she was old enough to handle the emotions that came with knowing you're adopted… that your aunt gave birth to you under duress and gave you up out of fear.

How do you explain that to a sixteen-year-old?

How do I explain her conception? How do I explain trying to kill myself when she was in my womb? Should I? She knew I'd been abused by a man in New York, but I never told her his name. I never wanted her to google him and see any kind of resemblance. She was nothing like him. She was all me. She was my twin. She was my child… she was my only child and she'd spent a lifetime calling me 'Aunt Winnie'.

I felt my mother's arms around me and heard her whisper in my ear, "stop crying, baby. This is gonna be hard, but we have to hold it together for River."

She was right. I straightened my shoulders, wiped my eyes again, and sat at the kitchen table, holding the DNA results in my hand as Damian led River into the kitchen with his arm around her shoulders.

She took one look at me and flew into my arms. I held her as a surge of motherly energy overtook me and wrapped us both in a protective shield. I would never ever let anyone hurt her. Especially Ian Boco. I would kill him first.

"It's okay, baby. I promise," I whispered into her freshly braided hair.

"Did you know?" she asked tearfully.

I couldn't bring myself to tell her another lie. "We'll talk about it when your mom and dad get here," I told her. "Just know… that everything you hear today… everything that happened, was done out of love. Promise me you'll remember that." I pulled back to look into her tearful eyes. "Promise me, baby," I pleaded, unable to hide the cracks in my voice despite my deceptively calm demeanor.

"I promise," she whispered.

I pulled her to me again, hugging her fiercely as I stared at Damian over the top of her head. I didn't know what to do. A wave of anxiety crept up my body, starting at my toes and systematically making its way through my being until I felt like I couldn't breathe. Damian recognized it and silently held my gaze as he took deep breaths in and out. His eyes lulling me into doing the same.

My breathing became less labored… the anxiety didn't disappear, but it hung back, allowing me to focus on the most important thing… the little girl crying in my arms.

Troy burst into the kitchen with Paris following closely behind. They both stared at me questioningly as they saw me cradling their daughter. I shook my head vigorously. I hadn't told her anything. It wasn't my place, and that was a devastating thing to admit to myself.

"Baby girl," Troy said softly, taking River's hand in his. "Sit up, baby. We need to talk to you."

"Daddy, I'm sorry. I should have listened. Please don't be mad at me."

"Now, how could I ever be mad at my little girl," he stood her up and put his hand under her chin, gently coaxing her to look up at him, "I don't care what that little funky piece of paper says. I'm your daddy."

"But —"

"There are things you don't understand… but we're going to sit here, as a family, and sort it all out today. We will answer all your questions. Nothing is off limits. Come sit next to me."

He walked around the table with her and put her in a chair between him and Paris as Damian moved closer to me, squeezing my hand underneath the table.

I pushed the DNA results to the middle of the kitchen table and took a deep breath, staring deep into Paris' eyes as I did so. I shook my head sadly. I couldn't start this conversation. As River's… mother… she needed to do it.

Paris cleared her throat and put her hand over River's, but River snatched away as if she'd been burned. This was gonna be a lot harder than we thought. Maybe if we had told her sooner. Maybe if she hadn't found out this way, she wouldn't be hurting the way she was hurting now.

"Did you cheat on my daddy?" River asked pointedly, staring daggers into Paris.

Tears filled Paris' eyes.

It would have been so easy to say, 'yes'. It would have been so easy to bear the brunt of River's anger to protect me, and the moment I saw Paris start to open her mouth… I knew that's what she planned to do. I couldn't let her do that. I couldn't let her risk the love of her child to protect my secrets. I wouldn't let her do that. Not for me.

"Your mother loves Troy," I said before Paris could respond. "She's loved him since middle school. She would never ever cheat on your father."

"Then how is that other man my father? Ian Boco. How can that be true? Did the DNA lie?"

At that moment, it was obvious to me she hadn't googled him. A simple google search would have told her everything she needed to know. She would have learned Ian Boco was a highly sought-after fashion photographer based in New York City who was arrested for assaulting his model girlfriend. Her name wasn't mentioned… but it was rumored to be Windsor Bradley, who dropped out of sight soon after his arrest. She would have seen his mugshot or pictures of him chilling on a yacht in the Riviera and searched his face for some resemblance to hers.

"River," I started and then stopped suddenly. I didn't know how to tell her. I didn't know where to start. I could feel Damian's hand squeezing mine tighter, sending me strength through osmosis. I tried again. "Remember when I told you about my time in New York?" I asked her.

She nodded.

"I told you about my modeling jobs and I showed you my portfolio, right?"

She nodded again.

"Do you remember what else I told you? About the bad things that happened… about the man who… hurt me?"

"Was it this man? This Ian Boco?" River asked quietly.

I nodded slowly.

My breath caught in my throat as a slow sense of realization settled in her eyes. She stared at me as if she was seeing me for the first time. In a way, she was.

Paris put her hand over River's… gingerly, as if she was afraid of being rejected again. This time River didn't pull away. She looked at Paris and whispered, "I'm so sorry, Mommy."

I don't know why… but hearing her call Paris 'mommy' hurt more, in that moment, than it did the first time she said it as a baby. I was silent, not knowing what else to say. River stared at me again. She opened her mouth to speak, but I could tell she was also at a loss for words.

"You didn't want me, Aunt Winnie?" she finally said, her voice full of pain.

"I wanted you, baby. I wanted you so bad, but… I couldn't. I was… fucked up… and I was scared. I tried, River. I kept you for two whole weeks. You slept with me… right here, on my chest, because I was afraid you'd stop breathing in your sleep." I put my hand on my heart for emphasis. "I breastfed you. I cocooned myself with you… but I wasn't healthy… mentally… and if he knew… baby, if he knew about you, he would have done everything in his power to take you away from me. I couldn't let that happen. I didn't want you to grow up like me. I didn't want you being forced to spend time with someone who could… do the things he did. I didn't want you to see it. I didn't want you to hear it. I didn't want you to think it was normal. I wanted better for you. Better than him… better than me."

I didn't realize tears were sliding down my face until I felt two sets of arms holding me. Damian and Mama. Damian slowly pulled away, giving my mother the room she needed to hold her youngest daughter. To comfort me in a way I couldn't receive 17 years ago when I was bruised and battered and suicidal. When I only allowed myself comfort in spurts while my shame kept me isolated from the world.

"You broke a generational curse the day you gave your baby to Paris," she whispered in my ear. "You did that. You refused to let your child see the things you and your sister saw growing up… the things I saw… the things my mama saw."

"Your mama and I… we couldn't have a baby of our own. So, when you were born… when your… when Windsor needed a good home for you… we took you," Troy said, his deep baritone slightly cracking as he spoke. "We didn't want strangers taking care of you. We wanted you with us. We wanted you from the moment we found out Windsor was pregnant. We were supposed to take you home from the hospital, but Windsor changed her mind. She wanted to keep you."

"When Windsor called and asked me to come and get you… I was so happy for me and daddy… but I was so sad for her. She loved you, River. She's always loved you. Please don't ever think she never wanted you. You were the most wanted baby in the world… by all of us," Paris added.

I was thankful for the way they told her how much I wanted her… even though it wasn't completely true. I would take my eagerness for an abortion and my failed suicide attempt to my grave. She would never know how much I resented being pregnant… how sad I was until the moment they placed her tiny body on my naked chest in the delivery room. When her skin touched mine, tying her to me for life. When her strong cries filled the space and her little eyes stared at me as if she knew I had what she needed to make everything better.

How could I not fall in love with her? How could I not see anything but beauty… even in someone born from such an ugly act. Seeing her now… emotionally traumatized over a decision I made… it had my stomach in knots.

I had to get out of there.

I stood up slowly, mumbled something about needing some air, and walked out onto the back porch, inhaling the wind like I would choke without it, as I all but choked on my raw emotions. I sat on the stairs leading down to my newly blooming garden and stared out into the depths of nowhere. I closed my eyes and listened as Leroy played his acoustic guitar, something he once told me he did when he had a lot on his mind. The slow haunting melody matched my mood as I ducked and dodged the skeletons running through my mind.

I don't know how long I was out there alone, but when I heard the creaking sound of the screen door opening and then soft footsteps on the deck behind me, I didn't have to open my eyes to know it was River. I scooched over to make room for her on the bottom step. We sat in silence, each lost in our own thoughts. I knew the chaos in my own mind, but I couldn't imagine the thoughts running through hers.

"I think some small part of me always knew," she said, breaking the silence between us.

I opened my eyes, afraid to look at her, but wanting to keep hearing the lyrical sound of her voice.

"I always thought it was strange… how much I looked like you. Even though I know it's possible… I mean, you look just like all those pictures of Great Aunt Maggie when she was younger so… I figured it was just the way our gene pool was set up. But sometimes…"

"Sometimes what?" I asked softly, finally able to look at her.

She was staring back at me with a sad smile on her face.

"It's the way you look at me sometimes. The way you're looking at me now," she whispered. "Like it hurts."

"That's because it *does* hurt, baby." I was trying so hard not to cry, but she wasn't making it easy. Not when she was looking into my soul and pulling emotions out of me I'd been fighting to bury her entire life.

"What did MawMaw whisper to you?" she asked quietly.

I picked up a roly-poly and smiled as its tiny feet tickled the back of my hand. We both sat there… watching it crawl across my fingers before I carefully dropped it in the grass.

"It's the roly-poly slide… wheeeee…" River sang suddenly.

We both broke out into a fit of giggles.

The Roly-Poly Slide was a song we made up together when she was four. The memory made me smile. We were sitting in the dirt and playing with the little bugs until they got tired of us and curled up into little balls. Then, River got a tiny piece of cardboard, propped it up on a rock. We rolled those poor little bugs down the "slide" multiple times while singing that silly little song.

River picked up another roly-poly and placed it on the back of her hand as we softly sang the song together. I held out my hand for it and placed it in the grass with its little friend.

"She told me I broke a generational curse when I gave you to your parents," I finally answered her question. "That's what MawMaw whispered to me."

River sighed sympathetically. "Does it hurt you to call them that?" she asked curiously.

"Sometimes," I said truthfully. "But the rest of the time I'm just glad you have them in your life. You know they love you more than anything."

"I know," she told me.

"I love you, ya know?" I picked up one of her box braids and twirled it around my finger.

"I know," she smiled.

"How do you know?"

"Because you always tell me," she said, tears winding down her cheeks.

"Don't you ever forget it." I told her.

She nodded and then said, "What do I call you now?"

It's something I'd never considered. I'd long ago given up the notion of anyone calling me mommy or mama or anything resembling that. I'd always just been 'Aunt Winnie.'

"You can call me whatever you want," I said, forcing laughter into my voice. "Just don't call me from jail."

She rolled her eyes with a grin. There she was. That was the River I knew. That was my baby. She grabbed my hand and squeezed so hard I thought both our fingers would break.

"I love you," she whispered, staring at me earnestly. "And I'm proud of you. You protected me. It just makes me sad because…" Her voice trailed off.

I understood what she was trying to say. I'd had sixteen years to get used to seeing my sister mother my child… and I never fully got over it. How could I?"

River just found out I was her mother. I gave birth to her and then gave her to Paris and Troy when the reality of my situation became too real. It was a reluctant gift from my broken heart.

River accepted my truth

Her truth.

Our truth.

I could no longer hold back my sobs as she leaned into my arms. We cried together, hugging each other tightly. For the first time in my life, there were no heavy secrets wearing me down and threatening to push me into a bottomless pit of despair. River knew who I was. She knew what she needed to know… and she still loved me.

It was all I needed to fill the tiny, empty space in my heart.

Chapter 33

Windsor Elaine Bradley

We weren't naive enough to think we had all the answers. We made the decision, together, to seek counseling for River. It's only been a few weeks, but it's helping. The heaviness that once altered her steps when she found out about her heritage... was slowly beginning to lighten. It wasn't going to happen overnight. It was something we all needed to recover from... but it was going to happen.

She wasn't sure what to call me now. Sometimes she called me, *Aunt Winnie*, while other times she just smiled, acknowledging my presence without calling me anything. She was still working through it.

She stared at me sometimes... with the same look in her eyes she told me I sometimes had when I stared at her... like it hurt.

Not anger, just... hurt... and curiosity.

What would it have been like to be her mother in every sense of the word?

What would it have felt like for her to be my daughter?

Did it matter?

We told ourselves it didn't, but... it did.

It did.

I shook off those thoughts and focused my mind on my immediate present and the party Damian and I were throwing to announce his book as Sandra K. Poole's most recent literary pick.

I created a brand-new scent for this day. River helped me. She stood at the white board writing formulas down as I carefully measured ingredients until, together, we created a scent unlike no other. It smelled like love.

She didn't know it yet... but I named it, *Windsor's River*.

It would be sold as a limited-edition soap, but first, it would be placed in the little gift bags Damian and I meticulously put together for our party guests. Each bag contained a full-sized soap and lotion and a copy of *Three First Names* with a brand-new cover and brand-new content from Damian's new publishing company, Daniel's Sun Publishing.

There was also, courtesy of Ms. Sandra K. Poole, a beautiful bookmark she'd had specially made for the occasion.

No one would receive their swag bag until the end of the party… but we planned on partying until dawn.

I stared at myself in the full-length mirror and smiled, daring myself to fully immerse myself in this day we'd spent weeks secretly planning… of course, with LeeLee around, nothing was fully a secret. She didn't know exactly what was going on… but she knew something was up. I had to laugh. She once told me she knew what she needed to know when she needed to know it. That she didn't know everything, and she didn't have all the answers, but when she received a message, it was her responsibility to deliver it.

It was hard to believe six months had passed since she picked me up, wobbly-kneed and dick whipped, from Damian's little house after our one-night stand. I started laughing at the memory and LeeLee looked over at me as if she could tell what I was thinking about.

"You really do look beautiful," she told me, standing next to me in the mirror and admiring herself in the classy, black silky jumper she was wearing.

"Me? Girl, you look fantastic in that jumper! I was beginning to think I would never see you in anything but your yoga pants and a hoodie." I said, turning so we were facing one another. I studied her thoughtfully. "I have the perfect thing for you," I told her.

I walked over to my dresser and opened my jewelry box, pulling out a pair of pearl earrings from a time in my life where diamonds and pearls were the norm for me. I'd sold most of the jewelry from that time. I'm not sure why I kept the pearls. Maybe it was because they reminded me of my grandmother on my father's side. Her beautiful silver hair was always perfectly in place, and her pearls were always on display.

She looked like she'd never seen a day of trouble or despair in her life… but looks could be deceiving. She'd endured more than most of us could imagine, but like Maya Angelou… she continued to rise until her death several years ago.

It was time for me to let go of the past. Time to let go of these pearls and give them to someone who could give them new life and new meaning.

"Windsor, I can't."

"You can, and you will," I gently pulled LeeLee's earrings out of her ears and replaced them with the pearls. I turned her towards the mirror and stood behind her with my hands on her shoulders.

"Gorgeous," I whispered with a smile.

"Thank you, Windsor," LeeLee said happily. "And thank you for inviting me to this party. I know it's for family and close friends only."

"You are family, Sis," I said sincerely. "You've been family since the day you showed up on my doorstep and convinced me to go get my man."

"And look at you now," she said, beaming with pride. "You got your man."

"Shole did," I laughed. "Let's head downstairs and see who else has arrived. I want you to meet Felecia."

"Damian's ex?"

"Yes. I think you'll like her…"

LeeLee and I made our way downstairs. I was in awe of the sea of beautiful black and brown people walking through my house wearing elegant all-black ensembles. The invitations had been specific. All-Black, after 5 attire and comfortable shoes. Only those named on the invitation were allowed to attend. We invited forty of our closest friends and family.

I sent Marissa an invitation… even extending that invite to her boyfriend, but I never heard back from her. Part of me wished the security guard Troy set up at the door would come to me and say, "there's a woman named Marissa at the door. She has an invitation, but I don't see her on the list."

It didn't happen.

My granny used to say, "everybody ain't gon' grow wit'cha… and everybody damn so' cain't go wit'cha!"

I never truly understood what she meant until now.

"Windsor," Damian stood at the bottom of the stairs, smiling at me appreciatively. I'd picked out this knee length, black cocktail dress with him in mind, it was the same dress I was wearing the night we met. The look in his eyes and the subtle way he licked his lips told me he remembered.

I blushed like a schoolgirl under his gaze.

"I remember that dress," he said proudly.

"I don't remember this suit," I said, admiring him in a tailored black suit that made him look like he belonged on the cover of GQ Magazine. His black shirt was open at the collar, exposing the hollow of his throat, one of my favorite places to kiss him.

"It's not every day a man gets to throw a surprise wedding and marry the woman of his dreams," he mumbled into my ear before discreetly biting my earlobe. "It's almost time to get this show on the road," he added.

"These people have no idea what's going on," I laughed.

"Winnieeeeee…" A tiny ball of energy collided with my legs, hugging them fiercely. I looked down to see Daniel with his arms wrapped around my legs, staring up at me with the biggest smile on his face.

My heart melted. I was still amazed at how quickly this little boy had taken to me. I picked him up and hugged him close as Felecia and Kelvin joined us.

"This is a beautiful party," Felecia leaned in for a hug. "Thank you for inviting us."

"It wouldn't have been complete without you," I told her. "Come on, let's go outside. Damian has an announcement."

Felecia raised an eyebrow. "An announcement?"

"You'll see."

Damian motioned to Ali Shaw, a local radio personality he hired to DJ the party. She nodded and then sent the music into a slow fade as she announced the party was moving into the back yard.

There were no April showers in the forecast, but Damian and I weren't taking any chances. This was Oklahoma. If you didn't like the weather, you only needed to wait a few minutes and it would change. A large tent, spanning from the back patio to the edge of the back yard, made sure no unexpected raindrops would disrupt tonight's festivities.

It was beautiful. An oasis in the middle of our suburban neighborhood. The collective chorus of oohs and ahhs as our guests made their way into the tent was music to my ears. This party, a gift from Sandra K. Poole herself, had to cost… shit… I didn't even want to think about it. She'd spared no expense for our special day, even when I confided in her the reasons why it was important for us to keep our ceremony private. I didn't want River filmed. I needed to protect her at all costs. Ms. Poole understood, shutting her producers down when they insisted on having camera crews at the party. This was her gift to us… no strings attached… and this gift would remain private, aside from a few, select pictures on the Sandra K. Poole website.

There was a huge projection screen at the rear of the tent, with neat rows of chairs in a half-circle pattern in front of it. As our guests took their seats, Damian and I sat on the front row waiting for the lights to dim. Daniel sat in my lap and put his little head on my shoulder. I glanced over at River. She was smiling at us. There was no malice. No jealousy. She'd taken a similar position in my lap throughout her childhood.

The lights dimmed and the DJ announced to the crowd that we would be watching a very special video. I held my breath. A hush of anticipation settled over the crowd. The opening credits of The Sandra K. Poole show started, and everyone erupted in applause when they realized the door Ms. Poole was knocking on… was ours.

I watched with pride as she interviewed Damian, telling him how much she loved the book and how honored she was to select *Three First Names* as the Juneteenth Literary pick.

"That's my baby!" Damian's mother shouted at the screen with tears in her voice.

Damian squeezed my hand and smiled as my face showed up on the screen, seated next to him on our patio, speaking to Sandra as if we were old friends. Another hush settled over the crowd as the interview continued.

"So, the two of you are recently engaged. How is wedding planning going?" Sandra asked us.

I looked over at Damian with a silly grin on my face. "Honestly, we haven't really started. I don't think I realized how overwhelming it would be," I said laughingly.

"Actually, I was thinking we could just do it tonight," Damian said with a grin.

"Tonight?" It was obvious I was confused, but like a model, I didn't allow my smile to falter.

"Yeah," Damian laughed, enjoying the way he'd totally caught me off guard. "We could do it right here… in the backyard."

"Tonight?" I asked again.

"Tonight," he said seriously.

"Can I come?" Sandra asked. "I'm ordained. I could marry you and then send you off on an awesome honeymoon."

"Wait. Wait. Wait. Wait." I held up my hands and Damian and Sandra laughed hysterically. "What's happening?"

"Just say, 'yes', baby," Damian said softly.

I stared into his eyes… trusting him completely. "Yes."

"Soooo, it looks like we're having a wedding… tonight," Sandra said, smiling into camera number 2. "I guess we should go change clothes. This is a very private ceremony, but there will be select wedding pictures on SandraKPoole.com tomorrow morning… and ten of my lucky viewers will win a copy of Damian's critically acclaimed book, *Three First Names*."

The picture on the projection screen faded, and suddenly, Sandra K. Poole, live and in person, stepped from behind the curtains as our party guests went crazy from the overload of surprises we'd just bombarded them with. A Literary pick? A Wedding? THE Sandra K. Poole? It was just too much for them to handle. There was laughter. There were tears. There were some people just staring from Damian and I to Sandra with shocked looks on their faces.

"Hey, everybody! I'm Sandra K. Poole," Sandra spoke into the microphone above the roar of applause, whistles and cheers. "Shocking, huh? Y'all didn't know what you were here for. You thought this was just a little get together, didn't you? It's a Literary pick reveal! It's a wedding!"

I handed Daniel off to Damian and quietly slipped away while the crowd's attention was focused on Sandra. I caught River's shocked expression and waggled my finger at her, motioning for her to sneak out of the tent with me.

Once we were outside, I grabbed her hand as we wordlessly walked back into the house. I led her upstairs and into my bedroom where my wedding dress had been laid out by Sandra's glam squad.

"You're really getting married? Tonight?" River asked, her eyes wide with excitement. "Did that just happen? Sandra K. Poole is at our house, and you and Uncle Damian are getting married? His book is her literary pick? He's gonna sell a million copies! Oh my God!"

She hugged me tight, jumping up and down with me like we were two toddlers playing dress up. One of Sandra's stylists unzipped my dress. I stepped out of it and she hastily helped me put on my wedding dress. My mother walked through the door just as my cathedral veil was being pinned to my hair.

She burst into tears.

"Oh, Windsor," she said softly. "Look at you."

I stared at myself in the mirror. I could hardly believe it myself. The ivory white dress looked beautiful against my dark skin. The bodice, encrusted with crystals, caught every light at every angle. Sheer floral lace appliques cascaded down the skirt while dramatic linear glitter shone from beneath. It was the fantasy dress I never knew I wanted until I saw myself in it for the first time. I was having the wedding I never knew I wanted until Damian proposed.

I was standing in my bedroom, with my mother, my baby, and a glam squad, on the night of my surprise wedding. What could be better than that?

"You look beautiful, Ma," River said softly, walking up behind me and staring at our reflection in the mirror.

Ma.

She slid her arm around my waist and laid her head on my shoulder. It was like looking at my present self and my younger self in a weird photographic manipulation… but it was real. This moment was real. We were real… mother and daughter, once removed, spiritually reunited as our relationship evolved with twinges of sadness for what was loss… but bountiful excitement for what was to come. I kissed the top of her forehead and closed my eyes, willing that moment to last forever.

But we didn't have forever. We only had a few more minutes, as the party planner gently reminded me, breaking into our moment, and bringing my psyche back into the room.

"You wanna give me away?" I asked River.

"Really?" she clasped her hands together, and she was suddenly that little four-year-old girl, singing about roly polys in the backyard, excited about everything under the sun.

I smiled. "Absolutely."

She looked over at Mama.

"What about MawMaw?" she asked timidly, not wanting to take an honor she felt belonged to her grandmother.

Mama put one hand on my cheek and the other on River's, staring at us through new eyes… eyes that no longer had to hide the truth.

"It should be you, River Elaine," Mama said with a happy smile.

"Well," River said, grabbing my hand. "Let's not keep Uncle Damian waiting."

I noticed Mama hung back a little and I turned to look at her over my shoulder. One of the make-up artists handed her a tissue. She dabbed her eyes and said, "I'm okay, baby. I just…"

"I know," I said, holding out my hand to her. "Me too."

And as the sounds of Leroy's acoustic guitar began playing the opening chords of Daniel Caesar's, *Best Part*, my daughter, and my mother walked me down the aisle.

June

Sometimes

A One-night stand

Is just…

A one-night stand,

But

Sometimes one night

Transforms into

A lifetime of nights

And a love

That spans forever.

A love that

Started in my loins

And settled in my heart

And

Somehow, she became

A permanent part

Of the life I didn't know I wanted.

I met her in October

I married her in April

It's never too soon

When you know...

Chapter 34

Damian Anthony Lawrence

I sat on the deck, watching as Rivvy sat cross legged in the dirt with Daniel, singing an offbeat melody about a roly poly slide as she propped a tiny piece of cardboard against a rock and gave each roly-poly a gentle nudge. I shook my head and chuckled, trying my best not to laugh out loud as Daniel squealed with apprehensive delight every time River put one of those little bugs in his hand.

"I'm so glad he figured out how to handle them with care." Windsor handed me a glass of lemonade and sat down next to me. "I'm not sure if I could have kept a straight face through another poly poly funeral."

"You ain't lying," I laughed loudly, causing Daniel to look up at us with a little frown on his face.

"The roly poly slide is serious business," Windsor whispered with a side-eye and a wink.

"I'll keep him quiet, baby," I called out to Daniel.

"Thanks, Mama Winnie," Daniel said with a grin and a wave. His little high-pitched voice tickled me.

I took a slow sip of my lemonade and admired the scene before me. This was Rivvy's last free summer before her senior year. She spent a lot of time with her friends, but she spent the majority of her time babysitting Daniel while I planned my book tour and Windsor fulfilled soap orders.

My phone beeped on the wicker end table and I glanced at it, trying my hardest not to pick it up while I was watching Daniel and Rivvy play. That phone could be a huge distraction, and I didn't want my summer with Daniel to be littered with vague memories of my son watching me as I dealt with any and everybody but him.

My phone rang. Sunday was our designated day off. I hated to answer my phone, but whoever it was wasn't taking no for an answer.

"Remember the last time you ignored a ringing phone?" Windsor reminded me, "You almost missed being Sandra's Literary pick."

"And today is my last free Sunday before we leave for Atlanta to do the Juneteenth show," I reminded her. "And then I'm going on the mini book club tour. Whoever it is can wait. Nothing is more important than this."

"Watching the kids roll roly polys down a cardboard slide?" Windsor laughed softly.

"Especially watching the kids roll roly polys down a cardboard slide," I said, leaning over to give her a gentle kiss. "Wheeeeee."

She started giggling, "I'm gonna go check on lunch, you want something from the kitchen?"

I handed her my phone. "Will you put this in my office?"

"Yep." She took the phone and then stopped short as she glanced at the screen.

"Babe, you might wanna take this," she said softly as my phone started buzzing in her hand.

"Who is it?"

"It's Sandra," she told me.

Sandra took her days off very seriously. If she was calling… it must be super important. I took the phone and could barely say, 'hello' before Sandra's voice came over the line.

"Well, hello, Mr. New York Times best-seller," Sandra's pleasant voice came over the line.

"Sandra! How are you? I'm surprised to hear from you on a Sunday," I responded with a grin.

I was still getting used to being called a New York Times best-seller. Well, it was more than being called one… I *was* one. Within a week of the literary pick reveal show, my book had sold so many copies my printer was working overtime. I couldn't produce books fast enough. It was a problem Sandra had already anticipated. The Sandra effect was real. Once she gave something her seal of approval… it could be hard to keep up with demand.

When Sandra suggested I bring Daniel's Sun Publishing under her umbrella, I jumped at the chance. I still ran my publishing company without having to worry about handling the printing of my books, and Sandra got a 20% stake in my venture. It was like getting an awesome Shark Tank deal without the threat of being stomped like a cockroach underneath Mr. Wonderful's heel.

"I just wanted to give you a head's up. We are flooded with orders… that's a good thing. You just sold your millionth book."

"I what?"

"Yep."

"You're serious?"

"Would I call you on a Sunday to joke around?" she laughed. "You might wanna check your bank account... there's a pending transaction there. Your author royalty payment... which has nothing to do with your profit as the president of your own imprint. Have you had a chance to look through more submissions? Seems like everybody wants to be associated with Daniel's Sun! Don't answer that question. We'll talk in-person next week when you and your family get to Atlanta. Tell Windsor I'll call her tomorrow about my soap order. That Windsor's River scent is beautiful. I can't wait to feature it in my magazine. Anyway... I'm late for brunch. I'll talk to you soon." And then she was gone in a whirlwind of good news, laughter and play auntie love.

I stared at the phone in my hand with a crazy grin on my face as Windsor stared at me with a puzzled expression on hers. She didn't ask me what Sandra said, just quietly went into the kitchen to check on lunch as I leaned back in my chair, afraid to check my bank account. Instead, I focused on Daniel, who was now propped up on River's hip as she carried him up the steps and gently dumped him into my lap before sitting next to me on the wicker sofa.

"Why are you smiling like that?" she asked bluntly.

"Smiling like what?"

"Like a cat that just caught a fat rat. I haven't seen you smile this hard since the wedding."

"Where's a cat?" Daniel asked.

"Your daddy's the cat," River laughed, taking Daniel from me, and standing up. "Let's go take a bath and put on some clean clothes. Then you can have lunch and... maybe a nap?"

"No nap." Daniel said solemnly.

River rolled her eyes and then laughed, "It was worth a try."

They went into the house and I waited until the screen door closed behind them to open my banking app and look at my pending deposits.

Shit!

I blinked several times... my mind filled with elation, joy, and... well... disbelief. I put the phone down and stared out into the back yard, lost in thought as I realized I was no longer a starving artist. I quit my job the moment Devin handed me the money from Daddy. It was seed money. He wanted me to step out on faith and stop being afraid of failure.

I did it.

The moment I decided to pursue my dreams full time...

Is that all I had to do? Step out on faith? Trust myself? Trust in my abilities to put my degree to work and market myself the way I marketed the clients my job provided? Making a rich man richer while I made… a decent living?

That decent living provided for my son. Provided for me. But it wasn't the life I wanted. It was just enough to keep me comfortable from paycheck to paycheck…. Helping other people instead of helping myself.

Helping other people market their dreams while I hustled my own dream on the side like an after-thought. Using vacation time and flying standby just to get to book conventions and speaking engagements…

I closed my eyes and remembered how good it felt to travel back and forth in Sandra's private jet as we put the finishing touches on the partnership we forged. I no longer had to wait for every paying passenger to board the plane and then pray my name was called for an available seat.

A slow smile took over my face.

"Lunch is ready," Windsor called from the doorway.

"Come here, wife," I said, motioning for her to join me on the couch. I pulled her into my lap and stared into her eyes. "If you could have anything you wanted… what would you ask for?" I asked softly.

"I have everything I need," she said with a smile. She was being sincere. It's what I loved the most about her.

"What if I bought you a warehouse so you could expand production of your soaps? Sandra said she's calling you tomorrow about her wholesale order. She's making the *Windsor's River* bar one of her favorite things."

"That is both exciting and frightening at the same time," Windsor sighed, "I'd definitely need a warehouse and more people to work for me and… it's all just so…"

"Overwhelming?" I finished for her. "I know. I just sold my millionth book."

"What?"

"Yeah," I said with a smile. "That's what Sandra was calling to tell me. She told me to check my bank account."

"Did you?" Windsor asked.

"I nodded."

"And?"

"And…" I kissed her softly. "We're gonna be alright." I slid my arms around her waist and squeezed gently.

"We were always gonna be alright." Windsor put her head on my shoulder and sighed softly. "There was never a doubt in my mind."

~The Beginning~

Epilogue

River deleted her Ancestry account, making the decision, on her own, that she didn't want to be contacted by Ian Boco or his family. Ian, famous for ignoring emails, found the notification in his messages a week later. He had a child. Curious, he logged into his account, only to find a blank space where his child's name should have been.

Was it a boy? Was it a girl? Was it a mistake?

For a brief moment he thought about Windsor and wondered if a child had come from their relationship. He hadn't seen her in years… there was still a permanent restraining order against him, but… had he known of a child… he would have found a way to truly punish Windsor for ruining his American dream by taking their personal business to the police. He shook his head. That was in the past. He still had a prestigious career and more money than he could spend.

Whatever became of her… he couldn't have cared less.

He never saw Amadi, bruised and bloodied, standing behind him with his gun, but the moment he heard the safety being released, he knew his time had come.

"I will die a great man and you will still be worthless," he sneered into the silence, not bothering to turn around.

He closed his eyes as the gun fired…

That was all. That was it.

Later, the newspapers would laud him as a highly sought-after photographer… the son of a diplomat… models and clients who worked with him would speak of him fondly… and his assault on Windsor and the subsequent revocation of his work Visa in the U.S. would be a mere footnote at the end of the articles.

Life had gone on for him and he lived it with no remorse or apology… until life ended amidst the violence he inflicted on, yet another young woman.

Windsor was in the basement cutting soap when she heard the news. She paused for a moment; her breath caught in her throat. A spontaneous tear slid down her cheek as she remembered the pain and abuse she endured at his hands… and then, with the sudden realization he was no longer a threat to her or her child… a slow smile appeared on her lips. She chuckled softly.

Windsor looked over at River, cutting soap on the other side of the table, and thought, "*I can't change the past… I would if I could… but it brought me you.*"

River looked up to find Windsor staring and made a crazy face.

"Why are you staring at me like that?"

"Because you're beautiful," Windsor said, with a loving a smile. "You're the most beautiful girl in the world."

River smiled and then shook her head in embarrassment. "Ma, you're such a weirdo," she said with a melodic laugh.

Windsor chuckled again, closed the browser window carrying news of Ian Boco's violent death, and took a long sip of sweet tea before singing along with India Arie as she went back to cutting soap.

About Damian's Windsor

Damian's Windsor is set in my hometown of Tulsa, Oklahoma with references to real, and imaginary places. *Phat Philly's Cheesesteaks* is a real restaurant in Tulsa, but *Claudine's*, a restaurant featured in *Erika's Diary* as well as *Damian's Windsor*, is a figment of my imagination. This fictional restaurant pays homage to *Soul Sisters*, a now closed, family-owned restaurant that was run by my best friend's family in the 1990's. *The Gathering Place* is a beautiful park in the heart of Tulsa, and now that I have three beautiful great-nieces, I imagine I'll be spending a lot of time there.

I also briefly mention a club called, *This is It.* I spent a lot of time in that club, drinking, dancing, waiting for them to play Indo Smoke so I could jump up on the stage and dance… with my no rhythm having self. Ohhhhh, to be young and free and leaving the club, going to *The Waffle House* on Peoria, and then going straight to work and falling asleep at my desk.

DJ Ali Shaw is a great friend of mine, and she is also the Musical Director for KJMM, an urban radio station in Tulsa, Oklahoma. Her Saturday show, *The Weekend Rewind with Ali Shaw* is extremely popular and keeps me grooving whenever I tune in.

There is no *Conversations with Sandra K. Poole…* but Sandra is a real person and we've been having conversations for over twenty years. She's my auntie… not by blood, but by choice, and I could *definitely* see her hosting her own talk show one day. Everyone who worked for Sandra in this book, are real friends of mine. Janita, my Cali cool friend, Kandyss, my STEM Dynamo, and Ron, our dearly departed "uncle" who had a wise spirit and a roving eye.

The Johnson Hotel in downtown Philadelphia, is a figment of my imagination, but *Kobalt Books and Entertainment* is a very real entity. The CEO, Cedric Mixon and his beautiful and accomplished wife, Holly, are real people who were instrumental in encouraging my literary career. It was important for me to include them in this book because I wanted to pay homage to the care and support Kobalt gives its authors. My very first novel, Slow Burn, was published through *Kobalt Books and Entertainment*. One phone call with Cedric about my future… and I found myself looking at an email with all my files and full ownership of my publishing rights. Much like Damian, regaining my publishing rights was a pivotal event in my writing career. Sometimes you just need that push.

Although Windsor Bradley is a fictitious character, writing her journey was therapeutic for me. I've heard about, seen, or experienced some of the desperate situations Windsor endured. It makes it hard to trust someone enough to stop waiting for something bad to happen… no matter how good things are.

Windsor was worthy of love.
I am worthy of love.
YOU are worthy of love.

Depression and anxiety are real. PTSD caused by mental, physical, and emotional relationship trauma… it's real. These horrible diseases can attack out of nowhere and bring you to your knees. If you find yourself in a desperate situation… if your mental, physical, or emotional well-being is in danger… if you're having thoughts of suicide… please reach out to someone who can help. You are not alone.

Acknowledgements

Steven, thank you for giving me the love and the space I need to write. Never in my life have I felt freer to be me and pursue this dream with no guilt.

Kannon and *Darrell III*, you are the most beautiful things I have ever created.

To my parents, *Albert* and *Patsy*, and to my sisters, *Kiona* and *Diona*, thank you for always encouraging my love of writing.

To my loyal beta readers, *Valerie, Janita, Kelli,* and *Sandra...* your true and honest feedback allows me to keep growing as a woman and as a writer. I don't trust my words with anyone else.

**I hate writing "*thank yous*" because there are always hurt feelings if someone is unintentionally missed. If you feel your name should be here... it should. Please charge it to my head and not my heart.

I appreciate everyone who has loved and encouraged me on this journey. Thank you for taking this ride with me. This is only the beginning.

About the Author

Ebony Farashuu is an award-winning author and owner of Metamorphosis Ink Publishing, LLC. In 2007, Ebony released her first novel, Slow Burn, via Kobalt Books and Entertainment. *Slow Burn* earned Ebony the 2007 Shades of Romance Magazine Reader's Choice Awards in the following categories: Best Multi-Cultural Fiction Book of the Year of the Year, Best Multi-Cultural Fiction Author of the Year, and Best New Multi-Cultural Fiction Author of the Year.

Ebony lives in Tulsa, Oklahoma, and she is adamant that all her titles take place in her hometown. As you read through her novels, you will recognize various landmarks and be treated to imaginary places that enhance the story.

After a series of physical and emotional setbacks, Ebony took a thirteen-year hiatus from writing. Ebony began a blog, SymplyEbony. Through SymplyEbony, she regained, not only her voice, but her passion for writing.

She picked up an old erotica project, locked herself in her home office, and began writing her comeback novel, *Erika's Diary*. *Erika's Diary* was self-published in January of 2020 and is the first project published under Metamorphosis Ink.

During that same year, Ebony decided to completely revamp her debut novel, *Slow Burn*. She made pertinent updates, taking into considerations the changes in technology from 2007 to 2020. She added bonus scenes, new poetry, a new cover and re-released it as *Slow Burn: Deluxe Edition*.

The release of *Orchid's Nectar*, the long-awaited sequel, to *Slow Burn*, solidified Ebony's literary comeback and fulfilled a personal goal. You are holding Ebony's sixth book, *Damian's Windsor*.

Ebony Farashuu

www.ingramcontent.com/pod-product-compliance
Lightning Source LLC
Chambersburg PA
CBHW071335250626
47159CB00004B/1611